Dec. 24 2014

PRAISE FOR
JOHNNIE COME LATELY

"The Kitchen family could be any wholesome All-American family, and like any family, they have secrets. In *Johnnie Come Lately*, Kathleen Rodgers brings to life an extended family that could be yours or mine. Their secrets will draw you into this book, and Rodgers' characters—from Johnnie Kitchen to her lovable chocolate lab, Brother Dog—will jump off the page, grab your heart, and not let it go until the very end."
—Terri Barnes, author of *Spouse Calls: Messages From a Military Life* and columnist for *Stars and Stripes*

"A beautifully crafted story about family secrets and second chances, *Johnnie Come Lately* is a guaranteed book club favorite. Former bulimic Johnnie Kitchen battles insecurity and doubt but never lets failure win. I loved her imperfections; I marveled at her strength. Reminding us of the true nature of courage, Johnnie is one of the best heroines I've met in years."
—Barbara Claypole White, award-winning author of *The Unfinished Garden* and *The In-Between Hour*

"*Johnnie Come Lately* is why humans have gathered for eons around the fires to listen to the Storyteller. Kathleen M. Rodgers masterfully unfolds the faded, damaged petals of her flawed characters to reveal their glorious essence in this gripping story about the soul's risk and its inevitable redemption."
—Parris Afton Bonds, *New York Times* bestselling author of *Deep Purple* and cofounder of Romance Writers of America and Southwest Writers Workshop

"*Johnnie Come Lately* evokes the pathos of family life—secrets, betrayals, misunderstandings, heartbreak, and just enough love and forgiveness to make it all worth it. Kathleen M. Rodgers treats her

haunted characters with keen insight and empathy, offering them the second, third, fourth chances that all of us flawed human beings need."
—Siobhan Fallon, author of *You Know When the Men Are Gone*

"The remnants of Johnnie Kitchen's childhood traumas threaten the life she needs and wants now—a deep and enduring love, children, and an orderly family life. Award-winning author Kathleen Rodgers has written a brave and uplifting novel that will move anyone who has faced a long, lonely road back from disaster and despair."
—Joyce Faulkner, past president of Military Writers Society of America and award-winning author of *Windshift* and I*n the Shadow of Suribachi*

"*Johnnie Come Lately* is a thoroughly compelling story of a family in crisis. Rodgers has combined humor, tragedy, and ultimately love in an uplifting story of the human spirit. There were times that I laughed and cried and shouted for joy, and I am not ashamed to say it."
—Dwight Jon Zimmerman, *New York Times* #1 bestselling and award-winning author, *Lincoln's Last Days*, radio show host, producer, and president of the Military Writers Society of America

"Kathleen M. Rodgers captures several life-changing events in Johnnie Come Lately with empathy, seriousness, and humor. Her characters are well-defined; her plot is very credible and her use of schemes to further her story all combine to make this a completely entertaining read."
—Katherine Boyer, retired librarian and book reviewer

"With *Johnnie Come Lately*, Kathleen Rodgers has crafted a story that hits every emotion and is, in many ways, cathartic. This deeply felt family drama resonates on multiple levels, ultimately leaving you inspired."
—Angela Ebron, former magazine editor and the author of *Blessed Health: The African-American Woman's Guide to Physical and Spiritual Health*

JOHNNIE COME LATELY

For
Claudia

Autographed by Author

Jan 2015

Kathleen M. Rodgers

JOHNNIE COME LATELY

∾

KATHLEEN M. RODGERS

Seattle, WA

CAMEL
PRESS

Camel Press
PO Box 70515
Seattle, WA 98127

For more information go to: www.camelpress.com
www.kathleenmrodgers.com

Cover design by Sabrina Sun

Johnnie Come Lately
Copyright © 2015 by Kathleen M. Rodgers

ISBN: 978-1-60381-215-3 (Trade Paper)
ISBN: 978-1-60381-216-0 (eBook)

Library of Congress Control Number: 2014946234

Printed in the United States of America

To my two handsome sons, Thomas and J.P.,
born in The Land of the Midnight Sun,
you continue to inspire me.

And in loving memory of Bubba Dog.
He was a healing balm to our family.
He made us better people.

ACKNOWLEDGMENTS

~

A HUGE THANKS TO MY publisher, Catherine Treadgold, and associate publisher, Jennifer McCord, at Camel Press, for their top-notch editing and for launching *Johnnie Come Lately* into the world. Thanks also to Sabrina Sun for her marvelous cover.

A round of applause for my hard-working literary agent, Jeanie Loiacono, who fell in love with my story and made sure Johnnie Kitchen and her family found a good home.

I am deeply indebted to Bonnie Latino, Drema Hall Berkheimer, Joyce Gilmour, Joyce Faulkner, and Dwight Zimmerman for their endless support and feedback over the six years it took to bring this novel to life.

I am grateful to my longtime writing mentor and friend, Parris Afton Bonds, who always encouraged me with the motto "trust the process."

Special thanks to my writing instructors Suzanne Frank and Dan Hale at The Writer's Path at SMU: you both were there when Johnnie took her first tentative breath.

Thanks also to my fellow writers who showed up on Saturday

mornings at the Writer's Garret in Dallas, Texas, and helped me hone my craft.

Big smiles to my dear friends Rhonda Revels (my inspiration for Whit in *Johnnie Come Lately*) and Elizabeth Ponder for always believing in me as a person, not just a writer, and for countless hours of phone and wine therapy.

To every teacher, professor, and college advisor who made eye contact and refused to let me fail. Thank you for helping me achieve my lifelong dream of earning a college degree.

Deepest gratitude to my husband Tom, cheerleader and soul mate for over thirty-five years, who refused to give up on me when we hit some rough patches.

And last but not least, a salute to our Armed Forces past, present, and future. Your dedication and sacrifice ensure that we have a free press.

PROLOGUE

~⌇~

Johnnie's Journal
December, 1979
Portion, Texas

Dear Mama,

I'M UP HERE AT SOLDIERS Park, hoping you might come swaying by with the breeze. Most of the leaves have dropped and it's getting cold. I asked the old soldier, the one you talk to from time to time, if you'd happened by here lately, but he just stands high on his pedestal, armed and ready, and gives me the silent treatment.

He's not about to give up your secrets—the secrets you pour into him from this bench. Dark things hidden behind bronze eyes that only seem to come alive for you. He won't tell me what you two talk about, or why you up and left in the middle of Thanksgiving dinner. One minute Aunt Beryl was talking about it being the sixteenth anniversary of President Kennedy's death, the next you were out the door so fast you knocked over your iced tea. When you didn't come back, me and Grandpa Grubbs drove here to the war memorial, thinking we might find you talking to your statue. By the time we got home, Aunt Beryl had already packed up and left for Salt Flat.

This is the longest you've been gone in a while. It's been three weeks now. Tonight, I thought if I put my words on paper, somehow they would find their way to you. Like when I was little and wrote letters to Santa. Somehow I knew when Grandpa and I mailed them at the post office, they would find their way to the North Pole.

Something's wrong with me. I tried to tell you at Thanksgiving, but you twisted off. Granny Opal keeps asking why her cakes disappear. Don't I know her business could suffer if she can't fill her customers' orders? How can I tell her that sometimes I cram down a whole cake at one time and then stick my finger down my throat? I've been doing this since Clovis died last summer … when I got so sick on those donuts. None of my friends know. I keep it hidden from everyone. Like you, I'm good at keeping secrets.

Today, after school, I ate all the leftover stew Granny saved for supper. I lied and told her I fed it to a stray dog that came by the house while she was out. She winked and said, "Maybe that stray dog has a sweet tooth, too?" I about died. We ended up eating cornbread and beans. Then I grabbed my notebook and jogged to the park.

I may be fifteen, but I still need you. And I need you to tell me why you said such hateful things when I was younger. One time you called me *sausage legs*, and I hid in the playhouse and wished I could disappear. I cried so much, my throat hurt for days. But I'm skinny now, Mama, just like you, and my legs don't rub together when I walk.

It's starting to get dark, so I better head back to the house before Granny sends out a search party. Before I forget ….

This past Sunday after church, Grandpa and I hiked down the path to the lake to hang the old Christmas wreath. The ribbon is so faded it's pink. A cardinal was perched on the dock, singing his heart out. Grandpa Grubbs stopped dead in his tracks and said, "Looky there, young lady. It's your *Uncle Johnny*. He's come back to sing you a Christmas carol."

I hear it might snow.

Johnnie

PS: In case you're lost, we still live at 8 Lakeside Drive.

CHAPTER 1

~~

Mid-March, 2007

JOHNNIE WOKE UP CHOKING. SHE coughed and wheezed, trying to catch her breath. Her throat dry, she struggled in the dark, thinking she might die.

Flinging off the covers, she bolted out of the king-size bed and groped toward the bathroom for a drink. Gulping down water, she heard her husband, Dale, calling from the bedroom.

"Johnnie. Is everything okay in there?"

"I'm fine," she answered after a moment, her voice raspy as she stood at the sink in a daze, staring at her reflection in the big beveled mirror, which Dale had recently installed. A nearby nightlight cast a milky glow over the marble-top vanity.

With a shaky hand, she fingered the loose strands of hair her mama once called the color of cinnamon, now a tangled mass around an oval face starting to show the fine lines of age. Drenched in sweat, her cotton nightgown clung to her slender, petite frame.

Carefully, Johnnie replaced the porcelain cup and steadied herself as she tried to make sense of what just happened. Her pulse throbbed as it all came back ....

SHE WAS AT A GATHERING at Granny Opal's house, stuffing her face with cookies and casserole and pieces of cake. People were everywhere, flocked around her in conversation. Then Grandpa Grubbs walked in, tall and lanky although he'd been dead for years. He walked straight up to her and frowned. "You're not Victoria. Has anyone seen Victoria?" She began to cry, her mouth full of cake. Was it her fault her mama had disappeared? The next thing she knew, she was hunched over a toilet, choking.

A RAP ON THE BATHROOM door startled her. "Johnnie?" Dale opened the door and poked his tousled blond head inside.

She turned away from the mirror. She'd been checking her face and hair for cake crumbs or vomit. Even in the dim light, she could see the concern in her husband's soft blue eyes.

"What's wrong, honey? Can't you sleep?"

She shook her head. "I thought I'd binged."

Dale opened the door all the way. "Honey, we've been through this before." He was clad in boxer shorts and a T-shirt, and she noted not for the first time that his compact, muscular body looked built for hard work. Men like him never struggled with eating disorders. "Come back to bed. You were dreaming."

Under the sheets, Johnnie curled up in a fetal position and hugged a pillow between her legs. "I'll be forty-three in two weeks." She stared at the clock on the nightstand. Four a.m. glared back. "I haven't binged in years. Why do I still dream about it?"

"I wish I knew." Dale snuggled next to her.

She took a deep breath. "What am I doing with my life?"

He nuzzled his face in her hair. "Raising our three kids."

She felt a twinge of sadness. "Jesus, they're practically grown." Her fingers crinkled the edge of her pillowcase, a soothing habit carried over from childhood. "They don't need me like they used to."

"I need you," Dale whispered. She felt the reassuring warmth of his breath at the nape of her neck.

Slowly, she turned into his warm embrace. He smelled of soap and shampoo from his evening shower and something else too, something deep and masculine.

She cupped his face in her hands. "How come you still love me after twenty-three years? I'm not a sweet young thing anymore."

"You've still got the goods," Dale murmured as his callused hands moved down to caress the curve of her hips. She snuggled closer, trying to block out the disturbing images from her dream. Encircled in Dale's arms, she felt safe and complete for the time being.

After a moment she whispered, "Maybe I should go back to college. Finish my degree."

Dale let out a huge yawn. "Honey, we've been over this before. We can barely pay for D.J. right now, let alone Cade and Callie Ann when their time comes."

"Maybe I could get a job."

"Unless it pays more than minimum wage, it would just put us in a higher tax bracket. Can we talk about this later? I've gotta get up in a couple of hours."

Her husband rolled over, facing the wall. She lay wide-awake in the dark, listening to the rhythm of his breathing as he drifted off to sleep. She'd given him the fruits of her womb— two sons and a daughter—and he worshiped her for it. He was her savior and she was his saint.

But she didn't feel like a saint. And Dale would surely reconsider his high opinion of her if he knew the secrets she kept.

Heavy secrets, like the weight of rocks on her heart. And because of these secrets she didn't push Dale about pursuing the things she really wanted in life.

Raindrops splattered against the bedroom window. In the back of her mind, in a place hidden away in time, she saw herself as a little girl, dancing hand in hand with her mama.

They were singing, "Rain, rain, go away. Little Johnnie wants to play."

AT THE GAS STATION THE next morning, Johnnie pulled up to the first available pump. She hurried to lift the nozzle and began fueling the Suburban. The metal felt cold in her hand. Wearing only a thin pair of sweats and an old T-shirt, she shivered in the chilly breeze. The clouds had blown away, and the smell of gasoline mingled with the leftover scent of the earlier rain shower. Spring in North Texas could bring a gully washer one day; then folks in Portion could go weeks without rain.

She glanced at the baby blue sky. Easter would be here in less than a month. By then she would be another year older, and after church they would spend Easter Sunday eating ham and lima beans at Granny Opal's. Johnnie longed for the days when she and the children spent hours dyeing eggs and Dale dressed up in a bunny suit.

While she waited for the tank to fill, she grinned at Brother Dog, the family's ninety-pound chocolate Lab. He stuck his head out the window behind the driver's seat and panted. Johnnie reached over to rub behind his ears.

"Can you believe what Callie Ann said to me yesterday when I picked her up from drill team practice?" Brother Dog wagged his tail, happy for the attention. She peered into his sympathetic eyes and talked about her fifteen-year-old daughter. "All I did was offer to take her shopping for a new Easter dress. You'd think I'd offered to buy her an itchy old girdle. She put her hands on her hips and said, 'Mother, please. You're joking, right?'"

Brother Dog whimpered, and Johnnie smoothed her hands over his satin face. "You're a good listener." She kissed the top of his head and continued.

"Then the other day Cade said to me, 'You're puttin' *what* in D.J.'s care package? Dude, his roommates will laugh their asses off.'" Johnnie put her finger to her lips. "Don't tell our stud baseball player I saw him stash those chocolate bunnies into his bag before practice."

She stiffened at the sight of a long black hearse barreling up to the pump next to her. Brother Dog growled. Johnnie glared at the black vehicle as if it were the Grim Reaper.

Then, feeling foolish, she leaned over and whispered to Brother, "I guess they've gotta get gas somewhere." Brother snorted, then turned his back on the hearse and stuck his head out the other side of the Suburban.

Chuckling, she focused on the numbers flashing by on her own pump.

"Mrs. Kitchen?" a male voice called out.

Slowly, she peeked around the pump. To her astonishment, her eyes focused on a tall, slim young man clad in a dark suit and tie, putting gas in the hearse.

"Morning." She greeted him with a cheerful wave. "My goodness, how long has it been?" She tried to conceal her embarrassment. He'd been to her home many times in the past, but she couldn't remember his name.

The driver's thin face broke into a familiar grin. "About four years. How's D.J. these days? Haven't seen him since graduation."

Hearing her son's name caused her to smile. "D.J.'s fine. He's working on an art degree. Remember all those awards he won in high school?"

The young man nodded and whipped out a hanky and wiped at something on the hearse's shiny black hood. "I've been working for Farrow & Sons when I'm not down at the armory," he offered, and she assumed he meant the National Guard Armory. "I'm still trying to figure out what I want to do."

She watched as he straightened up, folded the hanky, and stuck it in his back pocket.

"I'm either going to study mortuary science or auto mechanics." Grinning, he placed the nozzle back in the slot.

"Either way, I'll be working in a body shop when I'm not playing citizen-soldier."

She chuckled, studying his face. Was he always this funny? He had a nickname. What was it? After a moment, she gestured toward the hearse. "I bet your job can get tough at times. At the mortuary, I mean. Not that being in the Guard is a picnic, of course." She heard herself babble on, saying all the wrong things, and she could just imagine what the kids would think, especially the boys, if they heard her now.

The driver's pleasant expression turned somber. "There's talk my unit might get called up. I wouldn't mind seeing Iraq. But yeah, you heard about the Cooper kid, right?"

Instinctively, she placed her hand over her heart. "Oh, that was terrible." A dull pain settled in her chest at the mention of another teen suicide that had happened about a week ago. How many did that make? She'd lost track since the day she picked D.J. up from school in the eighth grade, and he said over the bulge of his backpack as he slid into the front seat, "Mom, one of my classmates killed himself last night." That day in the carpool lane, the two younger kids had been listening in the back. She worried that the news had robbed her children of some of their innocence.

That memory from eight years ago was still fresh. She shook her head and sighed at D.J.'s friend. "The Coopers used to go to our church. I heard he shot himself."

"Yeah, it was pretty grim. I was at work when the body came in. I felt sorry for his parents."

"Do they know why he did it? Cade didn't know him that well, but he heard he got busted for steroids, that he'd been bullied for being small."

The young man nodded. "That's the rumor." Then he glanced at his watch and adjusted his tie. "Well, I better get back to work. Got a funeral in a couple of hours. Great to see you again. Tell D.J. hi."

At last she remembered. Steven. Steven Tuttle. The boys called him *Tutts* for short.

She waved as Steven Tuttle drove away, the left rear turn signal winking as the hearse disappeared around a corner. Wrapping her arms around Brother Dog, she thought about their brief conversation.

A young person was dead because he took illegal steroids to bulk up, got caught, and killed himself. A quick glance at the back of her right hand—where tiny white scars were still visible from her own teeth sinking into her knuckles—reminded her how lucky she was. Both she and the Cooper kid had suffered from an unrealistic body image. He wanted to be bigger. She'd wanted to be smaller, to the point of disappearing.

* * *

Johnnie's Journal
Tuesday morning
March 27, 2007

Dear Grandpa Grubbs,

You've been gone so long, but I still hear your voice. Remember when we'd run errands and I'd say, "Where're we going, Grandpa?" You'd laugh and tease, "We're going up in the air to get red hair." I'd scrunch my chubby cheeks and say, "But I already have red hair." You'd pat my head and chuckle, "Then let's go to Timbuktu or Kalamazoo." I'd get serious and ask, "How are we going to get there?" Your whole face crinkled in a grin; you'd press the magic button on the dashboard of the Studebaker and say, "Why, young lady, we are going to fly."

And fly we did, right down to the grocery store, the bank, or wherever Granny Opal sent us. I tried to pass your sense of adventure on to my children. After school we'd chug a-chug-a on a make-believe train to Granny Opal's for cupcakes or bump along in a covered wagon to the museum or ride elephants to the zoo. Then we'd blast off to the moon to start homework. Nowadays my children are too old to pretend. So I take Brother Dog along and talk to him while he hangs his head out the window.

Tomorrow I'll be forty-three. Since Mama didn't keep a baby book about me, I looked up my birthday on the Internet. Was I in for a surprise! Turns out I was born the day after the famous earthquake in Anchorage, Alaska—March 28, 1964—on a Saturday between Good Friday and Easter Sunday. Maybe that explains why I feel caught somewhere between death and resurrection.

Where's that magic button when you need it?

Johnnie

CHAPTER 2

❦

Tuesday Evening

THIRSTY AND TIRED AFTER HER first shift at the new food pantry at Portion United Methodist Church, Johnnie waved to one of her new coworkers and took a long swig from a bottle of water she'd stashed in her purse. She wasn't used to being on her feet all day, but it felt good to be doing something useful for a change. Something with purpose, other than housework. And as much as she loved to journal, she needed something more. Would Dale ever understand this? Tonight, before going to bed, she planned to tell him, "Just one class. That's all I want for my birthday. Just one *lousy* class at the community college." They'd met at university before they both dropped out. Why was he so pigheaded about her going back to school now? Was it really about the money? Or was it something else?

She'd already done the research. The class would run around $150, plus books.

Before pulling out of the parking lot, she glanced at the old historical marker at the church's entrance. Back in sixth grade, during confirmation class, she could recite the whole thing by heart if she squeezed her eyes shut tight enough and pictured the words in her mind. Today, she'd be lucky if she could recall the opening lines:

> In 1851, the Reverend Jeremiah Harkins, a Methodist Circuit Rider from Tennessee, proclaimed to a small band of settlers: "On this portion of land, we will build a church." Out of this early settlement, grew the town of Portion, Texas ....

The sign was too far away for her to read the rest of the plaque, but she could make out the outline of a lone rider, sitting tall in a saddle, his few possessions stowed in two bulging saddlebags.

"A preacher man on a horse. Not exactly my idea of the Marlboro Man," her mama snickered the day Johnnie was confirmed, a rare Sunday when Victoria Grubbs graced the family with her presence. Church hadn't even been out five minutes when she paused in front of the marker to light a cigarette. Giggling, Johnnie had wrapped her arms around her mama's small waist, inhaling her scent of Jergens Lotion and clean cotton.

"Oh, Mama," Johnnie sighed at the memory, as if only seconds had passed since they'd stood in front of that marker.

Phoning home, she reminded Callie Ann to shove a turkey meatloaf in the oven and feed Brother Dog. Johnnie had just turned right onto Main Street and was about to call Dale when her phone rang.

"Hi there, ladybug. How was your first day on the job?"

Whit Thomas, Johnnie's best friend since she struck up a conversation with Whit at the grocery store fifteen years ago, owned A Second Pair of Hands, a company that catered to wealthy clients in the Dallas/Forth Worth area. Dale once asked, "What exactly does A Second Pair of Hands do?" And Johnnie had laughed and said, "Everything but sex," before she explained to Dale that Whit was basically a high-paid gofer.

She could hear Whit's radio in the background. "You know," she said, still haunted by the tragic faces that filed past her all afternoon at the food pantry, "there are a lot of starving people in our community." About this time, a Cadillac Escalade passed her going the opposite direction.

"Get outta here," Whit shot back. "In white-bread Portion?"

She let Whit's comment slide. "The hardest part was seeing the kids. A little boy about eight wouldn't even look at me when I offered him a package of peanut butter crackers."

Whit's radio went silent. "Sister Girl remembers those days. Mama always hated taking handouts. 'Stand there and play statue,' she'd tell us girls. That was Mama's way of saying 'look invisible.'"

Johnnie shifted the phone to her other ear. "Were you embarrassed? About being on welfare?"

It took a moment for Whit to respond. "Folks gotta eat."

Clearly, Whit didn't like talking about her past anymore than Johnnie did. But sometimes it couldn't be helped. "Whit, something's been gnawing at me all afternoon."

"What's that, ladybug?"

She wanted to tell Whit about her days as a troubled teenager, when she binged on bags of potato chips, cartons of ice cream, dozens of donuts, her belly so full she looked seven months pregnant and it hurt to breathe. She had no choice but to get rid of it, to purge. Be it a wooden spoon, the finger, the looped end of an extension cord jammed down her throat. Time stopped until she was empty, her throat raw, and she was vowing it would never happen again, until the next time, and the next.

Instead, she simply said, "All the food I wasted when I was younger. While people were starving, I—" She broke off.

A hint of sympathy entered Whit's voice. "You were sick. You couldn't help it."

"I know, but still …." Approaching the intersection of Main and Merriweather, Johnnie noticed a slim figure huddled by the stop sign off to her right, the person's head concealed under the hood of a sweat jacket: a day laborer most likely, somebody's gardener or housekeeper, waiting for a ride. She strained to see the person's face but it was hidden from view. *It's not her*, she told herself. *Too tall.*

"I don't mean to rush you," Whit cut in, "but I'm expecting a call any second so I'll make this quick. I know you don't want a big production, but let's do something fun on your birthday."

"Like what?" Glancing at the person one last time, Johnnie turned left onto her street of charming cottages and remodeled bungalows. With enough light left in the day, tall leafy trees and spring's earliest jonquils greeted her.

"Let's go roller-skating, like when we were kids."

"Roller-skating? At my age? I'd fall and bust my butt."

Laughing, Whit told her she'd discovered an old-fashioned rink in the area. "Whoops, there's my call. Gotta run."

After Whit hung up, Johnnie closed her phone and dropped it in her lap. Whit's comment triggered a memory, and Johnnie gripped the steering wheel a little tighter as her mind tumbled back thirty-seven years ....

ONCE AGAIN, MAMA WAS LATE.

"Grandpa, how far away is that college again?"

Sporting red suspenders, Grandpa Grubbs rubbed his chest as if in pain. Then he checked his watch for the millionth time and glanced toward the roller rink's entry. "She'll be here, young lady. She promised."

Granny Opal donned a party hat and a crooked grin, and pointed at the clown twisting balloons into weenie dogs. "I'd like to see him do *that* on roller-skates."

Children laughed and crowded around the fancy sheet cake fresh from Opal's Cakery. "Make a wish. Make a wish," they chanted. The heat from six candles warmed Johnnie's face as she bent over, teetering in a pair of rented skates, and prayed,

"Please, God, please let Mama hurry up and get here."

But Mama was a no-show.

As Johnnie barreled up the curved driveway of her dark red bungalow at 420 Merriweather, she realized that her mama's absence that day was the beginning of Victoria Grubbs' vanishing act. That year, 1970, her mama dropped out of college, a young infantry officer named Francis Murphy stepped on a booby trap in Vietnam, and Grandpa Grubbs suffered his first heart attack.

Spotting Dale's work truck parked under the red oak in front of the attached garage, Johnnie was certain of one thing: No matter how she tried to outrun the past, it would always be nipping at her heels.

Filing those thoughts away, she glanced at the logo on the side of Dale's truck:

Dale's Kitchens
Serving the Metroplex and Beyond

She remembered how D.J. had come home from college all full of himself, his thick brown hair pulled back in a short ponytail, after just one semester studying graphic design. At nineteen, he took Dale aside after work one day and offered his unsolicited advice: "Dad, your company's typeface, identity mark, and color scheme are seriously outdated. You do more than kitchens now. You renovate the whole house. Your brand has changed. Your logo should reflect that."

Rubbing his chin, Dale nodded at D.J. then turned to lock the large silver toolbox bolted to the bed of his truck. "Thanks for your advice, son. But I don't have the time or money to spend on some fancy ad agency."

D.J. chewed his right thumbnail. "Let *me* design it then."

Gripping his son by the shoulder, Dale said, "You concentrate on your studies. Let me worry about my company." Then he went into the house.

D.J. grabbed his smokes and headed down the driveway to sit on the curb. He'd done that since high school, advertising to the neighborhood that he smoked.

Johnnie observed all this from the corner of the deep front porch where she'd been watering plants. D.J. had been right that day two years ago—Dale needed to update his company's image—but he could be so darn stubborn at times. Now, as she slipped in the side portico entrance to focus on getting dinner ready, she wished she had come out of the shadows that day and cheered D.J. on. Instead, she hung back. Silent. Torn between her loyalties to her husband and son.

She dropped her purse at the computer center Dale built for her when he remodeled their kitchen two years ago. Hunched over the computer screen, Callie Ann barely looked up as Johnnie approached. Clad in running shorts and a T-shirt, Callie Ann had her long slender legs tucked under the computer chair. Brother Dog was curled around her bare feet.

"Hey, sis. What are you working on?" Johnnie bent to kiss the top of her daughter's silky blonde head.

Callie Ann moved in closer to the computer screen. "Nothing much."

A pair of amber eyes gazed up at Johnnie from the floor, and she reached down to scratch behind Brother Dog's ears. "Hey, sweet boy. Looks like you're working hard."

Straightening, she went to toss her sweater over the back of a kitchen chair.

Callie Ann twisted around. "Mom, Coach Brown called."

"Oh yeah?" Johnnie could smell the meatloaf in the oven. Her mind was on fixing dinner, not talking to Cade's baseball coach. "I suppose he's pushing his annual fundraiser again?"

"Cade's in deep doo-doo, Mom. He got caught drinking at some party. His picture's on the Internet."

Drinking? Cade? Johnnie was confused. What was Callie

Ann talking about? Rattled, she saw herself pull a bag of frozen broccoli from the freezer and place it on the granite counter. Then she stiffened and stared at her daughter. "But Cade doesn't drink."

Callie Ann rolled her eyes. "He's such an idiot. The whole school knows." She pushed away from the computer. "Look. Come see for yourself."

Johnnie moved away from the island and hovered over her daughter. She stared at an image of her youngest son on the computer screen. It was Cade all right, handsome and blond as ever, a beer can halfway to his lips. *How could this be?* she wondered, as she stared at the picture of her polite, loyal, affectionate, dutiful seventeen-year-old son, a pitcher for the Portion High School baseball team, with a beer in his hand.

"Who took this picture?" she snapped. "And why would they post it on the Internet?"

Callie Ann shrugged. "Some girl from another school in the area. At least that's the story I heard."

Johnnie clenched her teeth and spun around. "Where is he?"

Callie Ann gestured toward the back door. "He's out there with Dad, bawling his eyes out." Then Callie Ann's face crumpled and she burst into tears. "Cade's suspended from the next six games."

"There goes his baseball scholarship," Johnnie growled.

Brother Dog got up, shook himself off, and made a beeline for the back door. Johnnie was right behind him.

AT TEN O'CLOCK THAT NIGHT, after Johnnie got ready for bed, she went into the kitchen to start the dishwasher. Dale and Callie Ann had taken Brother Dog for a walk. She was exhausted from the discussion she and Dale had with Cade earlier in the evening. As she poured dish powder into the dishwasher, Cade walked in.

"Mom, are you busy?"

She glanced back at him. He had broad shoulders and stood

almost a foot taller than Johnnie. Even in the kitchen's dim light, she could see that he had been crying. His eyes were bloodshot, his lids puffy and swollen. She wasn't used to seeing him this way—eaten up with guilt, embarrassed.

Her shoulders tensed. "I'm headed to bed, honey. What do you need?"

Cade stuffed his hands in the pockets of his jeans. "Does Granny Opal know? I heard you talking to her on the phone after supper."

"No, honey. I didn't say a word."

Cade glanced at the floor. "It's okay if you tell her." When he looked up, his chin began to quiver.

Johnnie's throat tightened. It broke her heart how grownup he tried to act.

He kicked at something on the floor. "I called D.J. He sounded pissed. But he told me to hang in."

"I'm sure your brother's just worried about you."

Cade's jaw clenched. "I've let everyone down. Coach wouldn't even look at me when I came back from the office today. And Dad ...." His voice trailed off, and he began to cry.

"Look, why don't you try and get some sleep? It's been a long day." Reaching up to touch the side of his face, she felt tiny bristles where he needed to shave. "I'll call Coach first thing in the morning. Daddy and I'll go up to the school."

Cade slammed his fist on the counter. She jumped, startled by his outburst.

"I screwed up, Mom. I don't deserve to play. I hate myself. I hate my life. I wish I were dead!"

Gripped in fear, she froze as Cade's words set off alarms. Her mind flashed to the conversation she'd had last week at the gas station about the Cooper boy. Then today at the food pantry, before the clients shuffled in, somebody had brought up the statistic that suicide is the third leading cause of death among teens. She began to shiver. Cade was so wrapped up in his own shame. Could she reason with him? She doubted it.

She reached out to embrace him, to console him, but he pushed her away. He turned to leave.

"I hate myself," he cried, spinning around. Pointing a finger at his temple, he fired an imaginary gun.

At that moment, D.J.'s chilling words slammed into her head. *One of my classmates killed himself last night ....* She grabbed Cade by the shoulders. His muscles were hard and taut. He could toss her across the room if he wanted. She was on her tiptoes.

"Now you listen to me," she said, shaking him to get his attention. Her voice was slow and deliberate, and she was crying now too. "Look at me." She grabbed his chin, forcing him to look at her. His pupils were dilated, and his eyes were darting around the room like a crazy person's.

Before she could even think and stop herself, she blurted, "You think you're the only one who's ever done something you're ashamed of?"

That got his attention. He stopped crying long enough to look at her. Drunk with his own guilt, he laughed hysterically. "What did you do that was so bad?"

She released him and tried to leave the room. "None of your business, Cade."

"Tell me, Mom, what did you do?"

"Let it go."

Her temples throbbed as she fled the kitchen and moved into the laundry room. She grabbed a pile of dirty clothes off the floor and stuffed them into the washer.

Cade was at the door to the laundry room. "Mom," he demanded, wiping his eyes.

"Cade, I'm warning you. Drop it." She moved past him and back into the kitchen. She picked up a dishcloth and rubbed the countertops.

Relentless, Cade followed her and continued to speak. "Was it puking your guts out just to be skinny? Big deal. Girls do it all the time." Hulking over her, he stuck his finger down his throat and made gagging noises, taunting her.

His mocking stung her, cracking open an old scar.

A heat surged through her body. All the lies, all the secrets, churned in her gut: growing, intensifying, climbing up her insides, trying to escape. The words spewed from her lips, "I had an affair."

She shuddered and hid her face in the dishcloth. In her rush to save him, she'd made a horrible mistake.

When she looked up a second later, Dale was standing at the side entrance. She never heard him come in. His rugged face—normally ruddy and smiling—had gone pale and rigid with shock. Callie Ann dropped to the floor in a heap, hugging Brother Dog. Cade staggered back as if he'd been shot.

* * *

Johnnie's Journal
Outskirts of Portion
12:15 a.m.
March 28, 2007

Mama,

I wish I could stop the world from spinning. I am dizzy with grief. I need to talk to someone who won't judge me. Or Cade. God knows you're in no position to judge anyone. Your youngest grandson got caught drinking. Seventeen is considered underage. Maybe you'd know a thing or two about that. I heard you were hitting the sauce before I could walk.

Today's my birthday, Mama. I am officially forty-three. How many birthdays does this make that you've missed? Not that it matters anymore.

Missed birthdays are nothing compared to the atomic bomb I just dropped on my family.

Johnnie

CHAPTER 3

~~✼~~

A Quiet Place to Cry

UNDER THE GLOW OF THE Suburban's dome light, she read her latest entry one more time, then stashed the journal and pen in her purse. She had been sitting in her car, parked in the vacant lot of an abandoned building located at the edge of town. Now, easing out of the lot, she whipped a U-turn on North Dooley and headed south toward civilization. The last thing she needed was to get pulled over by a cop—a cop who might question why a woman her age was driving around after midnight with bloodshot eyes, dressed in her robe and slippers.

With nowhere else to go, she pulled into the entrance of Portion Cemetery and cut the engine. The lonely strains of a thousand crickets and frogs greeted her as she cracked a window for air. She slumped against the steering wheel. The skin around her nose and eyes was raw from crying. She had fled the house in disgrace, too upset to change clothes.

"What have I done?" she sobbed into the darkness.

At that moment, it was as if Grandpa was calling from his grave, reminding her of their long-ago conversation. Until tonight, she had tucked his disturbing words safely away. Now they surfaced, demanding her full attention ….

"I THINK YOUR GRANNY IS hiding something from me,"
Grandpa growled from his hospital bed, where he lay trapped
in a flimsy gown under a light blanket.

"A secret lover?" Johnnie teased. She was perched on the
edge of his bed, rubbing lotion into his chapped arms. She
regretted the impulsive remark the second it seeped out.

Grandpa gripped her hand, getting lotion all over the
blanket. For a man who'd just suffered his third heart attack,
he was surprisingly strong. And he was in no mood to joke.
"About Victoria. I think your granny knows where your mama
is."

Johnnie pulled away, too stunned to speak. Grandpa was
talking nonsense. Granny Opal wouldn't do a thing like that.
Johnnie started to stand up, intending to tell him he needed to
get some rest.

But Grandpa's gruff voice stopped her cold. "Young lady, I
think you're the one with a secret lover," he added, as if his gray
eyes could see straight into her soul. "I saw you down by the
dock with Old Man Cagle's son. About a year ago, right after
my second heart attack."

Just then Granny Opal breezed into the room, carrying a
basket of fruit. "Jonathan, aren't these lovely?" She smiled and
held up a banana. "The doctor says you need more potassium."

GRANDPA DIED THE NEXT DAY, and with him went his
revelation about seeing Johnnie with another man. That was
over twenty years ago, and Johnnie had wanted to rush home
from the hospital that day and tell Dale everything, confess her
sins as if Dale was the priest and she the sinner. But when she
stumbled into the tiny apartment, suffocating with shame, she
took one look at baby D.J.'s pudgy face and dark ringlets, his
grubby hands reaching for her, and she clammed up.

Wasn't Dale Junior proof that everything had worked out

for the best? When Johnnie rocked him to sleep, singing old familiar hymns and breathing in his clean baby scent, she felt born again, bathed in his goodness, as if the affair had never happened.

Now the secret was out, and she had no one to blame but herself. Wiping her eyes, Johnnie leaned back against the worn leather seat, trying to figure out what to do next. A weight pressed heavy on her chest; it hurt to breathe. The bile boiled in her throat.

Fumbling for the door handle, she pushed open the driver's door and retched. As her body heaved, she recalled the wounded look in Dale's eyes after she looked up from the dishcloth and realized he was standing in the kitchen, not ten feet away ....

HE LEANED AGAINST THE DOORJAMB, holding himself as if he'd been stabbed. The look in his soft blue eyes said it all: *Tell me it isn't true.* But when he opened his mouth to speak, all that came out was a thin raspy, "When?"

She grabbed the edge of the kitchen island to keep from falling. Fear gripped her body, and her words came out forced and slow as if she'd suffered a stroke. "Before the kids were born."

Cade and Callie Ann were still in the room. Cade paced back and forth, cupping his hands over his ears like a little kid who refused to listen. Callie Ann was still on the floor with the dog.

Dale glared at both of the kids. "Scram!"

They bolted from the room, along with the dog.

From the back of the house, Johnnie heard Callie Ann scream, "I hate you, Mom," before a door slammed.

After the kids left, all Johnnie's instincts told her to run, but something in Dale's eyes pinned her in place. His big generous mouth creased in anger. "Who was it?"

She had trouble breathing. "No, Dale," she pleaded.

His voice grew louder, more demanding. "I asked you, what was the guy's name?"

So help her God, she felt her face break into a smirk of self-loathing. After all those years of suppressed guilt, she was finally getting what she deserved.

Quickly, she looked away. She fixed her eyes on the hardwood floor that Dale had installed during a recent remodeling. He had wanted slate; she had wanted wood.

Something inside of her broke. "Dale, I never meant to hurt you."

"Just tell me his name."

"Jeral." She hardly recognized the sound of her own voice.

At first Dale blinked as if confused, then slowly the name began to register. His face twisted in disgust. "Jeral? Cagle? My God, Johnnie. That son-of-a-bitch tried to run me out of business." Dale pushed away from the doorjamb toward the back door.

She started to go after him, but halfway across the family room Dale threw his arm in the air as if to stop her. "Johnnie, just leave me alone. I can't deal with you right now." As he staggered past the big stone fireplace he built with his own hands, he paused one last time as if needing a moment to catch his breath.

Johnnie hated herself as she watched the life being sucked out of the only person in this world who had tried to save her.

HER CELLPHONE RANG, STARTLING HER. She fumbled through her purse for a tissue to blow her nose.

Cade sounded alarmed. "Mom, where are you? You've been gone over an hour."

She closed her eyes and sighed. "I'm at the cemetery."

Cade was silent for a moment. "What are you doing there?"

"Talking to dead people," she said dryly.

"Mom, Callie Ann locked herself in her room and won't open the door. I'm getting worried."

"Where's Dad?"

"He's sittin' out back, staring into space. I tried to talk to him, but he acts like he can't hear me."

Johnnie switched the cellphone to her left ear and started the Suburban. "Get a screwdriver and try to unlock Callie Ann's door. I'm on my way."

"Mama Girl?"

Johnnie swallowed hard. Cade hadn't called her that in years. "Yes, honey?"

"Mama, I'm sorry. This whole thing's my fault."

She took a deep breath and sped out of the cemetery. "Don't be ridiculous," she said. "I'll be home in a sec."

* * *

Johnnie's Journal
Purgatory
4:30 a.m.
March 28, 2007

Dear Lieutenant (a.k.a. Uncle Sam),

What you couldn't do for me in life, maybe you can do in death. I need a favor. First off, it should come as no surprise to you that I'm not perfect, given my start in life. I'd ask God, but I think He has turned His back on me. Every time I go to pray, all I hear is silence. A silence so big it feels like it will gobble me up. So, can you please send an army of angels to watch over Dale and the kids? Don't forget Brother Dog. He's the most innocent one in the bunch. And if you bump into Grandpa Grubbs while y'all are sittin' around playing harps—surely Catholics and Protestants mingle up there—tell him he was right. About seeing me at the dock.

You Know Who I Am

CHAPTER 4

～⁓

Happy Birthday, Johnnie!

"ARE YOU AND DADDY GETTING a divorce?"

Johnnie set her coffee mug in the cup holder and turned to face Callie Ann, who was leaning through the open passenger window.

The look in her daughter's eyes wasn't anger so much as fear. Johnnie had seen that look before. When Callie Ann was younger, she'd scurry into the master bedroom in the middle of the night, flip on the light switch, and dive under the covers, her whole body shaking as she burrowed deeper into Johnnie's ribcage, crying about how the Sandman would get her. Johnnie would hold her tight and tell her there was no such thing as the Sandman. And Callie Ann would look up at her with trusting eyes and believe her, until the next time she got scared. But this morning, something in her daughter's eyes had changed, and sadly, Johnnie realized Callie Ann no longer trusted her.

"Sis … I'm sorry about all this," Johnnie told her. "Look. Everything's fine."

Callie Ann impatiently flipped her ponytail back. "Then why did Daddy sleep on the couch last night?"

AFTER JOHNNIE RETURNED HOME FROM the cemetery, Cade met her in the driveway and reported that he'd found Callie Ann in her room, curled up asleep with the dog. When Johnnie peeked in on her moments later, Callie Ann was sniffling as if she'd been crying for hours. Leaving the door cracked, Johnnie had gone to check on Dale. She found him stretched out on the sofa in the family room, covered with a throw from the old leather chair by the fireplace. When she whispered his name, he didn't respond.

THE BELL RANG. JOHNNIE GLANCED at the clock on the dashboard then back at Callie Ann. "Honey, you better get to class …." Now was hardly the time for a deep discussion about last night.

Callie Ann glared at Johnnie a moment then hoisted her book bag over her shoulder and hiked off. As she walked across campus, heads turned. Watching her go, Johnnie recalled what Dale said last fall when Callie Ann was voted Most Beautiful Freshman at Portion High: "With your brains, little girl, that makes you the total package."

Brother Dog was waiting by the door when Johnnie got home. "I'm sorry you got left behind," she cooed, stooping to stroke his head. "Callie Ann was in such a bad mood, I thought it best you stay here." She dropped her purse next to the computer and walked over to plump up the sofa pillows and toss the throw back over the chair. A pair of Dale's socks poked out from beneath the couch. As Johnnie plucked them up and went to toss them into the laundry room, the muffled sound of her cellphone caught her attention.

What had Callie Ann forgotten now? Or was it Cade, needing her to come speak with the coaches? Or dear Lord, please let it be Dale …. Still clutching the socks, she dashed across the room and tore through her purse until she found her phone.

D.J.'s baritone voice greeted her. "Happy birthday, Mom." He sounded like he was walking in the wind and slightly out of breath.

Johnnie turned away as if he could see her through the phone. Sometimes, like now, she felt unworthy of his goodness. Even as a helpless baby, he'd given her what therapy couldn't: motivation to heal.

"Oh, honey …." she said at last. She pictured him walking across campus, tall and lanky in tight jeans and a polo shirt open at the collar, his back slightly bowed under the weight of a backpack, a cellphone jammed to his ear. Before heading into class, he would stop for a smoke.

D.J. hesitated. "Mom, I only have a sec. Cade called me last night. He told me what happened."

Something in D.J.'s voice alerted Johnnie that he wasn't referring to Cade's drinking incident. She stared straight ahead, not knowing what to say.

D.J. broke the silence. "Just tell me straight up …." He paused, taking a long drag on a cigarette. "Is Dad my real father?"

She closed her eyes, shocked. One little slip of the tongue had led to this. "Son," she gasped, slumping into the computer chair, "do you even have to ask?"

"That's all I wanted to know. I'll call you later. Chill."

Slowly, she pushed herself up from the desk. Like a blind person feeling her way around a room, she maneuvered around the kitchen island, one hand reaching out to help her maintain balance. She felt like she was walking sideways, her equilibrium off-kilter. In the laundry room, she dropped Dale's socks in the washer, along with some wet towels, and went to unload the dishwasher.

Picking up a metal bowl, she stared at her distorted reflection. It matched her mood. As she finished putting the dishes away, she couldn't stop thinking about D.J.'s question. Or the phone call that prompted it. She could just imagine Cade telling his big brother, "Hey, dude. Guess what? Mom cheated on Dad. Before you were born." And D.J., for his part, had probably stayed up half the night, tossing and turning, speculating, then deciding that maybe Dale wasn't really his father after all. Even though the truth was obvious: they both shared the same quiet demeanor and large, carpenter hands.

She needed to decompress. A power walk before her morning shower might help. Calling Brother Dog, she went to her room to change. She sat on the edge of the bed to lace up her walking shoes and spotted a pink envelope propped on the nightstand.

Holding it to her chest, she looked down at Brother Dog. His tail thumped against the nightstand.

"Daddy left for work without kissing me goodbye." She peered into the Lab's sorrowful eyes. "He's never done that before."

Brother jumped up on the bed and laid his head on Johnnie's lap. She stroked his rich brown fur as she stared at the envelope. "I never meant to hurt anyone."

Finally, she opened the card and read the message:

> Happy Birthday, Johnnie!
> You are my life,
> Dale

Pain and relief flooded her at the same time. Snuggling against the comfort of her dog, she wept. As Brother licked her face, she began to wonder: had Dale signed the card *before* or *after* last night's ordeal?

THE LINCOLN CONTINENTAL WITH A buttercream paint job sailed up to the curb at promptly seven p.m. Granny Opal blasted her horn and Johnnie sprang down the front steps to greet her.

"You look a little thin," Granny called out. She was wearing that loopy grin that seemed to grow more lopsided every year. She wore purple gauchos, a short denim jacket—to conceal her expanding waistline—and her trademark red cowboy boots. Big silver hoops looped through sagging earlobes dangled below her cropped hair.

Out of respect for her grandmother, Johnnie tried to appear cheerful, although a cloud of lead had fallen from the sky over 420 Merriweather. "Granny, I've been the same weight for years. Here, let me give you a hand with that."

Granny Opal placed a three-layer coconut cake into Johnnie's outstretched hands. "I may be retired from the business, but I can still bake a mean cake."

Johnnie smiled, taking care not to drop it. "I'm sure it will be delicious."

Early in her recovery, when she avoided sweets for fear they would trigger a binge, she refrained from saying anything derogatory every time her grandmother appeared armed with a dessert. Then one year, the year Johnnie was pregnant with Cade, she thought Granny Opal finally understood. After a meal of baked chicken and tossed salad, Johnnie's grandmother sailed into the dining room with a large head of cabbage on a crystal cake pedestal. Planted in the middle of the cabbage was a fat pink dinner candle. After everyone stopped laughing long enough to sing "Happy Birthday," Johnnie blew it out. When Johnnie quietly sighed with relief and started to open her presents, Granny Opal appeared in the doorway with a Texas sheet cake, much to the delight of a young D.J. and Dale.

Later that night, when they were getting ready for bed, Johnnie grumbled to Dale that Granny Opal was trying to sabotage her progress. Dale, to his credit, simply remarked, "Maybe she just likes baking cakes."

Granny Opal linked one arm through Johnnie's and together they mounted the steps onto the large porch. "Everything looks lovely," her grandmother commented as they entered the house.

Cade and Callie Ann were out back, playing fetch with Brother Dog. As Johnnie went to place the cake on the long farmhouse table that served as a room divider between the kitchen and the family room, she saw Granny Opal poke her head out the back door.

"Cade, when's your next baseball game? I'll come if it's not too hot."

Johnnie looked up, wondering how Cade would respond, but her grandmother had already stepped outside onto the deck and shut the door. A few minutes later, while Johnnie set out dessert plates and forks, the back door opened, and Granny Opal filed in, followed by Brother Dog. He trotted straight to the laundry room, where Johnnie could hear him lapping from his water bowl.

Granny Opal went to the sink and helped herself to a glass of tap water. "Cade told me what happened." She turned to look at Johnnie, who froze, afraid to look into her grandmother's dancing eyes. How much had Cade told her? A knot in her stomach, Johnnie watched herself pull out a chair and sit down across from her grandmother. The heady scent of birthday cake and vanilla candles filled the room. She felt a headache coming on.

Granny Opal removed one of her earrings and rubbed her earlobe. "Kids are going to drink, my dear. It's a fact of life. I told Cade I don't want to hear about him drinkin' and drivin'." She took a sip of water and set her glass in the sink. With her back to Johnnie, she added, "I know about the six games. He'll survive. In the meantime, I've got an acre of trees that need trimmin' and he's offered to do it. For free." She turned and winked at Johnnie then excused herself to go to the restroom.

Until that moment, Johnnie hadn't realized she'd been holding her breath. She dropped her head on the table and sighed with relief. She was still sitting there when Dale walked into the room. The moment he appeared, Johnnie felt like an intruder in her own home. Dale had been home for over an hour, had already showered, and yet they'd hardly exchanged two words.

Quickly, she stood and went to the sink, looking for something to do. Dale went around the island to get to the refrigerator. They moved about the kitchen, giving each other a wide berth.

His back to her, Dale finally broke the silence. "Do we have any sweet tea?"

In the background, Johnnie heard a toilet flush, then water running through the pipes. Granny Opal would appear in the kitchen any moment, and Johnnie didn't want her to know anything was wrong.

Johnnie's voice sounded wooden when she spoke. "No, but I'll make some." She turned to get the tea bags and start the water boiling.

Dale closed the refrigerator. Deep furrows lined his brow. "Johnnie …?" he started to say. Granny Opal appeared and he turned to greet her.

The old woman's eyes lit up when she saw Dale. "Hey there, handsome." She gave him a generous slap on the back. "I sure like those new countertops you installed in the bathroom."

A car door slammed in front of the house and Johnnie made a fast exit.

Leaning against the door, she watched as her friend, Whit, sauntered up the walkway, her long elegant skirt flowing as she made a graceful entrance in her strappy sandals. With her high cheekbones, caramel-colored skin, and short silver hair, she commanded attention every place she went.

"I still say we should've gone roller-skating." She held a bottle of Chardonnay in one hand and a balloon and goodie bag in the other.

Johnnie held the door open as Whit ascended the steps. "You look good in peach." She reached to give Whit a hug and took the balloon and goodie bag.

Whit turned to admire several baskets of flowers hanging from the eaves of the porch. "What a day! I dropped off dry cleaning for a client in Fort Worth then headed straight to

Dallas to hand-address five hundred wedding invitations for a lady in Highland Park." She grinned. "Next week I go clothes shopping at Neiman Marcus."

"Too bad you can't keep any of those clothes for yourself."

Whit laughed and breezed into the house, her perfume scenting the air as Johnnie followed her into the kitchen. Dale and Granny Opal were seated at the table, and Dale stood up when Whit entered the room.

Whit set the bottle of wine on the countertop while Johnnie fished through a drawer for the corkscrew.

"How's John Denver?" Whit teased, giving Dale a hug. She always said he looked just like the late folk singer.

"Oh, just rocky mountain high." Dale flashed his wide dimpled grin then sat back down.

Whit stared at him a minute and Johnnie realized her friend had picked up on the hint of sarcasm in Dale's tone. As Johnnie handed Whit the corkscrew, she glanced nervously from Whit to Dale then back to Whit.

Whit stood there a moment as if sizing up the situation. "A little tense in the house for a birthday party," she muttered.

About then, Brother Dog bounded into the kitchen from the laundry room. He rushed straight up to Whit, panting and demanding her attention.

Whit wasn't much of a dog person, but she stooped to scratch behind his ears. "Now don't go slobbering all over my feet," she warned. "I just had a pedicure."

After Cade and Callie Ann came in from the backyard, everyone sang "Happy Birthday" and they cut the cake.

As Whit went to open the wine, Johnnie took her aside and whispered, "Can you meet me for lunch next week? There's something I need to tell you."

Pulling her head back, she looked at Johnnie. "Okay, ladybug." She glanced around the room then poured a glass of wine and handed it to Johnnie. "You're not sick, are you?"

Johnnie shook her head. "No. Nothing like that."

Whit stared at her a moment, her mouth pursed in thought. Then she turned and offered Granny Opal a glass of wine.

"That would be lovely, Whit. I think we could all use a drink." Granny took the wine then pinched Cade on the cheek. "Except for you, hotshot."

Cade was hunched over a thick wedge of cake. He didn't look up.

Then Granny Opal turned her attention to Callie Ann, who had hardly touched her cake. "What's wrong, child? Don't you like coconut? You've always been my cake eater."

Callie Ann shrugged. "I'm still full from dinner, Granny. That's all."

Johnnie noticed how Granny sipped her wine and tried to act like her feelings weren't hurt. She was used to her great-granddaughter oohing and aahing over her creations, not turning her nose up and pushing her dessert plate aside.

Just then the house phone rang. Callie Ann jumped up from the table, scraping the floor with her chair. "I'll get it."

"Looks like *someone* lost their cellphone again?" Cade shoveled a forkful of cake in his mouth.

Johnnie rubbed her forehead. "Sis? You know we can't afford to keep buying you a new phone every time you turn around."

Dale took a swig of iced tea. "Your mother's right. Things are tight as it is."

Callie Ann jabbed Cade in the shoulder as she rushed past. "At least I'm not the one who got caught drinking." She seemed slightly disappointed when she glanced up from the Caller ID. "It's a payphone."

Johnnie put her fork down. "A *pay*phone? Who uses those anymore?"

"Inmates in jail," Cade belched, grinning back at his sister. "Is that your new boyfriend? Calling for you to bail him out?"

Callie Ann made a face then lifted the receiver. Johnnie nibbled her fingernail, not taking her eyes off her daughter. "You'll have to speak up," Callie Ann insisted.

Johnnie pushed her plate away and fiddled with the edge of her placemat. She'd just talked to D.J. that morning. Still ... *please don't let anything be wrong.*

Propping a hand on her slim hip, Callie Ann frowned. "Look, I'm sorry, but I can't understand a word you're saying."

Johnnie started to get up. "Callie Ann. Who is it?"

By now, Cade had twisted around in his chair, his broad shoulders squared off in a defensive position. Even Whit and Dale, who had been discussing the war in Iraq, stopped talking and turned to look at Callie Ann. And Granny Opal, Johnnie noted, had leaned back in her chair, her head tilted like a satellite dish as she, too, tried to listen in.

Callie Ann took on a superior tone. "You want to speak to *who*?" Finally, she cupped her hand over the mouthpiece. "Mom, you better take this. It's some wacko."

Smoothing her hair back over her left ear, Johnnie felt her heart pound as she took the phone from her daughter.

From the corner of her eye, she observed how her grandmother held the wine glass halfway to her mouth, her hand shaking so badly that wine sloshed out.

"Hello." She steeled herself for bad news. A sweet sickly taste filled her mouth.

The person on the other end coughed violently as if hacking up phlegm. "Johnnie Girl?"

For a split second, relief flooded her. The call wasn't about D.J. A moment later, she doubled over, overcome by what she heard: the raspy slur of a woman's voice. A voice she hadn't heard since her wedding day.

Gulping air, she tried to catch her breath as she swung around to face her family. "Mama? Mama? Where are you?"

By now, Granny Opal had struggled out of her chair and now stood by the phone, her usually rosy cheeks drained of color. "Victoria?" she gasped, her eyes wide with shock.

Before Johnnie could say another word, the line went dead.

Granny Opal gripped both lapels of her denim jacket and looked like she was going to faint.

In one quick move, Dale sprung from his chair and bolted across the room. Dropping the phone, Johnnie rushed to help him catch Granny Opal before she fell.

* * *

Johnnie's Journal
Front Porch Dispatch
Thursday 9:30 a.m.
March 29, 2007

Mama,

At least we know you're not dead. Ghosts don't call home from a payphone. A lot has happened since the last time you left. Grandpa Grubbs suffered two more heart attacks—the third time was a charm. After he died, Granny Opal started baking healthy cakes, but nobody wanted to buy them. When she put real eggs and butter back in, her business picked up. Later, I overheard her tell one of her best customers, "Jonathan's diet didn't kill him. Victoria did."

To hear Granny Opal admit this—you know how private she is—well, it made me question everything about our family and my very existence, which brings me to my next point.

I remember our secret trip, Mama. It was sometime before my sixth birthday. We boarded a Greyhound bus, and you made me swear not to tell anyone about our visit to the Army post. "Cross your heart and hope to die, Johnnie Girl. Don't you dare breathe a word about this to anyone. If Granny or Gramps asks where we've been, you tell 'em we went to Salt Flat to see Aunt Beryl." After the guards waved us on, I asked you why there was a star on every jeep and truck we passed along the way. Barely glancing at me, you said with a flick of your hand, "Oh, those belong to Uncle Sam."

Then we ate hamburgers at a picnic table with the tall

handsome officer you made goo-goo eyes at. As I polished off my French fries, he pinched you on the behind, and you giggled all flirty-like. Licking my fingers, I pretended not to see. Later, before we climbed on the bus, he bent to kiss me goodbye, and I asked, "Are you my Uncle Sam?" You let out a nervous laugh.

His smile vanished and he rubbed at something in his eye. At last he touched me on the cheek. "Be good for your mama. I'll see you when I get back."

I stuck a pigtail in my mouth and sucked on the loose ends. You always hated that, Mama. That day you yanked it out of my mouth so fast my teeth hurt. But it's what you said that caused my throat to swell. "Didn't you get enough to eat without eating your hair, too?"

About then, I heard him say, "Hey, Vic, lay off. She's just a kid."

For one brief moment, Mama, I hated you and loved him.

As the bus rolled through the night, you leaned your head against the window and cried. I stared up at the stars, asking God why everything had to be a secret.

It wasn't until years later that I learned the truth: his name wasn't Sam, he wasn't my uncle, and I would never see him again.

Johnnie

CHAPTER 5

~◆~

Lunch with Granny

"Have you been to the cemetery lately?" Granny Opal asked at lunch later that day.

Ida Lou's Tea House on historic Main Street in Portion wasn't Johnnie's favorite place to go—the food was bland and heavy on the mayo—but Granny Opal suggested it and Johnnie didn't want to hurt her feelings.

Taking a bite of her chicken salad, Johnnie set her fork down and hesitated before answering, "Yes, but I didn't get out of the car. Why?"

Her grandmother held a turkey sandwich halfway to her mouth. "There were flowers on your Uncle Johnny's grave when I stopped by there on his birthday last Sunday."

Johnnie leaned back in her chair and placed her hands on the linen tablecloth. "An old girlfriend, maybe?"

Granny Opal bit into her sandwich. "I think it was your mama." She stated the words as plainly as if she were commenting on the weather. "That phone call last night convinces me."

Electric tingles zipped up Johnnie's spine as she stared at her grandmother. After she and Dale had helped Granny back to her seat, Cade scooped the phone off the floor and kept calling the number back, but no one answered.

Johnnie reached across the table for her grandmother's hand. "It means she's been in the area."

Granny Opal's chest rose visibly as she said, "They were cheap plastic flowers, too. Probably scavenged from other graves." She patted Johnnie's hand, then picked up her sandwich and resumed eating.

Johnnie glanced at the half-eaten mound of chicken salad on her plate. She'd lost her appetite two nights ago after Dale found out about the affair, and now she felt queasy. As she took a sip of iced tea, one of Grandpa's dying remarks rolled through her mind for the second time that week: "I think your granny is hiding something from me."

She watched as her grandmother picked up a potato chip, studied it, then popped it into her mouth. After a moment, her grandmother seemed to notice she had stopped eating. "Ready for dessert? Ida Lou makes the best banana pudding."

"You go ahead, Granny. I can't possibly eat another bite."

Granny Opal gestured toward her midsection and winked. "It won't kill me to miss dessert."

After the waitress stopped by to refill their drinks, Johnnie folded her arms and leaned across the table. "There's something I need to ask you."

Her grandmother arched her penciled eyebrows. "Oh?"

Johnnie measured her words carefully. "Before Grandpa died, he told me you were keeping something from him. About Mama's whereabouts."

Granny Opal picked up a cloth napkin, dabbed the corners of her mouth, then dropped the napkin on her empty plate and leaned forward. "Guilty as charged. I won't lie to you, my dear. Shortly after your wedding, I received a handful of postcards from truck stops around the country."

"Truck stops?" A couple of diners glanced in their direction. Johnnie lowered her voice. "So Mama took up with a trucker?"

Granny Opal mumbled something under her breath and started brushing imaginary crumbs from her lap. She wouldn't look up.

Johnnie studied her a moment. All at once it became clear. "Wait, you think Mama was turning tricks?"

Reaching into her purse, Granny Opal pulled out a tube of lipstick. "Some things are better left unsaid, my dear." She began to freshen her lipstick.

Johnnie's chest tightened. She pushed her plate away and took another sip of iced tea. Surely she had known this about her mama, on some level, for a long time.

Granny Opal dropped the tube in her purse and looked up. "I had to protect you and your grandpa. Despite everything we'd been through, Victoria was still his little girl."

A slow anger burned inside Johnnie. "Do you know what Mama said to me at my wedding, right before Dale and I cut the cake?" *A six-tier wedding cake that could've fed half of Portion.*

Granny Opal suddenly looked tired. She pushed back from the table, her red lips half open.

Instantly, Johnnie regretted her impulsive remark. What good would it do now but bring her granny more heartache? "Never mind," she said as her mama's searing words flashed through her mind: *Johnnie Girl, every time I look in your face I cringe. I never should've let Poppy name you after my dead brother.*

"That's the last time I saw her," Granny Opal said, staring off. "She was standing there in the church parking lot, waving as you and Dale drove off in his dad's '57 Thunderbird convertible. She looked so pretty in blue taffeta."

Tears formed in Johnnie's eyes. Until this moment, she'd never stopped to consider her grandmother's memories of that day. Only her mother's painful, cryptic remarks.

As if unable to dwell too long in the past, Granny Opal turned to Johnnie and smiled. "Well, my dear. Your mama might have missed out on everything else in your life, but I will give her credit for one thing. She did make it to your wedding."

The waitress came with the check. After Johnnie paid the bill, Granny Opal fished some change out of her purse and left the tip.

Out on the sidewalk, Granny looped her arm through Johnnie's and they headed up Main Street, stopping every few minutes to admire something in a storefront window.

Finally, Johnnie turned. "Why do you think Mama hung up before we even had a chance to talk?"

Granny patted her hand. "Maybe she lost her nerve. Let's hope she calls back."

At Holy Grounds Gift Shop, a block away, they stopped to admire an Easter basket filled to the brim with bright plastic eggs. The aroma of freshly brewed coffee beckoned them inside. Standing before a rack of greeting cards, Johnnie heard her grandmother strike up a conversation with the shopkeeper as if she'd known the woman her whole life. They discussed everything from inflated gasoline prices to the drop-off in attendance at mainstream churches.

After a while, Johnnie found herself pulling out card after card and reading the messages. There were cards for anniversaries, birthdays, sympathies, and graduations. Even cards for pets. Finally, she plucked up a card that stated: *I'M SORRY FOR HURTING YOU.*

A sharp pain hit her in the gut and she stood there a moment, waiting for her vision to clear. While her grandmother finished shopping, she paid for the card and waited by the door. Mounted high on a plastered wall, a massive wooden cross made from old fence posts and adorned with a crown of thorns mocked her from across the shop.

A voice, like thunder, clapped in her ears: *you sinner.*

Feeling lightheaded, she stepped outside into the clean spring air.

AN HOUR BEFORE DALE WAS due home from work, Johnnie placed a crystal vase of cut jonquils on his nightstand. Years ago, right after they moved in and before Dale waved his magic hammer at the ramshackle house, she and Dale had spent an afternoon planting gnarled bulbs deep in the earth. Every spring they waited for the buttery trumpets to shoot up from their green stems and announce that winter was over. Standing back to admire the fragrant bouquet, she opened the card she picked up at lunch and wrote:

> Dale,
> A hundred years from now, I want to wake up with you and see the jonquils.
>
> Your Johnnie

LATER THAT NIGHT, AFTER SHE slipped into her nightshirt, she watched Dale sit on the edge of the bed and stare at the vase of jonquils. When at last she pulled down the covers on her side of the bed, Dale still hadn't bothered to open the card. Holding her breath, she waited for him to say something.

Instead, Dale stood, pulled off his jeans, and tossed them over the back of a chair. His broad shoulders sagged as he sat back down on the edge of the bed, his back to her.

Removing his reading glasses, he turned to face her.

"I've never been unfaithful to you." His blue eyes stared without blinking. "I've never screwed around on you. Not once." He turned away as if he couldn't stand the sight of her.

She picked up a pillow and hugged it to her body, an attempt to shield herself from his wrath.

His weight shifted on the bed. "How do I know that you'll never do it again?"

His words stung. She stared at the back of his blond head.

"Dale, it happened a long time ago." Her voice cracked. "I made a horrible mistake."

From the nightstand, the flowers filled the room with a sweet scent. For a moment, Dale turned and seemed to contemplate them and the unopened card. "Johnnie, I need some time. I'm trying to figure out how you kept this from me all these years."

With that, he picked up his pillow and left without a sound. Everything inside of her dropped as she listened to him make his way down the hall to spend another night on the couch. A floorboard squeaked. She heard Brother Dog come out of Callie Ann's room. His claws clicked against the hardwood floor as he followed Dale into the den.

She threw her pillow down and went into the bathroom to brush her teeth. Squirting toothpaste on her brush, she began to scrub. Thoughts of Dale and her mother filled her mind, and she brushed even harder. At some point, the bristles reached too far back on her tongue. She gagged. Utter terror shot through her as she fought the urge to vomit. The sensation lasted only a second, but it left her shaking.

When it passed, Johnnie looked in the mirror. "Okay, relax. You've made it. You've won."

But an inner voice, a voice she hadn't heard in years—except in her dreams—crept into her mind, interrupting her thoughts about Dale and her mother. It screamed, *Do it again!*

The urge to jam the toothbrush back down her throat to make herself vomit was so strong, she started to give in. She gagged once more, then froze in fear.

Looking up slowly, she glared long and hard into the mirror, staring down an old enemy.

"Go away!" she hissed as if another presence were actually in the room.

In the middle of the night, Johnnie woke and reached for Dale, only to find his side of the bed vacant. Foggy from sleep, she wondered if he'd gone to the bathroom, then she remembered he'd been sleeping on the couch.

She threw back the covers and padded down the hall to tell him to come back to bed. If anyone should be sleeping on the couch, it should be her. She was startled to find him sitting in the chair by the fireplace with the lamp on, a framed picture in his hand.

Dale glanced at her over his reading glasses. "D.J. didn't get his height from my side of the family." He held the picture up for her to see.

In the photograph, taken sometime before D.J. graduated from high school, their oldest son held up a largemouth bass. Next to him and shorter by several inches stood Dale, one arm thrown awkwardly around D.J.'s shoulder.

"Cagle was tall, wasn't he?" Dale said.

Her stomach dropped. He was connecting dots. She could see where he was going with this and it scared her. Her chin quivered. "The affair ended a month and a half before I got pregnant." Her voice caught in her throat and it came out a hoarse whisper. "D.J. got his height from Grandpa Grubbs. And from what I remember, my father was tall."

Dale glanced at the picture then back to Johnnie. "Since the other night, I've actually been wondering if D.J.'s mine."

Nauseated, Johnnie took a gulp of air. First D.J., now Dale.

After a long silence, Dale stood, gazed into the empty fireplace, and let out a weary sigh. High above the oak mantle, encased in a large frame, another picture seemed to capture Dale's attention. Tilting his head, he focused on an enlarged black and white photo of a pilot and his crew as they stood in front of a B-52 on the ramp at Carswell Air Force Base.

"I don't know which my father loved more: flying for the Air Force or getting hit on by all those women who flocked around him in droves." He paused. "My old man had a saying: 'What goes TDY stays TDY.' Les Kitchen may've been a lousy husband when he was away on temporary duty, but he was a good father when he was home. I swore I'd never treat my wife like he treated Mom."

Dale continued to stare at the photo as if Johnnie had left the room.

Tears streamed down her face. She wanted to run to him, but some small measure of dignity stopped her. She turned and went back down the hallway toward the empty bedroom.

* * *

Johnnie's Journal
Palm Sunday Service
April 1, 2007

Dale,

You smile at the little children as they enter the sanctuary, waving palm branches and singing "Hosanna in the Highest." It's the first time I've seen you smile in days. But you're not smiling at them, are you? You're smiling at memories.

I start to say, "Remember when," but you turn away, even in church. Today feels more like Judgment Day. And I am the criminal on the other cross, hanging on by a strap of hope.

What if Jesus had held a grudge? Turned a cold shoulder to the condemned man ....

What if forgiveness was nothing more than an April Fools' joke?

Johnnie

PS: Good thing we don't live in the Middle East. The Taliban would've stoned me to death.

CHAPTER 6

⁓⌐

Wednesday, April 4, 2007

A WEEK HAD PASSED SINCE Johnnie had invited Whit to lunch. Today, on their way to Olive Garden, they took a detour by Portion Lake. Far from the marina and dam, they huddled on the shore of a secluded cove, sheltered on one side by a high bluff.

Pushing hair of out of her eyes, Johnnie gestured to a line of trees high over her right shoulder. "In the fall and winter, when those trees are bare, you can see Granny's sprawling white house from here."

"Her property must be worth a fortune, just for the view." Whit turned her gaze from the bluff back to the water, and Johnnie marveled at her friend's profile. Whit's long, brown, elegant neck appeared as seamless as a young swan's. Though they were the same age, Johnnie thought Whit looked ten years younger. And there was no sign of the trauma Whit had endured decades ago at the hands of her drug-crazed mother. An injury that should have left her disfigured.

"You look so young and beautiful, Whit. How do you do it?"

Her friend laughed. "Oh ladybug, I was blessed with good genes. But so were you with that mess of auburn hair and creamy complexion." Without giving Johnnie a chance to respond, she pointed to a dilapidated structure sticking halfway out of the water. "I bet that old dock has seen better days."

Johnnie welcomed the change of subject. She wished she could see herself as Whit did. "I've been pestering Dale to replace the boards, but he always comes up with an excuse."

Whit buttoned the collar of her jacket against a brisk April wind. "So get Cade to do it. I bet he's good with a hammer."

Despite the noon sun, Johnnie shivered. "He got spooked one time when he and D.J. were down here night fishing under a full moon. Said he saw someone on the dock, then in the water. D.J. tried to tell him it was just the moon reflecting on the water, but Cade didn't believe him. He swore he saw a ghost."

Whit elbowed her in the ribs. "Sister Girl saw a ghost once. Good thing Mama's gun wasn't loaded. Turns out it was one of her good-for-nothing boyfriends trying to sneak in the back door."

They both laughed at Whit's attempt to lighten the mood. Then a long silence stretched before them while Johnnie gathered her thoughts. Her mind swirled with bits and pieces of the past and present and she wasn't sure where to begin.

Nearby, the leafy trees swayed in the wind, and she stuffed her hands in the pockets of her coat sweater. "Grandpa and I spent a lot of time down here. We used to sit on the dock and he'd stare out at the water as if he was looking for something. One time I asked him what he was looking for, and he said 'forgiveness.'"

Whit pressed a manicured finger to her plum lips but said nothing.

Hunched against the chill, Johnnie wiggled her knees to stay warm. "When I was about nine, I heard him and Mama fighting. She was still traipsing in and out of the house on a regular basis. She smarted off to him about something, and he lost his temper and yelled, 'If you hadn't gotten knocked up, your brother might still be alive.'" Johnnie closed her eyes for a moment. "I was too young to understand what he meant, but later, when we were getting ready for bed, I asked Mama if Grandpa was right about her getting knocked up and she smacked me so hard I wore her handprint for days."

Whit nodded as if she understood, then glanced away.

The smells of the lake, damp earth, and new vegetation brought back more memories. Johnnie picked up a rock, chucked it in the water, and watched the ripples move across the dark surface as the rock sunk to the bottom. Then she continued her story. "The next day at dawn, I woke to find Mama gone. In the hazy gray of morning, I snuck down here and found her still in her nightgown, standing there on the dock, staring out at the water. Sobbing. When she caught me spying through the brush, she flailed her arms and I took off running. As I scrambled up the path, tripping and skinning my knees, I heard her cry out in a strangled voice: "Stay away from this place. You hear? It'll bring you nothing but heartache."

Whit pulled off her sunglasses and stared straight ahead. "What's going on, ladybug? What happened here?"

As Johnnie pondered the best way to begin, a large airliner roared low overhead on its final approach into Dallas/Forth Worth Airport. She glanced up at its big silver belly and waited until the jet disappeared behind the treetops. After the thunder from the jet faded, her shoulders sagged and she turned to face Whit.

"Well, for starters, my uncle drowned here several months before I was born. That much I know."

"Your poor granny. I'm sure she still grieves."

"The circumstances around his death aré off-limits," Johnnie went on, "along with his old bedroom."

Whit's brown eyes darted swiftly around the cove as if some unknown danger lurked nearby. "Maybe it's just too painful for her to talk about."

Picking at the sleeve of her sweater, Johnnie confessed, "I

didn't bring you all the way down here to talk about my dead uncle."

"So why *did* you bring me here?"

Johnnie tried to ignore a dull pain in her chest. "I cheated on Dale," she said, her voice as stiff as the wind coming off the lake. "Here. A long time ago, when the trees were bare and you could see all the way up to the house."

Whit chewed on the stem of her sunglasses. "Does Dale know?"

Johnnie massaged her temples. "He does now."

Whit craned her neck and fixed a quizzical look at Johnnie. "How long has he known?"

At this point, Johnnie realized she was more afraid to tell Whit how Dale found out about the affair than about the affair itself. She glanced up at the sky, then over at Whit. "About a week. He found out the night before my birthday."

Whit narrowed her eyes. "The night *before* your birthday?" She paused, as if remembering something. "So, what made you decide to tell him now?"

Johnnie glanced at a blue heron perched on one leg in the water. "I didn't exactly tell him. He overheard it in a conversation."

Whit frowned. "A conversation? With who?"

Johnnie felt her lungs deflate. "Cade."

Whit pulled back, a huge crease forming across her forehead. "Cade?"

Johnnie nodded, sensing her friend's disapproval.

Whit wedged her sunglasses into her silver spikes of hair and studied her polished nails for a second. "Now why would you be telling your business to your son and not your husband?"

As her mind drifted back to that horrible night with Cade, Johnnie felt she had to defend her actions.

"Cade was freaking out," she explained. "Said he hated himself, wished he were dead." She shook her head as if she could dislodge the terrible memory. "I was terrified he might hurt himself. I had to let him know he could survive anything. It just slipped out. I didn't plan it."

She stopped to catch her breath and to gauge Whit's reaction.

Whit made a face. "I'm not sure if I follow you."

"When Cade told me he wished he were dead, I looked at him and said, 'You think you're the only one who's done something you're ashamed of?'" Johnnie let out a nervous laugh. "That poor kid. He actually thought the worst thing I'd ever done was stick my finger down my throat."

She finished the rest of the story about how Dale found out.

Whit looked at Johnnie long and hard. "How's Dale?"

Johnnie threw her head back and fought the urge to scream. "He's been sleeping on the couch for a week now. I don't know if it'll ever be the same between us. Whenever he walks in a room and I'm there …." She broke off, too drained to continue.

Whit brushed at something on her long skirt. "How are the kids?"

Johnnie's throat constricted, and her eyes filled with tears. Whit hunted in her leather pocketbook for a tissue.

"Callie Ann's hardly speaking to me," Johnnie sobbed.

Whit patted Johnnie on the back. "Sister Girl will come around. Just give her some space."

"And D.J. … well …." Johnnie's voice trailed off. She blew her nose into the tissue.

"So D.J. knows, too?"

Sniffling, Johnnie told Whit about D.J.'s phone call the morning of her birthday. "My God, Whit. I've made a mess of everything."

Whit nodded. "So, you wanna tell me about this fling of yours?"

Whit's question caught Johnnie off guard, but she kept a straight face. "His name was Jeral Cagle." As her story unraveled, she felt both shame and pleasure in the telling. "He was tall, tan, played on a men's softball team. The last time I saw him he came struttin' out of the bathroom like a male stripper in nothing but a jockstrap and a cowboy hat."

Whit's jaw dropped. "Lord Almighty."

Johnnie swallowed, wishing she'd brought along a bottle of water. "The man was built, Whit. And he had the merriest blue eyes ...."

Whit flung her hand in the air. "Stop right there, ladybug. I'm gonna need a cold shower or a confessional booth."

Johnnie went silent.

Whit pursed her lips. "Look, I get that the guy was hot. But that's not reason enough to have an affair. What was really going on?"

Johnnie forced herself to breathe. "I've been asking myself that for years. All I can figure is this: Grandpa had just suffered his second heart attack. By then Mama had disappeared for good, and Dale was out of town on a big commercial job and couldn't come home. He was working so hard to make a name for himself. Although I'd been in therapy, I was still messed up and vulnerable. I bumped into Jeral shortly after we brought Grandpa home from the hospital. Despite my better judgment, I fell under his spell. First we went to his condo, but his roommates asked too many questions. I couldn't take a chance at the apartment so we started meeting here."

She mashed the tissue against her nose. She looked Whit square in the eye. "Where Dale was careful and steady, Jeral was wild and adventurous."

"Did they know each other?"

Shame surged through her body. "Dale used to work for Cagle Construction before he went out on his own. He liked Old Man Cagle but he never had any respect for his son. He said Jeral acted entitled. When Old Man Cagle retired and handed things over to Jeral, Dale left to start his own company. Jeral did everything he could to run Dale out of business."

"Guess it didn't work. Any chance they could run into each other?"

Johnnie shook her head. "Nope, he's been dead for years.

He wrapped his Corvette around a tree right after his second divorce."

Whit lifted an eyebrow. "But why here? Seems to me this place is off-limits."

Johnnie stuffed the shriveled tissue in her pocket. "I've been drawn to this place my whole life. I come here looking for answers and leave with more questions."

Whit looped her arm through Johnnie's and they began to stroll along the shoreline. "I think you brought that fellow here to thumb your nose at something."

"Like what?" For a fleeting second, Johnnie felt small and insignificant next to her tall, regal friend.

"You tell me."

"You mean God?"

"Not necessarily."

Johnnie closed her eyes as the heat of truth fired through her body. The words formed on her tongue and spilled out. "You mean all that heartache Mama warned me about?"

"Yes, ma'am!" Whit clapped her hands with conviction.

They stopped and stared at each other then resumed their stroll.

Johnnie spoke first. "There's been so much information withheld from me all my life. Then I went and did the same thing to Dale. But my biggest concern now is to take care of my family. Make things right again."

"Absolutely," Whit shot back. "Just don't forget to take care of yourself in the process."

This last remark made Johnnie flinch, and right away she recognized the need to tell someone she trusted about her fear of a relapse. Normally, she would tell Dale these things, but that was out of the question now.

"Whit, all of this upheaval has triggered something in me. Since last week, I've had the urge to make myself sick. To jam a toothbrush down my throat every time I brush my teeth. It happened again this morning."

Johnnie glanced down at her hands, then stopped abruptly and held her right hand out. "See these scars? These are the leftovers."

Whit steered them toward an old log where they could sit down.

"I'm scared," Johnnie admitted. "I've come too far to give in. I've worked too hard."

Out of compassion, Whit took Johnnie's pale hand in hers and lightly brushed her fingertips over Johnnie's knuckles. "You and I both know about scars."

Johnnie jerked her head up. Her concern shifted from herself to her friend. "Yeah, but mine were self-inflicted. What your mother did to you was horrible." She trembled, but it wasn't from the cold.

Gently, Whit dropped Johnnie's hand. "I had just turned sixteen. I had a big track meet coming up. I was hoping to qualify for state."

Whit looked off into the distance, and Johnnie knew she was remembering the day her mother threw a pan of boiling water on her, leaving Whit with third-degree burns on her left arm and breast. Miraculously, the burns on the left side of her neck and lower jaw healed completely.

"I missed the track meet, of course. I was in no shape to run. But the worst part," Whit added, her mouth working as if she were trying not to cry, "the worst part is that Mama never apologized."

After a while, Whit shifted on the log. Her eyes held the look of someone who had tried to make peace with the past. She picked up her pocketbook. "Now listen here, about that *urge* you've had ... to make yourself sick. You better nip that thing in the bud. Don't you dare let that ol' devil get the best of you."

Hearing the word *devil* made Johnnie's skin prickle.

For a moment she was sixteen again, alone in the hall bathroom, a window cracked open to air out the stink. Huddled over one of Mama's amber-colored ashtrays, she was trying to set fire to the wooden spoon she'd just used to make herself hurl. Only moments ago, she'd jammed the spoon too far. The curved end lodged at the back of her throat. She couldn't pull it out. Terror ripped through her body. She thought she was choking to death.

Suddenly the spoon broke free. She gagged and spit up bile with traces of blood. Once she'd stopped shaking enough to collect her thoughts, she decided she must destroy the spoon, and hopefully, the dark, evil thing that had taken over her body. How else could she explain the strange urges that seized her, the urges she was powerless to stop, no matter how hard she prayed to Jesus to make them go away?

Fumbling with the handle of the gnawed spoon, she took her mama's cigarette lighter and held the spoon over the flame. The damp wood smoldered. Just as she commanded, "Get behind me, Satan," Grandpa's voice roared through the closed door.

"Johnnie Girl, what the hell is going on in there? Are you trying to burn the house down?"

Whit's voice cut into Johnnie's thoughts. "This bark's hurting my butt." A gust picked up and Whit stood and slipped on her sunglasses. "C'mon. I'm starving."

Her teeth chattering, Johnnie pulled herself up off the log and followed Whit. "Hot soup sounds good."

As they headed toward their cars, something caught Whit's eye and she hiked off down the shoreline toward the dock. "Does Granny Opal come down here often?" she called over her shoulder.

Shielding her eyes from the sun, Johnnie watched as Whit stooped for a closer inspection of the dock. "No. Never," she answered, stepping over a dead fish that had washed up on the muddy bank.

Whit motioned for Johnnie to come closer.

Squinting, Johnnie saw a faded plastic rose tied to the dock by its stem.

Her stomach lurched, and she began to shake as she glimpsed

around. "It means she's been here, too."

"Who?" Whit tugged off her sunglasses and stared at Johnnie.

Johnnie felt her breath being sucked out of her lungs. "Mama," she whispered.

LATER THAT NIGHT, JOHNNIE DECIDED to face Dale straight up, as D.J. would say, and do whatever it took to get him to open up and talk to her. The biggest obstacle: Dale's inability to forgive. She would have to work to regain his trust. She turned off the kitchen lights and headed to the bedroom.

Cade was at the library, and Callie Ann had gone to the garage to work out on an old exercise bike. After Callie Ann made drill team, Johnnie noticed an increase in her daughter's workout routine. Despite her own past, she tried not to let this worry her.

Dale had just come out of the bathroom when Johnnie entered the room, locking the door behind her. Dale started to walk past her, but Johnnie reached for his arm.

"Dale? We need to talk."

He stood there still dressed in jeans and the T-shirt the kids had given him for Father's Day. His breath smelled of mouthwash, and he had tucked his leather shaving kit under one arm. He shrugged, making no further attempt to go around her. "What's there to talk about? The damage is done."

She stood before him, hearing the pleading in her own voice. "I've told you a dozen times how sorry I am. I'll do anything you ask, Dale. Just don't shut me out."

Without thinking, she dropped to her knees and grabbed hold of his legs, clinging to him as if her life depended on it. She realized she was groveling, but she didn't care. This was the first time they'd really touched in over a week. She craned her neck, peering into his blue eyes.

At first Dale stood frozen, looking down at her, unmoved by her sudden and unexpected gesture. Then something in his face broke, and his eyes seemed to soften. He blinked, as if in surrender. Finally, he placed one hand on top of her head like a minister about to offer a blessing.

Grateful for his touch, Johnnie buried her face against his thigh. After a moment, she untucked his shirt and reached for his belt, but Dale stopped her. He showed no interest. She heard his quiet exhale of breath, then felt him give her a dismissive pat on the head as if she were a small child or a friendly dog. She didn't move. In all the years they'd been together, she had never known Dale to turn away from sex.

After a long silence, he lifted his hand and walked out of the room, leaving her there on her knees, feeling like a rejected whore.

Pushing herself up off the bare floor, she gathered her pride and went after him. "Dale, where are you going? You can't just walk out. We need to talk."

"I'm going where I can get a decent night's sleep."

* * *

Johnnie's Journal
(hardcopy sent snail mail)
1:30 a.m.
April 5, 2007

Dear Abby:

I am the wife of a carpenter. You should see what my husband can do with his hands. He can turn a piece of plywood into a thing of beauty. A pile of river rocks into a welcoming hearth. A falling down house into a showplace. What he can do with his hands he can't do with his heart. He can't find the tools to forgive me.

I was his rough piece of plywood, his pile of unpolished rocks, a work in progress when we met. A young woman at war with herself, battling an enemy—bulimia—that had invaded my life and held me captive since puberty. My husband took me into his home and heart, and he got me the help I needed to mend. But I was young and foolish, and I cheated on him shortly after our wedding. The affair only lasted a few weeks, but I kept it from him for twenty-three years.

All I can figure is I wanted to be with someone who didn't know I was broken. Who wouldn't try to fix me.

Now the secret is out. My husband is hurt and confused, my children are caught in the middle, and it's all I can do to keep the walls from falling down around me. On the one hand, I'm glad it's out in the open. The guilt can eat you alive. On the other hand, a giant wrecking ball has taken a swing at my marriage.

Living In A House Divided

CHAPTER 7

~∽

1984
Pecan Grove Apartments

IN THE APARTMENT HOUSE JOHNNIE shared with Dale at the start of their marriage, Johnnie had needed to choose her binging times with care. It was 11 a.m. and Dale had been gone for two hours.

Johnnie eyed the first batch of warm cookies as if she was looking for something, someone, in each tempting bite. As she slid the spatula under another golden morsel, her mouth watered. She listened to the sound of children's voices filtering in from the preschool behind the apartment as she shoved another cookie into her mouth, feeling her senses overwhelmed with the texture and flavor of butter, flour, and sugar. In her haste to mix the dough, she'd left out the vanilla and almond extract, but she barely noticed the missing ingredients. Granny Opal would have been scandalized.

With each bite, her panic mounted. The children's voices grew louder, their playground chatter coming through the ceiling vents. Her heart raced as she glugged two glasses of milk and downed three more cookies. The walls of her stomach expanded. Her gut hurt but not enough to stop. Not yet. She would know when. When her body rebelled. When she could no longer stand up straight. When she had to double over just to breathe. The timer dinged and the heat from the oven hit her in the face as she removed the second pan.

Reaching for another cookie, she flipped on the exhaust fan over the stove to try to drown out the noise coming in from the outside, the happy noise of life going on around her. She glanced again at the clock. Eleven-fifteen. She'd been in the tiny kitchen bingeing ever since Dale left at 9 a.m. Already she dreaded the appointment with the shrink in two hours and she still needed to work out. Blocking all this from her mind, she crammed down another cookie.

By now, she had stopped tasting.

A knock at the door startled her. Her heart pounded and she spit a glob of half-chewed cookie into the sink. My God, who could be at the door this time of morning? Please don't let it be the sweet elderly woman two doors down who needed Johnnie to carry her groceries in from the car. Or Granny and Grandpa, stopping by unannounced. Or dear God, a policeman, right there in the middle of a binge. There to inform her they'd found her mama's body. Strangled or stabbed. Naked in a ditch. Cut up and dumped in a suitcase. Not now. Not like this. Not with food all over her face and in between her teeth and gums, her hands greasy from cookie dough. Her unwashed body smelly and in need of a shower. The air in the tiny apartment reeked with the heavy aroma of baking.

Johnnie held her breath and crept to the front door in her socks. Peeking out the peephole, she cradled her bulging stomach in her right forearm and imagined this is what it felt like to be pregnant. She would only open the door if it was a cop.

Two young men in skinny black ties and white dress shirts were already walking away. Relief flooded her. The Mormons could go save somebody else's immortal soul today.

Back in the kitchen, she dumped the greasy cookie sheets and mixing bowl in the dishwasher, wiped down the counter, lit a candle, and headed down the hall toward the torture chamber.

As she turned on the faucet and bent over the commode to heave, Dale's voice invaded her thoughts. She slammed the bathroom door and tried to block his words from her mind.

Last week, he'd come home in the middle of the morning to pick up some tool he'd forgotten. She never heard the front door open. He caught her in her ratty nightgown, frying up a pound of frozen hamburger meat. She stared at him in disbelief. She might as well have been caught stealing.

His blue eyes unwavering, he clenched his fists at his sides.

Trapped, exposed, with nowhere to run, all she could do was cover her face with her hands and mumble, "Don't look at me."

Ignoring her plea, he walked up and kissed her on the forehead.

His voice was so quiet and calm. "Johnnie, why aren't you better yet? After all the money I've spent?"

She half-shrugged, trying not to choke up. What could she say? Even she didn't understand why she did what she did.

He started to leave. "Don't you have an appointment later?"

Nodding, she turned the stove off and stared at the skillet full of gray hamburger meat.

"By the way, I'm taking off early today. There's an old house I want to show you over on Merriweather—a rambling brick bungalow that's just come on the market. Needs a lot of work. Nothing I can't handle on weekends."

It was all she could do to speak. "I can't wait to see it, honey."

A house. A house that hasn't been tainted with her sickness. A bathroom she hasn't thrown up in. A kitchen where she will wear pretty aprons and cook for Dale.

CHAPTER 8

~✺~

Thursday Morning, April 5, 2007

"YOU PUT DALE WHERE?" JOHNNIE clutched the phone and peeked out the kitchen window at her new neighbor, a portly airline pilot who had just moved into the neglected gray cottage across the street.

The house had sat vacant for years, except for an occasional renter. Then last week, overnight it seemed, a SOLD sign went up and the pilot moved in. No moving van, no pickup truck full of furniture or boxes. Only a faded red VW Bus in the skinny driveway, a couple of foldout lawn chairs on the front porch, and two cats sunning themselves on the windowsills. In his gray uniform and pilot's cap, he reminded Johnnie of a younger Captain Kangaroo, minus the mustache.

While she watched the man poke his small puffy hand in the mailbox, she tried to concentrate on what she was hearing on the other end of the line. It was just too unbelievable.

"Well, I couldn't very well put Dale in your old bedroom, now could I?" Granny Opal's voice sounded as crisp as the buttered toast Johnnie imagined her granny had served Dale earlier that morning.

"But Uncle Johnny's bedroom is off-limits," Johnnie

protested, more irritated than betrayed. She took a slug of coffee and watched her new neighbor linger at his mailbox, the flap still open. He kept one rubber-soled shoe propped on the curb.

"The man has ladies' hips," she whispered to Brother Dog, curled nearby. She studied her neighbor's round backside and recalled something Grandpa Grubbs said to her years ago: "Never trust a man whose butt is bigger than his shoulders." Despite her bad mood, she laughed aloud, a horsey laugh that sent Brother Dog scrambling to his feet for the back of the house.

Granny Opal's cheerful voice twittered on. "Well, it seems so silly now, doesn't it? It is just a room, after all."

"Yes, but …." Johnnie caught herself. How many times had she explained to her girlfriends on sleepovers that the closed-off room was a shrine to her dead uncle? Her grandparents might as well have posted a sign on the door that said: KEEP OUT.

"I told Dale he could stay here as long as he liked, while you two work out your differences."

Differences. As if she and Dale had merely had a spat. Telling Whit about the affair was one thing, but Granny Opal? Forget it.

Johnnie hesitated. "Granny, what did Dale tell you?"

"I didn't ask for the gritty details, my dear. He just said you two had a disagreement."

"Did he tell you he's been sleeping on the couch for over a week?"

"Yes. He's having back problems because of it."

"Granny, didn't he tell you *why* he's been sleeping on the couch?"

"No, my dear, he did not. That's between you kids. You're both adults. You need to work it out."

And just like that, Granny Opal hung up.

With the hum of the dial tone in her ear, Johnnie tried to

digest the news that Dale had spent the night in her dead uncle's old bedroom. In a daze, she continued to stare at the new neighbor, who now ambled over and stood in the middle of the street, waving his arms like he was trying to flag someone down. He had such small hands for a man of his girth. She craned her neck to get a better look. There were no cars coming either direction that she could tell. She felt bad she hadn't introduced herself. But after all that had happened last week, she hadn't felt too neighborly.

She hung up the phone and went to dump a full pot of coffee down the drain. She'd made it early that morning, positive Dale would return to fill his thermos before heading out for the day. Until Granny Opal's cheerful announcement, Johnnie had no idea where Dale had spent the night. She'd assumed he'd checked into a motel, not hit Granny Opal up for a place to stay.

The pilot stopped waving his arms. They hung limp at his sides. His whole body seemed to slump, and the bill of his pilot cap covered his face. He looked like he could use a friend.

Picking up the coffeepot, she grabbed two mugs and rushed out the front door.

"Good morning." She flew down the steps and headed toward the street. "I've got a pot of coffee and no one to share it with."

The man looked up, startled at first.

Johnnie motioned at his dull gray uniform. "Are you coming or going?" She realized she'd intruded on something private but now it was too late to retreat. Her eyes followed a trail of crumbs from his chin to his jacket lapel.

His small mouth twitched into a cautious smile. "Hello there, Miss." He stuck out a doughy hand and took the mug Johnnie offered. "Eugene Marvel. Pilot for hire." He laughed as if this was a standard line. But it seemed to Johnnie that he was trying too hard to sound cheerful.

She introduced herself and poured his coffee. "Are you

looking to remodel? My husband's company specializes in older homes." She glanced at the crumbling gray cottage, seeing its potential.

Mr. Marvel tipped his hat back as though deep in thought. He took a sip of coffee. "I'm looking for something, Mrs. Kitchen. But I'm not sure it requires paint."

AFTER HER CHAT WITH MR. Marvel, Johnnie ran to the grocery store to pick up a few things. As she unloaded a tub of Dale's favorite brand of pimento cheese onto the conveyer belt—in the hopes that he'd return home soon—an old familiar voice rang out over the store's sound system: Karen Carpenter, singing her upbeat megahit, "On Top of the World."

Johnnie hadn't thought of this song in years, but the singer's smooth voice triggered a memory. A memory of the day she heard that Karen Carpenter had died. After she paid for her groceries, she rushed home, let Brother outside, stashed the cold stuff in the fridge, and headed down the hallway to her bedroom.

On the top shelf of her closet, buried under a stack of old textbooks and journals, she found the green spiral notebook she'd carried with her all over campus her freshman year at college. After rifling through some pages, she found what she was looking for.

* * *

Johnnie's Journal
Feb. 5, 1983
Campus Library
North Texas State University

Dear Miss Carpenter,

Mama's voice cracked over the phone in my dorm room this morning when she broke the news. She said you died yesterday ... of complications from anorexia. Granny Opal must have been hovering nearby because I heard her say, "Victoria, it's Saturday morning. Let the child sleep in." Mama kept shushing Granny, telling her to be quiet, that what she had to say was important. Then Mama took a drag on her cigarette and blew into the phone. "Is that what's wrong with you, baby girl? You got this *anorexia*?"

The back of my throat stung at her question. Dizzy, I turned to face the wall, keeping my voice low. "Mama, I can't talk now. My roommate's still asleep."

Mama coughed and said, "She was only thirty-two. Two years younger than me."

"I'm sorry," I started to say, but she'd already hung up.

As I placed the phone in its cradle, I thought about all the times Mama used to grab a hairbrush and sing along with your records. She'd close her eyes and pretend she was you, Karen Carpenter—internationally known American pop singer—crooning out songs like "Close To You" and "Rainy Days and Mondays." Sometimes I'd warble along, but clearly, Mama was the star. One time "We've Only Just Begun" came on, and Mama plopped down in front of the old upright piano and started bawling. I stopped singing and asked, "What's wrong?" and she told me to shut up and keep singing. Your silky voice filled the room. Mama pounded her fists on the ivory keys as if playing louder would make the lyrics come true.

No sooner had I hung up with Mama, than Aunt Beryl called from Salt Flat. Not sure how well you know your geography, Miss Carpenter, but Salt Flat is a ghost town out in West Texas. Although most of the townsfolk have died off or moved away, Aunt Beryl still haunts the place—and us—from a distance when she's not parked here on her broom trying to stir up trouble. You'd think I'd be better prepared for my great aunt's snipes, but this morning she caught me off guard.

"You still throwing up?" she started right in. "I just heard on the TV about the death of that wholesome young singer your mama likes, the one used to sing with her brother …. She just keeled over from starvation or some cockamamie thing."

Well, I have to tell you, Miss Carpenter, my jaw tightened and I started shaking. Before I could think of a comeback, I slammed the phone down. My roommate groaned and shoved a pillow over her head. I told her I was sorry. There'd be hell to pay later for hanging up on Aunt Beryl. She'd probably already phoned home to report my rude behavior. Knowing Mama, she'd bite right back. That's one thing I'll say for Mama, she doesn't take crap off Aunt Beryl.

So, Miss Carpenter, did you ever throw up after eating? Did you ever feel like a freak around food? I still can't believe you're dead. If someone rich and famous like you could get sick, then how can a nineteen-year-old college girl like me get well? I don't starve myself like you did. I have something else, dark and ugly, and it's been taking over my life since my first boyfriend was killed in a bus crash after I turned fifteen. His name was Clovis. He was cut in half when he went through a window. We don't talk about it. After his funeral at the Catholic Church, I bit into a chocolate donut and couldn't stop.

Hours have passed since I learned of your death. I'm at the library, supposed to be taking notes for a paper that's due next week, but I decided to write you instead. I have a food hangover from last night's binge because I couldn't barf up all the junk I ate. My hands are swollen and clammy, my mouth is dry as cotton candy, and my belches are making me sick. I call them egg burps because they smell like rotten eggs and hurt coming up. Hope nobody in the library notices. Gas pains are sharp today, like someone's stabbing me in the gut with a butcher knife. Maybe if I fart I'll feel better.

I'd been good all week. Then yesterday afternoon, I walked by this grand old building a few blocks from campus. The place Aunt Beryl told me about when I was ten. The sidewalk is buckled in places and weeds are growing through the cracks. As I stared at the boarded-up windows and front door of what used to be the Denton School for Unwed Mothers, I imagined my mama as a scared teenager with a bulging belly and no place to go.

On my way back to the dorm, I stopped by the convenience store and bought a bag of chips, three fried pies, and a small carton of ice cream. I polished off the ice cream while my roommate went to do laundry. After we went to bed, I got back up, crouched alone in the stairwell, and crammed down the chips and pies. Then I crept to the bathroom that everybody shares and locked myself in the last stall, praying no one would get up in the middle of the night to pee. Some girl came in right after I stuck my finger down my throat. I could hear her slippers sliding along the hard tile floor. The stall clicked shut, and then she started crying. I couldn't stand it. Hearing her cry made me cry; I don't know why, but I tried not to make any noise. Finally she left and I kept trying to throw up, but I couldn't after that.

I have to be good the next few days because I have a date next weekend with a hunk named Dale. My roommate keeps talking about his broad shoulders and the way his muscular thighs fill out his Levis. She has a crush on him, too. He's a few years older than we are. We met him at a frat party last weekend. He said he was only there for the free beer. His eyes are the color of bluebonnets in the late afternoon when the sun hits them just right and their colors fade. But it was his hands that I noticed above all. They were large and rough, yet the way he cupped his beer …. I imagined them cupping me.

Mama doesn't know about him yet. She'll get all weird and start giving me the big lecture like she of all people has any right to talk. She has nothing to worry about, considering I'm still a virgin.

You must have felt this way about a guy once. Lots of guys, probably. You cranked out a few love songs in your day. I sure hope your death doesn't send Mama on one of her benders. It's not like she knew you or anything. Still … she told me one time, "People are always dying on me."

I told her, "Mama, I'm not dead." She grabbed me and held on tight.

So I guess you're "On Top of the World" now, like you used to sing in your song. Is there a special place in heaven for famous people like you? Or is everybody just clumped together like marshmallows, weightless souls floating through space?

> Daughter of your most
> devoted fan,
> Johnnie Grubbs

CHAPTER 9

~⌐

Thursday Afternoon, April 5, 2007

A SLOW DRIZZLE FELL AS Johnnie rocked back and forth in a slatted rocker on the Craftsman-style front porch. She'd fallen in love with that porch in 1984. With its square tapered columns and no railing to obstruct the view, it offered her the perfect vantage point. What better place to while away an afternoon or to spy on a new neighbor, in company with her best friend Whit? Inhaling the fresh scent of rain, she watched the pilot hoist a shovel from the back of his VW Bus. Still clad in his uniform, he shambled across the small, unkempt yard and stopped a few feet from the curb. A tiny orange flag marked the spot where he started digging.

Johnnie pitched forward in the rocker, paused, then glanced over at Whit. "You'd think he'd at least change clothes. Or wait until the rain stops."

Whit kicked off her sandals and pushed back on the porch swing, her broomstick skirt billowing at her feet. "So that's Mr. Marvelous, huh?"

Picking up her mug from the wicker plant stand, Johnnie blew on her tea. "This morning he stood in the middle of the street, flapping his arms like one of those inflatable waving men you see down at the car wash."

Whit took a sip of Chardonnay. "So you think he flies for one of the commuters? I don't mean to sound ugly, but he looks too fat to fit in a cockpit." She twirled the wine stem between her fingers.

Johnnie recalled the trail of crumbs she'd seen on Mr. Marvel's lapel that morning. "I'm not really sure what airline he works for, or if he's even employed. But I do know he's digging a hole in his yard in the middle of a rain shower. In his uniform."

"Maybe he's got a dead body stashed in the back of that beat-up old bus."

Johnnie made a face and shook her head at Whit's humor. "Right, and he's going to bury it in broad daylight. Out in his front yard while we watch."

A muffled bark roused her from her seat. "Keep an eye on Mr. Marvel. I'll be right back." Cupping her mug in one hand, she went to let in Brother. His whole body wagged when she opened the back door. He trotted through the house and slouched next to Whit, his lips flat against her bare foot.

Settling back in the rocker, Johnnie took a sip of her tea, then told the dog, "Brother, if you didn't have any bones, you'd be a puddle of chocolate."

Whit gave him the eye. "Well, so much for swinging." She reached down and gave him a perfunctory pat on the head. He craned his neck, staring at her in complete adoration.

Johnnie chuckled. "That dog worships you."

Whit adjusted her skirt. "Wish I could find a man as loyal as Brother."

Johnnie glanced at her friend. Despite Whit's exotic beauty, a string of broken relationships stretched behind her. "You will. He's out there somewhere."

The smell of wet dog drifted toward her. "Guess I should towel you off, huh, Brother?" The dog continued to stare at Whit.

"Brother loves me 'cuz I'm brown like him." Whit ran her

polished nails through Brother's shiny coat.

After a few moments, Mr. Marvel dropped his shovel and clomped inside. The soft rain continued to fall.

"Maybe he's out of breath. I would be too if I was hauling around all those pounds," Whit remarked. "You know what they say … 'Behind every fat person is a skinny person dying to get out.'"

Johnnie didn't comment. She had her own theory about overweight people. Their fat was simply a fortress: walls of flesh to hide behind or shut others out.

Swirling wine around in her goblet, Whit turned to Johnnie. "So how are you and John Denver getting along? Is he still sleeping on the couch?"

Johnnie had been dreading this question since Whit showed up after work for her free glass of wine. "Actually, he spent last night at Granny's place."

"Say what!" Whit's dark eyes flashed with what Johnnie took as criticism. "Now why would your husband be spending the night at your grandmother's house? Ladybug, that's messed up." Whit pursed her lips and brushed at something on her lap.

Johnnie felt the sudden need to defend Dale. "Well, he had to sleep somewhere. You know how tight he is. He probably didn't want to spend money on a motel."

"So, he's just gonna camp out over there. Is that it? And you're okay with that?"

Brother stretched out as if he'd grown bored by their conversation. He rested his chin on his front paws, crossed in that elegant pose Johnnie loved. "I don't see that I have much of a choice, considering I'm the reason he left."

Whit's expression softened. "Have you heard any more from your mama? Has she tried to contact you again?"

Johnnie drummed her unpainted nails against the side of her mug. "Nope. And I'm not sitting around waiting, either." With that, Johnnie dismissed the subject. *Mama knows where to find me, damn it.*

Glancing at her watch, she realized Callie Ann should have been home by now from drill team practice. It was 5:30 and Johnnie tried not to worry. But the roads were slick, and now she wished she'd picked Callie Ann up herself, instead of entrusting her daughter with some older girl fresh out of driver's ed.

"Call her if you're that worried. Maybe they stopped by Sonic."

Once again Whit had read her mind. "No, I'm not calling her. I'm trying to give her some freedom. Lord help me when she starts driving." Taking a deep breath, she pocketed the worry for now. She was good at putting up a front. She'd learned it from Granny.

Mr. Marvel returned in tan coveralls. He picked up the shovel and resumed digging. A small mound of dirt began to pile next to a hole.

"Whatcha digging for? Buried treasure?" Whit called out, the wine loosening her up.

Mr. Marvel looked up, one foot on the shovel, and waved. "Good afternoon, ladies."

Johnnie wanted to duck. Instead, she returned the wave. "Hi there, Mr. Marvel. This is my friend, Whit. She's a regular comedian."

Whit snickered and took another sip of wine.

Mr. Marvel bowed with a flourish. "Pleased to meet you, Miss." Then he went back to digging.

Moments later, the rain stopped and the sun broke through a hole in the clouds. The wet pavement glistened under the blinding rays.

A squeal of tires caught Johnnie's attention. Whit jumped from the swing, both hands clutching her empty glass.

A jacked-up Jeep with oversize tires came careening down the street from the east.

Mr. Marvel heard it too because he stopped digging and turned toward the sound.

As the Jeep approached, he headed straight for the street, wielding the shovel. He moved fast for a man of his girth.

Brother looked up, his head tilted in full alert. Johnnie bolted out of the rocker and grabbed Whit's arm. In shock, they watched Mr. Marvel fling the shovel right in front of the speeding Jeep.

The Jeep screeched to a halt. A teenage boy jumped out and stalked toward Mr. Marvel. "Hey, buddy, whatcha do that for?"

That's when Johnnie saw Callie Ann slink out of the passenger seat, lugging her backpack and gym bag.

So this was Callie Ann's ride home from drill team practice. A hotheaded rooster with wavy black hair, his arm muscles bulging from his sleeveless T. The creepy new boyfriend Cade had tried to tell them about.

The shovel lay crumpled beneath the front wheels of the Jeep.

Brother spotted Callie Ann and galloped down the steps. Johnnie and Whit were right behind him.

"You just hit a kid." Mr. Marvel's voice echoed like shock waves up and down the street. Big fat tears squeezed out of his eyes.

Johnnie didn't know whether to slug him or hug him.

The boy appeared stricken, as if he fully expected to see a child lying dead under his Jeep. But then his shock turned to anger. "You could've killed us. What if it had gone through the windshield?"

Mr. Marvel looked shaken. His jowls jiggled as he said, "Son, you better slow that thing down. Or I'll slow it down for you."

Bending, he retrieved the shovel and stomped off. Right before he went inside, he stabbed the earth with the mangled blade.

The shovel stood there like a warning.

High overhead, a red-tailed hawk circled, looking for supper. A train whistled in the distance. A large jetliner took off from DFW Airport.

Then Callie Ann started sobbing, and Brother danced in front of her, trying to help. Whit threw a protective arm around her and ushered her inside. The boy took off in his Jeep, peeling away from the curb.

Johnnie stood in the middle of the rain-soaked street, shaking her fist at the back of the Jeep as it headed west. She hoped that little shit got an eyeful of her in his rearview mirror.

Turning, she glanced at the area where Mr. Marvel had been digging near the curb. The small mud-hole reminded her of the miniature lakes the boys used to make for their GI Joes.

A shaft of sunlight cast an eerie glow on the tiny orange flag upended in the weeds. She bent to get a closer look.

Written in chunky black marker on one side of the flag: the word **EDWIN**.

CHAPTER 10

~✺~

Wednesday Evening, April 11, 2007

"WHO FARTED?" CADE'S VOICE BOOMED over the hum of the microwave.

Johnnie turned in surprise. "You're home early." The microwave dinged, and she lifted the hot dish and set it on the counter.

Cade flashed his Pepsodent grin, the one he'd been charming her with since he cut his first teeth. "I love the smell of broccoli in the evening," he declared, twisting the line from *Apocalypse Now*.

She kept a straight face. "I thought it was napalm and morning."

"Oh, Mama. You can't take a joke." He dropped his backpack and bent to give her a kiss. "I love all your smelly vegetables, especially when you smother them with cheese."

Chuckling, she let him peck her on the cheek. Her eyes took in his white polo, slouchy jeans, and flip-flops. "How come you're not in your practice clothes? Don't you still have to suit up ... even though you're benched?"

Cade strode to the refrigerator and grabbed a bottle of Gatorade. He chugged half of it before he looked at her. "What else are we having? Besides *broccoli*?"

"Turkey cutlets and whole wheat rolls." If she could get away with it, every meal she prepared would be healthy and lean.

"Good thing Daddy's not here. You'd never hear the end of it."

"Yeah well …." She shrugged. Dale hated turkey, except at Thanksgiving and Christmas.

"Mama, seems like since Daddy moved out, we've been having a lot more turkey. Turkey sausage. Turkey bacon. Turkey fingers … gobble, gobble, gobble. You think we could have some beef every now and then?" He pinched her side and mooed like a cow.

She slapped him away and told him to wash up. "And tell your sister dinner's ready."

A few seconds later, she heard Cade howl from the back of the house, "Holy shit, baby sis has a hickey."

A door slammed and Cade roared with laughter.

As Johnnie slid the skillet off the stove, the image of a cocky boy in a Jeep sped past her mind and slammed against her heart. The day she'd been dreading for fifteen years had finally arrived. She and Callie Ann would have to have another talk, a franker discussion than those early ones when Callie Ann was twelve. Johnnie would warn her that even the nicest boys get horny and try to sweet-talk a girl straight out of her convictions—along with her underpants.

But when it came to her own boys, well … that was different. She liked to believe they were honorable.

A few minutes later, Cade strode back into the kitchen in gym shorts and a T-shirt. He stood at the sink, washing his hands.

"What's with Mr. Marble? That shovel hasn't moved in a week, and that hole's not getting any deeper. But the clown bus is gone again."

"Marvel," Johnnie corrected him, setting plates on the counter, "like the comic book."

She didn't know whether to feel sorry for Mr. Marvel or report him to the police. Earlier that day, on a quick pass through the grocery store to pick up milk and toilet paper, she'd spotted the man in uniform, standing in the middle of the kids' cereal aisle. Whipping her cart around, she stopped at the far end of the aisle and watched him lean down to pick up a box of Captain Crunch. Or was it Lucky Charms? She couldn't tell. Rubbing a plump hand over the box, he studied the front side for what seemed like forever. Then he kissed the box, hugged it to his chest, and stuck it back on the shelf. She shivered and shoved her cart toward the dairy case, hoping he hadn't seen her.

On the way home, she spotted the tomato red bus parked in front of the old elementary school. The tall metal slide still stood erect, but the rest of the playground had been bulldozed and the building half demolished. A lone round man stood among the ruins, his jacket flapping in the breeze.

As she cruised by, she wondered how this seemingly gentle man could turn violent and lash out at a stranger speeding down the street. A stranger with bulging biceps and a lip-lock on her daughter.

"Mama? Earth to Johnnie."

She flinched, unnerved by Cade's voice in her ear and his hand waving in front of her face. She closed the silverware drawer and glanced at him. "What?"

He grinned, flashing his dimples. When he was young and wanted his way, all he had to do was tilt his head and say, *Mama, how can you deny these dimples?*

Cade held his stomach. "I'm starving. Can we say grace without her?" He glanced toward the hallway. "She might be afraid to come out."

Johnnie stared at Cade. "How big is it?"

"What?" he said, looking innocent.

"The hickey," she hissed, irritated now.

Callie Ann slid into a chair as Johnnie placed the platter

of cutlets on the table. The first thing she noticed was her daughter's hair parted straight down the middle, spilling down both sides of her neck onto her chest. *She's covering up*, Johnnie thought, used to seeing Callie Ann's hair pulled back in a ponytail after drill team practice. Johnnie took a seat at the end of the table and placed a paper napkin on her lap. "Well, let's dig in."

Cade rubbed his hands together. "Looks good, Mama."

Callie Ann stared at Johnnie, her dove blue eyes questioning her every move. "Aren't you going to say grace first?"

Johnnie tried to act like nothing was wrong. Dale's empty chair loomed in front of her. D.J.'s spot on the other side of Cade seemed even more vacant tonight. Her family of five had dwindled down to three—at least at the table. She folded her hands and closed her eyes. "God is … God is …." she started, but the words would not come. The prayer she'd been reciting their whole lives had suddenly vanished. She fell silent.

Cade reached for the platter. "Good food. Good meat. Screw the prayer. Let's eat."

Callie Ann rolled her eyes. "You're such a caveman." She spooned broccoli onto her plate then helped herself to a cutlet. "No wonder you don't have a girlfriend."

Cade chomped a mouthful of food and winked at his sister. "The reason I don't is simple, baby sis. Girls empty your pockets then break your heart."

Johnnie passed the basket of rolls and waited until her children were served before she filled her plate. She couldn't help but wonder if Cade's remark was somehow directed at her. She listened to them banter back and forth, exchanging barbs.

Brother walked into the room and sniffed his way around the table until Cade gave in and slipped him a bite of turkey. "Hey, Labster." Brother inhaled the turkey and waited for more.

"Daddy hates it when you do that." Callie Ann held her fork

in the air and stared at Cade. "He says you've taught Brother to mooch."

Johnnie gazed at the back of Brother's brown head, his body in a perfect sit. *You have better manners than all of us,* she wanted to say.

Cade rubbed the top of Brother's head and told him to lie down. "Yeah, well, Daddy's not here, is he?"

Her son's words stung. Brother's warm body pushed against her feet. He stretched out and sighed as if he carried the weight of the family on his back. The only sounds in the room were the scraping of forks on plates.

After a moment, Cade picked up a roll and stared across the table at his sister. "Looks like lover boy's been busy."

Callie Ann's face reddened. She stopped chewing. Her hand flew up to her neck. The movement caused the curtain of hair to part, and in that split second, Johnnie caught a glimpse of the ugly bruise. The warm roll she'd just bitten in to, with the savory butter flavor, stuck in her throat like raw dough. She tried to wash it down with a glass of water.

Cade made a whistling noise then resumed eating.

Johnnie hadn't planned to discuss the hickey at dinner, but Cade's words left her no choice. "Callie Ann. It doesn't look good. People might think …. Well, you need to think about your reputation. One thing can lead to another. Then another. And then before you know it …." Her voice trailed off. She couldn't bring herself to say it.

"What Mama's trying to say," Cade cut it, cleaning his teeth with his tongue and clearing his throat, "is she doesn't want you to get preggers … like Queen Victoria."

Johnnie dropped her fork with a clang. "Queen *who*?" But even as she asked the question she knew. *Mama!* She glanced back and forth at her two youngest children. "How long have you been calling her that?"

Cade and Callie Ann exchanged smirks. Finally, Callie Ann spoke up. "Since we were kids. D.J. started it."

Johnnie leaned back in her chair. "Why am I not surprised?" As far back as preschool, D.J. had exhibited an adult sense of humor.

Cade's eyes lit up. "Well, it all started one time when D.J. asked Granny Opal a question about that old black and white photo on the top of Granny's piano. You know, the one where your mama is walking along in heels and a dress, swinging a string of pearls."

"Yes, Mama looked like a movie star in that photo. Back in the day, professional photographers used to camp out on Main Street. They'd snap your photo for a nominal fee," she told the kids.

"Well, all he did was ask Granny Opal if your mama was out on a date. He said she sure looked sexy."

Johnnie chuckled. "And what did Granny say?"

"That's the thing," Callie Ann chimed in. "She snapped that photo out of D.J.'s hand and told him to 'watch his mouth.'"

Cade looked over at Johnnie. "D.J. was pissed. From then on he called her Queen Victoria because it seemed like everyone was protecting her like she was royalty."

Johnnie took a bite of her cutlet. "Tell me about it. I had to live with her."

Cade got up to pour a glass of milk. "Remember that time D.J. got stopped by that cop up on Main Street? For doing 'The Lady Walk'?"

"Oh my God, that was hilarious," Callie Ann laughed, clearly happy to have the attention deflected off of her. "We were walking home from the movies. It was summer."

Johnnie smiled, remembering D.J.'s act. "We'd just left the Palace Theatre. It was still light out. At thirteen, your brother was tall and gangly from a recent growth spurt. The next thing I knew, he went strutting up the sidewalk ahead of us, swaying his hips from side to side and swinging a string of imaginary pearls. That's when that cop rolled down his window and yelled, 'Hey, kid, you a little light in your loafers?'"

As she finished the story, she realized the connection between D.J.'s prancing walk and the photo.

Cade turned to her, flashing his trademark grin. "And that's when you ripped that cop a new one, Mama."

She looked at both of her children then down at Brother Dog. "Damn straight, and I'd do it again. Just next time, somebody clue me in on your inside jokes."

Cade reached for the meat platter. "Anybody want that last piece?" He speared the cutlet, leaving a trail of brown juice on the table.

SHE HEARD HIS LOUD SNIFF, the rattle of tags. Rolling over, Johnnie peeked out from under the covers. Silhouetted against the dim glow of a nightlight, Brother Dog stood by Dale's side of the bed, his chin resting on the comforter.

"What are you waiting on, an invitation?" She motioned for him to join her. "Come on up."

With one quick jump, he was on the bed. Nudging her with his nose, he curled up on Dale's pillow and let out a wheezy sigh.

She gave him a pat and rolled over. A second later, she heard the bathroom door shut, then the click of the lock. Probably Cade taking one of his late night showers. She tried to drift off to sleep to the sound of running water, but those two phone calls right before bedtime played on her mind.

The first came as she was taking off her makeup.

"Hey, Mom," D.J. said. "Just checking in."

She set her cell down and turned it on speaker. "Queen Victoria and 'The Lady Walk,' huh?"

"Wait, so …." He paused for a second then chuckled. "Which one of your darlings ratted me out?"

"Doesn't matter. The name fits, you know. I kind of like it."

"Yeah, well… I just figured she needed a nickname, considering she walked out on everyone."

Once again, his insight took her by surprise. At times like

this, she missed him more than ever. She started to tell him about Callie Ann's hickey but figured Cade had already beat her to it.

"So, who's the creep messing with my little sis? You want me to come bash in his face?"

She laughed and told him to get some sleep.

The second call came moments later as she turned off the bathroom light and headed to bed.

"I have just one question for you, Johnnie. Where would you be without me?"

Dale's words stung, and she had no comeback. A second passed between them; then Dale spoke again. "While I was paying for your therapy, providing you a home, giving you my heart, you were out screwing the *bastard* who tried to run me out of business."

Dale had never spoken to her like this, not in all the years they'd been married. He'd always held back, been such a calming force in her life; the strong sturdy trunk rooted to the spot. She'd been the swaying leaves, changing colors to fit her moods.

Before she could think of what to say, he hung up.

* * *

Johnnie's Journal
The *Mourning* After
April 12, 2007

Jeral:

After twenty-three years of lockdown, this adulteress has come out of the closet.

No banging doors or broken dishes. No shouting matches or slamming bodies. Only the ear-shattering silence of a phantom husband. A husband who keeps moving through this house, his work boots clopping down the hall, his body sighing into his leather chair to take the weight off the morning before he heads out. When I look up, no one is there. The paper is still out by the curb. The aroma of coffee is yesterday's news.

And I'm stuck with the memories of that winter night so long ago, when Dale had been out of town for weeks, overseeing a new job site in East Texas. By then he'd left Cagle Construction to start his own business, and you couldn't stand the idea, could you? Sober and craving company, I sashayed into the Slingback Saloon and spotted all six-foot-four of you against the bar. You looked surprised I'd come alone. Those jolly blues, a-shimmer and up to no good, took all of me in. *Come here*, they summoned. Your lips curled in a sly grin, and you crooked your finger, reeling me in. Two magnets pulled toward each other and nothing to stop us.

Smelling like cedar and spice on a cold Christmas night, you twirled me around, then whispered in my ear, "Wanna dance, pretty lady? And later, make puppies?"

I laughed so hard I forgot myself. That was my downfall— giving in to your mischief.

That night on the dance floor, you let me know your body was my banquet. Together, we could feast on each other's flesh and never get fat. Or old. Or wrinkled. Because the table set before us wouldn't last.

We'd have a good time, call it a night. A week. A month if we were lucky. When I was with you, I simply stashed Dale behind a closed door, the same place I stashed God whenever I flipped on the exhaust fan to shut out the sound of my own retching.

I was fine until the night the fever broke and I saw us for what we were—two lonely animals, tangled together, humping.

You were like a sickness, one I've been trying to purge from my thoughts all these years. Until last week, I thought I'd done a pretty good job. But now you're back in my head, taking up space in my home, in this sanctuary Dale and I worked so hard to build. Good thing you're already dead. Dale would be halfway across town right now with a sledgehammer.

Get out of my mind before I lose it. I'm not the person I was back then.

In closing, I want you to know I always hated it when you called me by my maiden name, "Hey, Grubbs," like I was one of the guys on your softball team. Guess you felt less guilty that way. Goodbye, Jeral.

Johnnie

CHAPTER 11

~◡◠~

Thursday Evening, April 12, 2007

L ATE IN THE AFTERNOON OF the next day Dale called again,
urgency in his voice. "I found two old photos and a letter
taped to the underside of a drawer in your uncle's nightstand.
You might wanna hustle over here while your granny's still at
the store."

Johnnie stiffened. Dale's tone told her these weren't just *any*
photographs. "Who are they of and what's the letter about?"
She stared at the pound of lean ground beef, golden yolks, gray
oats, and ketchup unmixed in the bowl. Tonight Cade was
getting *real* meatloaf.

"Just hurry. Before she gets back."

"Can you bring them here? I'm in the middle of making
dinner."

"They're not mine to take." He clicked off.

Dale. Always the good guy.

Setting the phone down, she plunged her hand into the
gooey mess, squishing the lumpy ingredients together before
folding them into a loaf pan. After washing her hands and
placing the pan in the oven, she glanced at the clock, took one
look at Brother, sleeping upside down on the braided rug in

the den, and tiptoed out the door.

As she cranked up the Suburban and headed up Main Street toward Granny's place, one question went through her mind: who would go to all that trouble to hide a couple of photographs and a letter beneath a drawer in her dead uncle's bedroom?

Less than five minutes later, she wound her way around Lakeside Drive. Surrounded by towering oaks and pecan trees, the sprawling white house with the large picture window sat back off the road, past the bend. The tires crunched the gravel as Johnnie pulled into the narrow driveway, past a faded metal sign that swayed in the late afternoon breeze: *Opal's Cakery: All Occasions.* Granny hadn't baked for profit in years, but she insisted on keeping her sign.

The long front porch with its metal glider and potted geraniums beckoned her inside. Before she got to the steps, she noticed Dale's truck parked around the side of the garage. It was almost hidden from view, with only the back end visible. This was her first visit back to the house she'd grown up in since Dale took up residence. Granny's yellow Lincoln was nowhere in sight.

Far to her left, nestled under a red oak in the side yard, the old playhouse, with paned windows and cloth curtains, called to her across the years. Here, in this sacred place, she scribbled in her diaries, giggled with the fairies, and rocked her baby doll with corn-colored hair and lake-water eyes.

Oh, sweet, blessed childhood…. Johnnie sighed. If only she could crawl back, even for a day.

Mounting the steps, she pulled open the storm door and stepped inside.

The confectionery aroma of a cake shop filled her senses as she adjusted to the light. Even years after Granny retired, the warm scent of sugar, vanilla, and almond extract clung to every fiber in the rugs, upholstery, and drapes. "You have the best smelling house in town," a friend in junior high once raved, adding, "My house smells like bacon grease."

The living room was dim as she made her way past the upright piano. Her mama had poured her soul into that instrument every time she'd played it. The piano sat silent now, transformed into the family shrine. Framed pictures and figurines competed for space.

"I'm back here," Dale called from the other end of the house.

Breathe, she told herself, gripping the shoulder strap of her purse. She hadn't seen Dale in a week. Not since he'd moved out … if you could call it that. All he took with him was his shaving kit, his laptop, and a few clothes.

As she turned to go down the gloomy, dark-carpeted hallway, she stopped and caught her breath. Something was different. Something she'd never seen before in all the years growing up here.

The hallway was bathed in sunlight.

A brilliant beam came through the open door of Uncle Johnny's bedroom.

She almost cried.

When she rounded the corner, Dale looked up from the edge of the single bed. Behind him, the heavy drapes were peeled back from the big window that faced west. The glass sparkled. Someone had cleaned the window, inside and out. The once forbidden room was aglow with light. Even Dale's pale hair seemed blonder today. For a second she was nineteen and meeting him for the first time at a frat party.

"Thanks for coming." He motioned for her to sit down.

Dropping her purse on the floor, she sat near the foot of the bed and waited for Dale to show her the photos. Her eyes took in the room. The long oak dresser had been cleared off and dusted. Dale's wallet and keys rested in one of Granny's crystal relish dishes. A row of green and cream-colored encyclopedias lined a small bookcase by the door. Near the ceiling, an L-shaped shelf wrapped around two walls, lined with sports trophies and an old train set. A yellowed football pendant tacked to the wall proclaimed: Portion Bandits—State

Champions—1963. Next to the pendant, a young man in a cap and gown smiled confidently from a framed photo. Her uncle had her coloring, Johnnie noted, auburn hair and a pale complexion. The chin, with a hint of a cleft, resembled hers as well. Someone had handwritten *Valedictorian* across the bottom.

"I used to sneak in here sometimes when no one was home," she said, "but I never snooped."

Dale turned toward her, his reading glasses halfway down his nose. "I wasn't snooping. Granny asked me if I could fix the drawer on the nightstand. It's been stuck for years."

The small drawer, about three inches deep, rested between them on a bedspread Johnnie didn't recognize. The drawer's musty scent mingled with Dale's cologne.

He handed her a tattered envelope. "This is the reason the drawer wouldn't open."

Inside the envelope were two faded photographs and a letter from West Point, dated April 1963. The letter was addressed to Johnny Grubbs, 8 Lakeside Drive, Portion, TX. Her eyes scanned the opening line: *We are pleased to announce that you have been accepted as a cadet into the class of 1967 at the United States Military Academy at West Point.*

Dumbfounded, she put the letter down and blew out a lungful of air.

She gazed again at the young man in cap and gown whose smile held so much promise. "So he got accepted to West Point .... I never knew that. Sad he didn't get to attend. He died that summer." She shook her head and pulled out the two photos.

Her heart skipped ahead of her. She closed her eyes for a moment. Taking a deep breath, she concentrated on one photo at a time.

In the first picture, black and white, two young men stood side by side. The guy on the left was easy to recognize. In Bermuda shorts and a white V-neck T-shirt, Uncle Johnny leaned forward on crutches, a cast on his left leg. He stared straight ahead, handsome but unsmiling, a younger version of Grandpa. Next to him, even taller and more dashing, was a dark-haired young man with deep-set eyes and a sheepish smile. His arm was thrown over her uncle's shoulder. A pen dangled from his hand as if he'd just signed his friend's cast.

Johnnie held the photo closer, her heart quickening at the realization. "My God, Dale. It's him, Francis Murphy. Why, they must have been best friends in high school." She flipped over the photo. Scribbled in pencil on the back: Johnny and Francis, June 1963, right before Francis left for West Point.

She handed it to Dale. "That's Mama's handwriting. I'm positive."

Dale nodded. "I bet she's the one who hid the photos and letter. But why?"

She turned her attention to the second photo, saving it for last.

The colors had faded with time, but the image was clear. A tall, good-looking Army officer in uniform grinned for the camera; dark eyebrows framed his piercing eyes. Her father, Francis Murphy, *The Lieutenant*. Behind him, off to the side, past the edge of a picnic table, a young chubby-cheeked girl in pigtails peeked out from behind a tree, squinting at whoever took the picture.

She stared at the image of herself as a young girl. "I think I was five here. Mama and I snuck away on a bus to visit him. He must have left for Vietnam right after that."

She studied the handwriting on the back: Francis and Johnnie, Fort Hood, 1969. "I have no idea if he loved me, but I remember him being kind."

Dale cleared his throat. "D.J. favors him. He has your dad's eyes as well as his height."

The eyes of an old soul …. she reflected. She was staring at her dad but thinking of her son.

At the bottom of the drawer, a flash of red caught her

attention. Folded between layers of wax paper was a child's Crayola drawing of a bird. She picked it up and turned it over in her hands.

"The cardinal was his favorite bird."

Johnnie jumped at the sound of Granny Opal's voice. The old woman appeared in the doorway, pinching her cardigan together with both hands. "He'd stand out in the yard for hours and mimic their calls. One time Victoria nearly broke her neck running to get me. I was mopping the kitchen floor when she came hollering that her brother was talking to birds. As she went skidding across the wet floor, taking the mop bucket with her, I heard her cry out: 'One just landed on his shoulder.'"

In that instant, Granny's voice faded away....

JOHNNIE WAS FOUR OR FIVE, walking hand in hand with Grandpa along the bank of Portion Lake. Grandpa stopped to fish his hanky out of his back pocket to blow his nose.

She got the giggles. "You sound like a goose honking."

Grandpa swiped his nose and chuckled.

She skipped on ahead. That's when she saw him at the edge of the shore, his red plumage, his tiny black face and beady eyes, staring at his reflection in the water. He turned his head to look at her.

In a series of fluty whistles, she heard him call her name. "John-neee.... John-neee."

She'd never heard a bird talk.

Her mouth open, she glanced back at Grandpa. "A little bird talked to me."

The old man caught up with her, stuffing his hanky in his pocket. "What did he say?"

She reached up and tugged at his arm. "He said my name, Grandpa. He said, 'John-neee.... John-neee.'"

Grandpa stooped to inspect the bird. It blinked and took a couple of steps on its skinny legs.

Grandpa's cracked lips twitched and his tongue rolled around inside his mouth as if he had a lollipop stuck in his cheek.

He cleared his throat. "That's not just any bird, young lady. That's an angel bird, flown straight down from heaven."

Johnnie gulped. "Let's tell Mama and Granny."

Grandpa jerked her arm. She'd only known gentleness from him. "This is our secret. Little Bird talking to you …."

He held her hand and they watched the red bird dart off, disappearing into the trees.

"JOHNNIE, WHAT IS IT?" DALE'S voice startled her.

She looked up. Granny was gone. She could hear pots and pans banging around out in the kitchen, but a part of her was still back at the cove with Grandpa.

"I was remembering something. From a long time ago." She took a deep breath and clasped the drawing to her heart.

Dale turned to face her. The mattress shifted under his weight. "Something sad? You're crying."

Shaking her head, she swiped at her cheek. "No. Something magical." She stared at Uncle Johnny's senior portrait on the wall. *You came to me that day, didn't you? Even Grandpa believed it. What were you trying to tell me?*

Her cellphone rang, jarring her senses. She reached for her purse to answer the call.

Dale took off his glasses and stood to stretch. The two photos lay face down on the bed where he'd dropped them when Granny appeared in the doorway.

"Mother, where are you?" Callie Ann started in. "You ran off and left the oven on. Brother was going nuts when I walked in the door. Don't you know that oven timer hurts his ears?"

Johnnie fiddled with the edge of the wax paper then placed the drawing back in the drawer. No need to disturb the red Crayola bird anymore. She shifted the phone to her other ear. "Can you cover the meatloaf with foil and turn the oven off? I'll be home in a minute."

Callie Ann grumbled something and hung up.

Dale retrieved the two photos and handed them to Johnnie. "You might want to slip these into your purse. Something tells me Opal doesn't know about them. I saw a total look of innocence on her face when she walked in on us."

Leaning against the doorframe, Johnnie glanced at the two photos one more time before she stashed them in her bag, along with the letter. She started to leave.

"Dale?"

He turned from the window, where he'd been watching sailboats out on the water. "Yeah?"

When are you coming home? Are you coming home? she wanted to ask. But all she could muster was a simple "Thanks."

Nodding, Dale picked up the drawer and slid it back into place in the nightstand.

Beyond the window, the sun began to set over Portion Lake.

CHAPTER 12

~✧~

Wednesday Afternoon, April 18, 2007

"How come you're not at practice?" Johnnie unplugged the vacuum and rolled it into the hall closet.

Cade took a swig of bottled orange juice and let out a loud belch. "Mama, can I ask you something? Don't get mad at me, okay?"

Already her defenses were up. Why did he keep dodging her question, only to replace it with one of his own?

Every day for the past week he'd come home early, dressed in street clothes. Today he wore pressed jeans and a baby blue polo that showed off his powerful arms. When he started lifting weights in middle school, he'd flex his muscles for Johnnie and say, "Mama, check out my guns." Then he'd make her squeeze his biceps to prove how strong he was.

She shut the door and glanced at him. "What?"

"This old Vietnam Vet came to talk to our class today. He asked if we had a parent or grandparent who served in the military." Cade paused to guzzle more juice. "That's when I realized I could yap about Colonel Kitchen carpet-bombing in his B-52, but I know jack about The Lieutenant … except that he got killed in Nam."

Leaning against the closet door, she struggled to find the words. "Well … there's not much to tell. Until I was your sister's age, I only knew him as some unknown guy who got my mama pregnant. Turns out I met him once, when I was five, but I thought he was someone else." She crossed her arms and studied the rows of hardwood planks that lined the hall floor.

"So … who did you think he was?" Cade twisted the bottle cap back and forth on the plastic rim.

Her eyes focused on a small clump of dog hair she'd missed with the vacuum. Yet her mind traveled back to the Army post and all those stars Mama flicked her wrist at as if she were swatting at flies. *Oh, those belong to Uncle Sam.*

Johnnie massaged a cramp in her shoulder. "It doesn't matter. What matters is Mama led me to believe he was someone else." She took a deep breath and looked at her son. "Anyway, he was Catholic. He went to West Point. And when I was six, he was blown to bits … on the seventh anniversary of JFK's death."

Cade winced, crossed his arms around the empty juice bottle. "So who told you? Granny Opal? Your grandpa?"

"Nope. Aunt Beryl. Grandpa's sister."

Cade took a step back. "You mean the lesbo from West Texas?" His eyes twinkled with laughter.

"Who told you she was a lesbian?"

"Granny Opal."

Johnnie rolled her eyes. *Frigid was more like it.* "She was an old maid ranch woman. About as affectionate as a tumbleweed. I tried to stay on her good side. Mostly."

"So how come Aunt Beryl told you?"

"I think she did it to spite Mama. Those two were like flint and steel. Rub them together and sparks flew."

"I don't get it." Cade shook his head. "Why didn't they just come out and tell you who your father was? What was the big secret?"

"It was a different time back then. People didn't talk about things like teen pregnancy."

"Did she tell you on the phone? Over dinner?"

Johnnie scratched an itch on her scalp. "Not exactly. She wrote me a note. Stuck it in a Christmas gift she mailed from Salt Flat. After she and Mama had a falling out that Thanksgiving, Aunt Beryl stayed away for a long time."

"What did the note say?"

At this moment, Granny Opal's voice echoed in her head. *Some things are better left unsaid, my dear.*

Johnnie reached down and picked up the clump of dog hair. "Pretty much what I told you. His name, rank, when he was killed."

She ducked in the hall bathroom to throw away the hair.

She would not tell Cade how she unwrapped a box of tampons and found her great aunt's note tucked between the rows of cotton missiles. Twenty-eight years later, Aunt Beryl's words were still implanted in her brain:

To My Favorite Niece,

Tampons and a doctor's speculum are the only things that should enter your vagina at the tender age of fifteen. Don't make the same mistake your mama did and get pregnant. It will kill your grandpa. Instead of silly bath salts and smelly perfume, I decided to give you the gift of truth. Your father was a lieutenant in the United States Army. He was killed in action on November 22, 1970.

The note, plucked from her hand by Mama, had caused Grandpa to fume and grab his chest. Mama left the room and made a long-distance call to Salt Flat. Granny had been left in a dither over when to serve brunch.

CADE'S VOICE INVADED HER THOUGHTS as she came out of the bathroom. He was waiting for her by the door.

"So where's he buried?"

"Arlington." She was still rattled by the memory. "Virginia. Not Texas. I've never been."

Cade tapped the empty juice bottle against his palm. "We should go sometime." He started down the hall toward his room.

Surely she had mentioned this before. Told the kids where their late grandfather was buried. Then again, maybe not. Maybe it was genetic—an omission gene that ran in her family.

"Hey, Cade?"

"Yeah?" He turned to look at her.

"I have something I need to show you."

Cade followed her into the kitchen. At the desk, she rifled through her purse and found the envelope she'd been carting around since last week.

"Your dad found these hidden in Uncle Johnny's old bedroom. They were taped to the bottom of a drawer in the nightstand."

"That's twisted."

Cade set the empty juice bottle down and examined the color photo taken at the Army post. "Dude, if you shaved D.J.'s face and head, he could pass for your dad. They even have the same eyes. This'll blow him away when he sees it."

Nodding, she rested her head on his shoulder. "Pretty uncanny, huh? Your dad thought so, too."

Cade held the photo up for closer inspection. He elbowed Johnnie and chuckled. "And who's the little porker in pigtails, hiding behind the tree?"

Johnnie pinched him. "You sound like Aunt Beryl." She passed him the other photo.

He stared at it for a long time. "How did Uncle Johnny break his leg?"

She shrugged. "Sports, maybe? Remember, until last week,

I'd never seen these photos. I had no idea they even knew each other."

"Mama, why is our family so screwed up?"

She looked up at Cade but had no answer.

His question weighed heavily on her mind, along with the image of her uncle on crutches, his solemn expression haunting when compared with her father's sheepish grin. A grin that seemed to say, *I've got a secret.* From the moment she'd laid eyes on the date scribbled on the back, she'd done the math. Her mama would've already been pregnant that June in 1963.

ON A LAZY AFTERNOON a few days after Dale discovered the photos, Johnnie drove down to the cove, rolled up her jeans, and dangled her feet over the side of the dock. Pulling the black and white photo from her purse, she stared at the image of her uncle. "Okay, bird talker. Start talking. Did you know that your friend was messing around with your sister? Did you know about me … before you died?"

At that moment, a shiver went up her back. She felt someone walk up behind her, but when she turned, she saw nothing but a long shadow from a tall pine tree.

"What happened here?" she cried out to the water, trees, and wildlife—the silent witnesses to an unspeakable tragedy that stunned a family to silence.

But only one answer came: the sound of water lapping against the dock.

CADE'S VOICE JARRED HER. "MAMA, I need to tell you something." He jammed his hands in his pockets, his arms stiff and unnatural.

She stared at him hard, her fractured thoughts regrouping. She knew what was coming. "Don't tell me, you got kicked off the team?"

He frowned, shaking his head. "No, Mama. I quit."

"Quit?" Her gut twisted like she'd been kicked. She walked

over and sat on the couch. "This is going to kill your dad."

Cade gripped the back of a kitchen chair. "Um, Daddy already knows. I told him last week."

Last week? She rubbed the spot between her eyebrows. "You've kept this from me this whole time?"

She heard him sigh.

"We thought you'd freak out, Mama. You have enough to worry about without worrying about me."

The late afternoon sun filtered in through the window over the kitchen sink, filling the room with natural light. "And your coaches? Did they freak out?"

Cade turned the chair around and straddled it. "Screw the coaches. The truth is, I've been tired of baseball for a long time. I've been playing for everyone but me. I'm ready to move on."

"Move on? You still plan on going to college, right?"

He shrugged. "First I gotta get a job."

"Doing what?" She pictured him bagging groceries, flipping burgers, cleaning toilets at the local truck stop. Jobs he'd held each summer since he was fifteen.

"I'm working on it, Mama."

She grabbed a sofa pillow and picked at the piping. "Well, I guess you better break it to the others. Best that they hear it from you and not me."

Cade rose from the chair and quietly slid it into place. He cleared his throat. "Actually, Callie Ann and D.J. already know. So does Granny Opal."

The air left her lungs. She couldn't bear to look at him. She fixed her gaze on the stone fireplace, but her eyes were drawn up to the mantel where Cade grinned back at her from his senior portrait. She shut her eyes against the image of a tuxedoed young man, too handsome for his own good. "So I'm the last one to know?"

He came toward her. "I'm sorry, Mama. I was just trying to protect you."

Her head spun around. "Protect me from *what*?" She could

imagine how old and ugly she looked to him right now. *Mama, you look like a monster,* Cade had told her one time when she lashed out at him over some childhood prank.

He bent over the back of the couch. "From being disappointed in me." He hugged the back of her neck and left the room.

Brother scratched at the back door. She didn't budge. A moment later the muffled sound of country music crooned up the hallway. Brother scratched again, gave a high-pitched yelp.

It took everything in her to get up off the couch and let in the dog.

* * *

Johnnie's Journal
The Witching Hour
April 19, 2007

Dear Dad,

My spirit is sore. I am like a prizefighter in a ring with no visible opponent. Ducking my head, I dance around waiting, dodging the blows that never come.

And all I end up doing is swinging at ghosts.

Your daughter,
Johnnie

PS: I no longer eat hair. Thanks for sticking up for me that day at the Army post when Mama yanked my pigtail out of my mouth. You were my hero that day.

CHAPTER 13

❧

Saturday Morning, April 21, 2007

THE LOW GROWL STARTED AT the back of Brother's throat. Johnnie stirred, sensing something was wrong. She reached for her cell on the nightstand. No missed calls from Cade. The last time she talked to him was around 2:30 a.m. He was on his way home from the senior party. Said he was at the lake, wasn't drinking, and needed to drop off a buddy first. When he didn't show by 3:00 a.m., she called again. His phone went straight to voicemail. She must have dozed.

By now, it was 5:45 a.m. and Brother had worked himself into a frenzy. Growling, he lifted his head, thrust his nose forward, and leapt off the bed and out the door. Johnnie was jolted straight up. Fear pressed against her chest as she threw back the covers and struggled out of bed.

Brother's barks ricocheted through the house. Grabbing her robe, Johnnie made her way up the hall past Callie Ann's room. Callie Ann had spent the night at a friend's; no need to glance in there. When she got to Cade's door, she held her breath, hoping to find him curled under his covers. Fingers of light slipped through the open blinds across the empty bed. Her boy had not come home.

She threw on her robe and tried to breathe as she hurried up the hall. Maybe Brother had heard one of Mr. Marvel's cats prowling about the yard. They'd already killed a couple of birds, a robin, and a blue jay, leaving a few feathers and fuzz scattered on the porch.

Maybe Dale had come home. But Brother wouldn't make such a fuss at the front of the house. He'd be at the side door, tail wagging, whining and dancing with glee.

No, his barking had grown into an agitated yelp, and he paced, looking back at her to make sure she was coming. Her heart misfired. Her mind raced ahead like a scout on patrol.

Belting her robe, she cinched herself up against whatever waited on the other side of the door: a police car, a uniformed cop, making his way up the sidewalk to tell her Cade had been killed in a car wreck. Or had choked on his own vomit, had lain dead on some sofa while his asshole buddies slept off a night of binge drinking. Or D.J., injured after being jumped by thugs between buildings as he trekked home across campus late at night from the library. Or a madman, standing on the porch, waiting to attack the moment she opened the door.

Gulping air, she peeked out the side window.

"Oh. Lord. Jesus." The words amplified in her ears, rushed out of her. She'd spotted a black hearse next to the curb, the passenger door open, the front seat empty.

Her mouth dry, she pressed against the wall to steady herself.

Then she spotted two familiar figures, one bent over the flowerbed by the front porch. The other, Steven Tuttle, stood a few feet away, brushing his dress slacks and checking his polished shoes.

Suddenly Cade's blotchy face came into view. He straightened and wiped his mouth with the back of his forearm. He glanced over his shoulder, as if surprised his brother's friend had stuck around.

Johnnie threw open the door.

Anger surged through her, a rage more powerful than she'd

ever felt. She wanted to smack him, kiss him, beat the living daylights out of him.

She swooped down the steps and lashed out, "I thought you were dead!" Brother Dog charged past, clamoring for Cade's attention.

"Sic 'em, Brother!" she hissed, and stared hard at her son. By now she was shaking.

"Hey, boy." Cade's arms flailed as he reached and missed Brother's head. He stumbled, tripped.

Johnnie's instinct was to catch him. Instead, she closed her eyes and let him fall. He was still drunk.

Panting from excitement, Brother raced over to greet Steven while Cade pulled himself up.

Steven rubbed Brother's ears then gave Johnnie a sheepish grin. "Good morning, Mrs. Kitchen." He kept a respectful distance, as if he understood that she was a woman caught in her bathrobe, and it didn't matter that she was old enough to be his mother. "I was hoping to get him home without waking you up." He glanced at the hearse. "Didn't mean to scare you."

Johnnie ignored the remark and motioned to where Cade had gotten sick. "I hope he didn't kill my jonquils."

Brother trotted over to the hearse, hiked his leg, and peed on the rear tire.

She started to apologize, but Steven chuckled and shook his head. "Don't worry about it. I'm headed to the carwash anyway after I gas up." Hands in his pockets, he turned to go.

Johnnie caught a whiff of Cade as he lurched forward. "Hey, Tutts, ol' buddy. Tanks for the lift."

Steven backed away, his palm out in a half-wave. "No problem, man. I didn't want you to get picked up for public intoxication. I've seen it happen before in this town."

Johnnie glared at her son's face, puffy from drink. "Where's your truck?"

Cade frowned. He teetered, unbalanced. "Uh, at the lake."

"It better not be anywhere near Granny Opal's place."

Cade's bloodshot eyes barely met hers. "We weren't at the cove, Mama Girl."

She froze, too angry to cry. Her temples throbbed as she kneaded the sides of her head. "Don't *mama girl* me. Get in the house." She hated the venom in her voice.

After Cade staggered up the steps, Brother on his heels, Johnnie turned to Steven. "I owe you one."

"Don't be too hard on him, okay?" He looked around. "I better get this buggy rolling. Don't want your neighbors to freak out."

She watched him shut the passenger door and disappear on the driver's side. Right before he ducked his head down, he called out over the roof: "My guard unit's been activated. We'll be deploying to Iraq. Give D.J. a holler."

"Will do. Be careful." She thought of his mother, a woman she'd never met.

His face broke into a broad grin. "Always."

He had the kind of face people talk about when they say "good bones." Though a tad on the thin side, he could model for *GQ*. He waved one last time, long slender fingers moving in a fluid dance. He had the hands of an artist, a musician. Hands like D.J.'s. But Steven Tuttle's hands spun the wheel of death.

As the hearse pulled away, she listened to the tires rub against the curb. The morning paper caught her eye, but she left it for later. Nothing in the headlines took precedence over what she had to say to her son.

Taking a deep breath, she climbed the front steps and went inside. Brother danced around, waiting to be fed. She retrieved his dishes from the dishwater and filled one with food, the other with water. She set them down in the laundry room.

"There you go, big dog." Brother crunched and gobbled, content in his world of eating. At that moment, Johnnie loved him more than anyone in the world.

She went to make coffee.

After Brother finished eating, he rolled around on the

braided rug in the den, wiping his mouth and snorting. He grabbed a toy and wanted to play but Johnnie wasn't in the mood. "In a minute, big dog. First, I need to talk to Cade."

She found him in the hall bathroom, staring at himself in the mirror. By now he'd sobered up a bit. Their eyes met in the glass.

"I'm sorry. I'll never do it again."

Her own words bit back at her from the lips of her son. For a second she was Cade, leaning against the sink, staring in the mirror. Same promise. Different poison.

She reached up and kissed the back of his bristled scalp. He reeked of alcohol, sweat, vomit, and day-old cologne.

"Cade, I think you need help. I think you have a problem."

"No, Mama. I'm fine."

"You lost your scholarship, Cade. Because of underage drinking."

He averted his eyes, turned on the faucet to drown out her words.

"Cade, look at me. Don't you care?"

His eyes, darker and bluer than Dale's, glared back at her from the mirror. "I fucked up, Mama. But I'm going to make it right. One day soon, you'll be proud of me."

"I am proud of you. Just not at the moment."

For a second the only sound was the water running in the sink and Brother plopping down on the cool hardwood floor outside the bathroom.

Cade splashed his face and grabbed a hand towel. He stood up, towering over her.

Their eyes met once again in the mirror. "No, Mama. I mean *really* proud of me. Just you wait and see."

CHAPTER 14

∿

April 24, 2007

THE FOLLOWING TUESDAY, ON A slow afternoon at the food pantry where Johnnie did her volunteer work, a familiar voice caught her attention.

She looked up, startled by the young man in camouflage. Her eyes cut straight to the nametag on the right chest pocket of his uniform: TUTTLE.

"Steven? Uh, I mean …." Seeing him in his National Guard uniform threw her off. She didn't know what to call him. "I'm sorry, I'm not good with military ranks." Just because the man who'd fathered her had been in the Army and Dale's dad was an Air Force colonel—a *full-bird* colonel at that, Lester Kitchen always reminded everyone, patting both shoulders where his eagle insignia used to sit before he got fat and retired to Florida. Despite all that, she didn't know how to properly address a person in the military.

Steven held a black beret in his hands, "I'm a specialist, ma'am, an E-4. But just Steven to you."

He'd had a haircut since Saturday. His short hair emphasized his exquisite cheekbones. For a second, Johnnie remembered Steven and D.J. in high school. They were the kind of boys whose good looks were less noticeable because of the length of their hair and the style of their clothes. They were clad in skinny-girl jeans and black T-shirts emblazoned with the names of heavy metal bands. Their aggressive music pulsed from the attached garage where they jammed with other angst-ridden teens in D.J.'s band, War-4-Money.

They were all such pacifists back then. Now one of them was going off to war.

"What brings you here?" He appeared taller, more filled out. "Squared away" as Colonel Kitchen might say. He'd looked sharp on Saturday when he dropped Cade off, but this uniform set him apart. Transformed him into someone different, more formidable.

Steven's voice took on an edge. "We deploy in a few days. Had a cookout at the armory on Sunday for the families staying behind. We have a lot left over and our commander wants it put to good use. Plus, we had to clear out the snack bar. Can't take it with us." He gestured to a dolly weighed down by several boxes.

Johnnie came around the counter and did a quick inventory of the items—coffee, bottled water, sports drinks, frozen hamburger patties, hot dogs, buns, industrial-size cans of pork 'n beans, energy bars.

She glanced up and grinned. "Pop Rocks?"

Steven chuckled. "Our last commander liked them."

Several folks ambled in the door and smiled when they spotted the young soldier. The other customers in line and a couple of Johnnie's coworkers seemed to stand a little taller in the presence of a man in uniform. One man smoothed back his hair and sucked in his gut.

At this moment, Johnnie longed to talk to her oldest son. She wished he and Steven had stayed closer after high school. This past Saturday, she'd waited until noon to call D.J., giving him time to sleep in before she told him how Steven had dropped Cade off that morning.

"Wait, so Tutts is driving a hearse now?"

"I thought I told you. I ran into him at the gas station a few weeks ago."

Johnnie mentioned that Steven had joined the National Guard and was deploying to Iraq. That set D.J. off. He went into a rant about the time his sophomore year that he got bullied by a bunch of redneck jocks because he spoke out in class about being against going to war with Iraq. The next morning, as he headed out to work the Saturday breakfast shift at the Cottonbelt Café, Johnnie heard his anguished cry: "Mom, get out here." Rushing outside, she found D.J. in the middle of the yard, surrounded by dozens of for-sale signs planted like gravestones. By the curb, a homemade sign declared: "DIE PUSSY. AMERICA! LOVE IT OR LEAVE IT!"

D.J. had tugged at his ponytail. "Those assholes."

The look in his eyes had crushed Johnnie's heart. She'd called the cops but no one was ever caught.

The memory was still painful all these years later. She wanted to ask Steven if he remembered, but now wasn't the time.

"Guy," she directed one of her coworkers, "would you give Specialist Tuttle a hand?" Together, Steven and the short, squatty fellow with a thick neck slid the boxes off the dolly and stashed them against one wall.

An elderly woman came in the door and giggled the moment she saw Steven. "Oh my, I just love a man in uniform." The woman behind her nodded in agreement.

A big burly man with a scruffy beard walked up and started pumping Steven's hand. "Young fella, thank you for your service."

Steven appeared apologetic. "I haven't even deployed yet."

A Hispanic woman approached, touched his left shoulder. "You remind me of my grandson. He's already been to Iraq and back. Twice." She seemed so proud. "But he's a *Marine*."

Steven gave her a sly grin. "Yes, ma'am. I'm glad he made it back." Johnnie detected a twinkle in his eye.

When they finished the paperwork, Johnnie walked him to the door. She gave him a hug. "I'll be praying for you." But even that seemed inadequate. What if he was like D.J. and no longer believed in prayer? Or God.

Turning, he put the black beret on his head and flashed her a smile. Her hand over her mouth, she watched him march toward an Army Humvee parked in front of the church office.

"Wait!" she called, stepping outside to wave one last time. "What's your mother's name? I thought I might check on her from time to time."

He hesitated. "Her name is Beth. Give her a call." He stuck his camouflaged arm in the air and returned her wave.

She went back inside and tried not to cry. Everything about Steven reminded her of D.J. Everything but the uniform.

CHAPTER 15

~⚬~

May 8, 2007

A WEEK LATER, GRANNY OPAL called Johnnie at the food pantry, her voice chipper as usual. "I've been spring cleaning and found a card you made for your mama ... 'back in the day,' as the kids would say."

With her phone jammed to her ear, Johnnie excused herself and ducked outside, past a line of tired-looking souls waiting for their weekly grocery allotment.

"What kind of card?" She stood near the entrance, hugging herself as the scent of a nearby honeysuckle swirled around her. With each breath, she willed herself to be still. Out in the parking lot, a car door slammed and the church pigeons took off in unison.

Granny sounded slightly out of breath. "Well, my dear. It's a Mother's Day poem you penned when you were eight. It's dated May 14, 1972." She paused, then added with a chuckle, "You were always such a stickler for dates, even at a young age. You used to drive your grandpa batty, asking him every morning what day of the week it was, what month. Guess that's when Santa started putting a calendar in your stocking each year."

Johnnie's eyes followed a convoy of ants marching across the sidewalk. She had the urge to grind them to smithereens. Instead, she took a deep breath and leaned into the side of the building, turning away in case someone walked by. "Read it to me."

"Right now?" the old woman said, her voice faltering.

"Yes." A wicked smile tugged at the corners of Johnnie's mouth. If it was important enough for Granny to interrupt her at work, it was important enough for her to read it. "Now."

"Okay, here goes." Granny cleared her throat and began to read: "Dear Mama."

Johnnie closed her eyes and pictured the poem scrawled in unsteady cursive with Crayola tulips decorating the page. She let her grandmother's soothing voice wrap around her like a protective shawl.

> You are pretty and sweet
> and have small feet.
> If I was rich I'd buy you a crown
> and a princess gown
> and build you a castle
> so you'd never leave town.
> In case you forget, we still live at 8 Lakeside Drive.
>   Love,
>   Johnnie

When her grandmother stopped reading, Johnnie tried to peel herself off the bricks of the building but she couldn't move. She could hardly breathe.

A part of her was back in her eight-year-old body, pudgy and unsure of herself, longing for winter when she could hide under her coat and pretend she was thin. Thin like her friends who had mothers who drove them to ballet and tap and attended every school party smelling of perfume, their hair sprayed and teased.

"Sweet child, are you still there?" Granny's voice burbled from the other end of the line.

Johnnie's throat ached. "Yes, I'm here." A sprinkler kicked on in the flowerbeds and the scent of water and mulch filled her nostrils. But she might as well have been back in third grade, making up fairytales and marking off the days on her calendar, wondering if today was the day Mama might stagger in the house with whiskey on her breath and dark circles under her eyes. And Grandpa Grubbs would be transformed from his good-natured self into someone she didn't recognize.

"I was going to drop this by tomorrow," Granny went on. "I thought you might want to frame it."

Just in time for Mother's Day, Johnnie thought. "Listen, I gotta get back to work. I'll see you tomorrow. Thanks again."

Stashing the phone in her pocket, she went inside. A haggard-looking woman lugging a boxful of food passed her in the hallway. A small child skipped beside her. Johnnie searched the woman's face and saw the same tired and beaten down expression her mother had so often worn. She tried to smile, but the woman averted her eyes. Would she ever stop looking for her mother in every stranger she passed?

Her phone vibrated again right before she picked up her clipboard to help the next customer. She signaled to a coworker that she needed to take this call.

"Yes, Cade. If it's about graduation—"

"Mama, I just left the recruiter's office."

"The recruiter's office?" She turned away from the counter and stared at a stack of canned meat. Something in Cade's voice told her this had nothing to do with college baseball.

"Yes, Mama. I'm going to enlist … in the Army."

THE STENCH OF UNWASHED BODIES followed her from the building to her Suburban. Right after she'd hung up with Cade, a ragtag family of greasy-haired children and their bedraggled parents trudged in the door, asking for food and clothing. They were passing through on their way to somewhere, and Johnnie and her coworkers didn't have the heart to make them fill out the paperwork proving their lack of income. You couldn't fake this kind of misery.

Despite their rancid odor and the pain of Cade's announcement jack-hammering through her heart, Johnnie put on a warm smile and fussed over the family. Making small talk, she doled out food and clothing then walked them to their car, a mismatched pile of junk on wheels.

"You're pretty," the little girl in a tattered yellow dress said as she twirled around Johnnie.

For a second, Johnnie thought the girl was talking to someone else. She reached down and cupped the child's dirty face in her hand. "So are you." The little girl blinked then climbed into the car with the others.

"Thank you for your kindness, ma'am." With his scruffy beard, tattooed forearms, and western-style cowboy shirt stretched tightly across his thin chest, the father couldn't be much older than D.J. "My lady and I appreciate everything."

The young woman, in low-slung jeans and ballet flats, buckled her seat belt and stared straight ahead. Johnnie couldn't blame her for the snub. Even poverty has its pride.

After they left, Johnnie rushed inside to grab her purse and keys. Guy said he would lock up. She wondered if he'd noticed how rattled she was after talking to Cade.

Now, with the air conditioner blowing hot air in her face, she stared out the windshield as the import of her youngest son's phone call began to sink in.

"Mama, I'm going to enlist … in the Army."

"What? No, Cade. You're not old enough."

"I only need one of y'all to sign for me."

But even as she'd argued against it, she'd realized he had already slipped from her grasp. Once that kid made up his mind about anything, he was halfway there.

In her mind, she saw the blast, the bloody mist spray from

the place where he'd been hiding. Or riding in a Humvee. Or handing out candy to a child. Her beautiful blond boy, blown to smithereens in an instant. Just like her father, The Lieutenant. The man she thought was her Uncle Sam. The man waving goodbye at the bus station.

Her phone jangled, jarring her from her trance. She was still in the parking lot, hadn't budged. The engine idled; the AC blew cold air now.

Dale's voice cut through the horror. "Johnnie?"

She started to blurt out about Cade, but the urgency in Dale's voice stopped her short.

"I'm up here on Main. I think I've spotted your mama … parked on a bench in front of the war memorial."

Chills ran up her back. "Oh my God. Are you sure?"

Dale's words were precise, measured, but they still came at her too fast. "I'm positive. Looks a little gaunt. A lot older. But I'd know that face anywhere."

A face they hadn't seen in twenty-three years. A hollow-cheeked beauty who could look you square in the eye while her spirit seemed to be someplace else.

Johnnie's breathing came in rapid bursts. "I'm leaving the church. Don't let her get away."

After fumbling with her phone, she dropped it in her lap and varoomed off in the direction of Soldiers Park.

"Mama!" She smacked the steering wheel with a violent thump. Her anger took her by surprise. She focused on the road, the stop sign ahead, but her thoughts veered back and forth between her mother and Cade.

Turning down the AC, she breathed deeply, trying to settle her racing pulse. A sour smell left behind by the transient family she'd helped clung to her hands and clothes. A smell she knew all too well. The smell of hopelessness, despair, the smell her mama brought into the house on those rare visits home when Granny placed a towel and a bar of soap in her hands. "Go wash up, Victoria. Before Poppy gets home."

Other times she'd appear all glammed up, smelling like the perfume department at Dillard's.

Turning right on Church Street, Johnnie zoomed south past the back side of the park, a long rectangular expanse of green that took up a whole city block. She searched for a woman in blue taffeta, or rags, or God knows what. But the hedges that bordered this side of the park had grown tall, and she couldn't see past them. At the next intersection, she hung a left, raced past the south end of the park, made another left, and sped north on Main.

She spotted Dale's truck by the curb, across from the war memorial, and lurched to a halt behind it. Dale climbed out of the cab and came toward her. He tucked his shirt in his faded jeans. Before she could reach the handle, he yanked open the driver's door and held out his hand.

"Hurry up. I think she just left."

Together they crossed the street and headed toward the center of the park where the statue of the soldier stood guard. Johnnie had to race to keep up with Dale's longer stride. The shade from the big oaks and pecans blocked out most of the sunlight this late in the afternoon.

She scanned the area around the war memorial. *Please be here, Mama.* The bench was empty.

Johnnie remembered all the times she'd played here as a child, skipping along with Mama, Granny, and Grandpa. Then one day in late fall, around Thanksgiving, Johnnie and Mama and Grandpa went for a stroll in the park. Everything seemed fine until Grandpa said something to Mama. Then Mama pushed him away, started wailing, and took to the bench. Johnnie tried to make her laugh by climbing up on the base of the monument. "Look at me, Mama. I'm almost as tall as the soldier." And as Johnnie climbed higher up the statue, Grandpa stashed his hanky in his back pocket and scolded, "Get down, young lady. That's disrespectful."

Johnnie's throat tightened at the memory. *Why had they kept so much hidden from her? Why didn't they just tell her that her daddy had been killed?* The ground rose toward her and she reached for the bench to steady herself.

Dale's voice echoed in her ears. "She must have seen the sign on my truck and got spooked."

Johnnie plopped down on the bench, out of breath. "Maybe you were seeing things. I'm always looking for Mama."

Dale circled the area, looking in all directions. He spun around and glared at Johnnie. "Bullshit. I saw her. Plain as day. Sitting right there." He pointed at the bench. "I know what I saw."

She shivered and turned from Dale to the bronze soldier high on his perch. "How 'bout you, Mr. Statue? Did you see her, too?" *No sense getting her hopes up. After all, Mama had a history of coming and going.*

Dale shook his head and started to walk away.

Johnnie stood up. "Why didn't you chase after her? Stop her from leaving?"

Dale walked back toward her. "She disappeared while I was calling you, before I could get out of my truck."

They stood inches apart in front of the monument. This is the closest they'd been to each other in a long time. Dale ran his thumb along her cheek. She started to give in to the coarse touch of his hand, the scent of him alluring even after a long day of work. Maybe he was ready to call it a truce. To forgive and forget. To come home.

All at once, she felt shy, and she glanced away. Something at the base of the statue caught her eye. What in the world? She moved closer.

Her stomach lurched. There, spray-painted in dark green graffiti: WAR-4-$$$

Dale saw it too. Their eyes met. He bent to get a closer look. "Do you think D.J. did this?"

Johnnie stared at the words. She didn't want to think that her oldest son would deface a memorial built to honor the war dead. Yet after all these years, she could still hear the angry music scream from D.J.'s guitar, see the permanent scowl he wore for months after being targeted by bullies.

"Maybe it was already here," she said. "Maybe this is where D.J. got the name for his band."

Dale pulled off his gimme cap and ran his hand through his hair. "Maybe. Look, I've had a long day. I'll meet you back at the house. Cade asked me to stop by. Says he has something he wants to discuss."

CHAPTER 16

∾

Go Army!

"**Y**OU MIGHT AS WELL STAY for supper." Johnnie moved around the kitchen, aware that Dale was eyeing her butt. She'd worn her favorite jeans to work, the ones that showed off her slim but shapely figure. At her age, it was difficult to find comfortable jeans that fit well.

Dale leaned against the granite island, the brown and cream polished slab he'd spent a whole weekend installing for her birthday two years ago. "Top of the line, Johnnie Girl," he had winked. "No builder's grade for you." And then he'd nuzzled the back of her neck. "When would you like to break it in?" They'd giggled like teenagers in front of Granny Opal and the kids, hiding their private joke.

How had they come to this? This awkward dance between two lovers who'd been living apart, neither one knowing when to make the first move.

"When did you get that blouse?" His attentive eyes seemed to take all of her in as he stood with his arms crossed. "I like that color on you. Peacock blue."

Heat rose in her face. How could she have ever cheated on a man this good? A man who recognized the color *peacock blue*.

She glanced down at the peasant blouse she'd picked up at last week's sidewalk sale. "Thanks. I only paid fifteen bucks for it." Avoiding his eyes, she took a box of whole grain pasta and a bottle of olive oil out of the cupboard and set them on the counter.

Dale went to the sink to wash his hands. "Any idea what Cade wants to talk to me about?"

She studied the way Dale's shoulders flexed as he worked up a lather. She had the urge to sneak up behind him and bury her face in the middle of his strong back. She could hide there forever.

He grabbed a wad of paper towels and turned to look at her. "He's probably going to hit me up for a job since he hasn't said anything about college lately. At least he hasn't to me." He wiped the back of his neck and forehead. "I could use an extra hand. Guess I haven't told you. I won the bid on the old Dooley Mansion."

She lifted the plates from the cabinet. "The Dooley Mansion? You mean the *witch lady's* house? That old place has sat vacant for years. I didn't know you put in a bid."

"Yup. The new owners want to turn it into a bed and breakfast. Should help keep us afloat for a while."

Us. He'd used the term as if nothing had gone wrong between them.

She put a pot of water on to boil. Dale walked around the kitchen and den, running his hands over everything. He paused in front of the stone fireplace. "This is one of the first improvements I made. Remember?"

A puff of hot steam hit her in the face as she dumped the pasta into the boiling water. She turned from the stove. "Of course I remember. I helped you haul the rock."

While they waited for Cade, she basked in the warmth of having Dale home, even if it didn't last past supper. At the sink, she rinsed a handful of cherry tomatoes and stared out the window as the last bit of sun dipped behind the horizon.

When Dale gutted the kitchen two years ago, he'd placed the sink on the north wall so she could see out front and feel less hemmed in. Her mind drifted to the empty bench in front of the war memorial a few blocks to the west. She imagined a woman, limber and lithe, making her way to the bench. Once seated, the woman tilted her head and said something to the soldier. Then the birds scattered and the woman rushed away, leaving nothing behind. As if she'd never been there.

"What are you thinking so hard about?"

Startled, Johnnie turned from the window and caught Dale gazing at her.

The cherry tomatoes were still cupped in her hands. Water dripped everywhere. She swallowed. "Mama."

"I'm sorry she ran. My guess is she's somewhere in the area."

Johnnie set the tomatoes on a cutting board and picked up a paring knife. "Why can't Mama just come home?" The blade sliced through the flesh of one tiny tomato after another. "Why can't she and Granny work out their differences?" Her words seemed to bounce back at her off the cutting board. She might as well have been talking about her and Dale. Why couldn't they work out their differences? Why couldn't Dale just come home?

About then the pasta boiled over and Brother scratched at the back door.

"I'll get him." Dale strode toward the door as if relieved to have something to do.

Setting the knife down, Johnnie flipped the burner off and dumped the pasta into a colander in the sink. She grabbed a dishtowel to wipe up the mess on the stove before pouring the pasta back in the pot and drizzling it with olive oil.

Brother charged in, whining and dancing around Dale. "Hey, big brown." Dale roughhoused him to the floor. The dog snorted with joy.

Then he made a beeline for his water dish, and Dale stood in the middle of the den, unsure of what to do next.

Johnnie heard Cade's pickup come up the driveway and park next to Dale's. As she put the bottle of oil away, she told herself to stay calm. Dale would put a stop to Cade's foolish ideas. Talk some sense into him.

When she turned from the cupboard, Cade was framed in the doorway. Time stopped as she gaped at her *All American* boy in his best khakis, a crisp white dress shirt opened at the collar. His hair looked different too. It had been cut shorter on the sides and spiked on top.

Grinning, he strode over and gave Dale a man hug. "Hey, Daddy." She noticed that he was wearing black dress shoes.

Then Johnnie saw the plastic bag. The one that said *Go Army.*

Dale saw it, too. "Whatcha got there, hotshot?"

Cade lifted the bag. "Stuff the recruiter gave me."

Dale took a step back, scratched his ear. "What recruiter?"

"The sergeant down at the recruiting station."

The muscles in Dale's jaw clenched. "Now hold on a minute. You went and talked to a recruiter?"

Cade looked at Johnnie. "You didn't tell him, Mama?"

She shook her head. "I figured that was your job."

Dale glanced at Johnnie then back at Cade. "There's no need to rush into anything, son. Why don't you give yourself time to think about it? You can come work for me until you figure things out. Maybe take a few classes at the community college."

"I want to serve my country, Daddy." He pulled a coffee mug and some ink pens from the bag. "Here, Mama. This is for you."

Gulping back fear, Johnnie took the mug and stared at the logo: *Proud Army Mom.* She squeezed the mug and searched Cade's determined face. "Son, I don't want you to get killed in some stupid war."

"Mama, you've had all three of us kids dying since the day we were born. It's my decision." He took one of the pens and stuck it in Dale's shirt pocket. "Sorry, they were all out of mugs for dads."

At that moment, something seemed to shift in Dale. Johnnie

saw a fire ignite in his blue eyes.

One question pounded at her temples: What would make Cade suddenly want to join the Army? He'd never once mentioned it until today. Then she remembered Steven. "Did Steven Tuttle put you up to this? Plant this cockamamie idea in your head that morning he brought you home?"

Cade rolled his eyes. "Tutts is a Guard puke, Mama. You don't even know the difference. He's a weekend warrior. I'm talking about going full-time. Active duty."

God, he was already sounding military.

Cade's eyes cut to Dale. "And Daddy, I know how you worry about money. After I serve, I can use the GI Bill to go to college." His voice softened. "All you'd have to worry about then is Callie Ann." He looked at Johnnie. "And Mama, I know you've wanted to go back to school."

Johnnie almost choked.

Dale walked to the window and stared at the backyard. It was already dark out. "So, what do you need from me? My blessing?"

Cade's voice took on a hard edge. "I need one of you to sign the consent form."

Dale took a deep breath. Johnnie could hear it all the way across the room. "And if we don't?"

This conversation is not happening, Johnnie screamed inside her head. She found her focal point: a framed photograph on the wall taken when the kids were ten, five, and three—the boys in their wool buffalo-plaid caps and Callie Ann in a cream knit beanie tied at her chin. All three had their heads thrown back and were catching snowflakes on their tongues.

Cade's voice broke through her memory of that long ago snow day. "I'll be eighteen in two months, Daddy. I won't need your consent then."

"Is this what you really want to do?"

Their voices swirled around her. She wished she could walk into the old photograph and go back in time.

"Yes. I want to do it now, while I'm still young. I don't want to look back someday and regret that I never served."

Even in the photograph, Cade had his mouth opened the widest, his head thrown back the farthest. He was always the adventurous one. Her pulse throbbed in her ears.

Dale let out another sigh. "Okay, then. I'll sign."

She wheeled around, stunned. "You'll do *what*?"

Dale rubbed the back of his neck. "He's going to enlist anyway. Be it now, or two months from now."

"My son is *not* joining the Army." There, she'd said it. She'd built a barricade of words, as if they could stop a tank from barreling down on top of her.

Cade threw up his hands. "Mama, it's always about you. I knew you wouldn't understand." He stomped out, slamming the door behind him. Seconds later his truck went careening down the driveway, a pair of headlights glaring through the side door.

After a moment, Dale moved toward her. "He's going to enlist. With or without us. He needs to know we are on his side."

Shaking, she groped for the right words. "I swear Dale, if you sign …."

He went to calm her. "He's almost eighteen. We have to let him go."

All her anger, all her fear, boiled up. She rushed at Dale, pushing him even though he outweighed her. "If he gets killed, I'll never forgive you."

Dale's face grew crimson as he tried to regain his balance.

She beat her fist against his chest. "You have no right to sign those papers. You didn't serve."

Until that moment, Dale's lack of military service had never come up.

He grabbed her wrist and held her. Their faces were inches apart. "Oh, I served plenty, Johnnie. Every time my dad got orders. Every time I started a new school. Every time a plane went down and Mom waited for the knock at the door."

He moved her aside. "Your son is a grown man. The quicker you accept that, the better."

He left, not even bothering to close the door behind him.

ALONE IN THE KITCHEN, SHE stared at the pot of pasta, cold by now. Out of fear for Cade, she'd said ugly things to Dale. It never mattered to her that Dale hadn't served in the military. She wished she could eat her words.

She continued to stare at the pasta.

The urge came on at once, commanding her to attack the food, cram it down, numb herself. Her mouth watered, she grabbed a fork, hacked into the pasta, and shoved a cold chunk into her mouth. She started to chew.

The old voice ordered her to gorge until she hurt. Don't think. Don't cry. Just cram it down. Forget about Dale. Forget about Cade. Forget about that tragic little family at church.

Forget you ever lived.

Then terror shot through her. What if she couldn't stop once she started?

A violent rage exploded inside her. She lashed out at the invisible presence. The one that was always there, lurking over her shoulder.

"I won, you hear me? I won!"

She flung the fork down and heaved the pasta into the sink. In one quick move, she flipped the switch and fed the pasta into the dark hole. The only sound in the room was the angry growl of the disposal's blades grinding the pasta into mush.

When the sink was empty, she staggered to the den, dropped to her knees on the braided rug, and wept.

CHAPTER 17

~∾

Wednesday, May 9, 2007

Leash in hand, Johnnie and Brother headed east on Merriweather. At the first telephone pole a block from the house, Brother stopped to pee.

"Okay, big dog, let's move before it gets too hot." She gave a gentle tug on his leash, and Brother fell in beside her. At Dooley Street, they turned north and settled into a fast clip.

By noon, the roads and sidewalks would scorch the pads of Brother's paws. But at eight in the morning, the sun was still half-asleep, the air dry. Her face and chest slathered in sunscreen, Johnnie wore a pink visor, lime green gym shorts, and matching sports top. In the old days, before they got Brother, she'd powerwalked to music piped in her ears, a house key tucked in her sock. Nowadays, she never left the house without her cellphone and keys tucked in her fanny pack.

"Nobody'll bother you with that little butt purse strapped to your hips," Dale had teased her one morning as he backed down the driveway. "They'll think you're packin' heat."

He'd caught her in a frisky mood after their spontaneous romp in the sack. She'd patted the bulge and grinned, despite her fear of guns. "Yep, me and my trusty baggie. In case Brother drops one. We'll stop an assailant for sure."

Was that the last time they'd made love, their last tender moment before life had started to throw curve balls?

She picked up her pace, and Brother followed suit. With each stride, the memory of her last words to Dale chipped away at her heart. *If he gets killed, I'll never forgive you.*

Hours after Callie Ann had come home from the girls' softball game, Cade finally showed up. He'd tapped on the bathroom door where Johnnie was washing her face, her cheeks blotchy from crying.

"Mama, I'm sorry I stormed out. I've been over at Granny Opal's talking to Daddy. He told me what you said after I left. About him not serving. But he's not mad at you. He said he understands where it came from."

She blotted her face with a towel, wishing she could hide. "What do you mean?"

"You know, 'cause of what happened to my granddad. The Lieutenant."

BROTHER'S ABRUPT HALT TO SNIFF at something in the grass jerked Johnnie back to the present. Her eyes fixed on a brown clump inches from the sidewalk.

"Leave it," she commanded and yanked on the leash. "You don't need to be sticking your nose in another dog's business."

Brother lifted his head and they started moving again.

They passed a small wooden bungalow with a tidy yard. Two men leaned over a car in the single driveway, their upper halves hidden beneath the open hood. Brother snorted and one of the men, a young guy in overalls, looked up and waved.

"That's a nice lookin' dog you've got there. Is that a Lab?"

"Yeah. He's ninety pounds of chocolate love." She smiled and kept walking. When had compliments about her dog replaced the hoots and wolf whistles?

To her right, a big-bodied jet nosed skyward, taking off from DFW Airport. The roar from the engines reverberated over the blue skies of Portion and filled Johnnie with wonder. She'd been ten when the airport opened, and she and Grandpa Grubbs never grew tired of sitting on the dock, watching the jets fly over. Living this close to a major hub, she sometimes had to stop and remind herself to listen. Today, she welcomed the noise, like a clap of thunder in the middle of a drought.

A burst of adrenaline kicked in and she called to Brother, "Come on. Let's race it." They took off trotting, Brother's ears flat against his head, his retriever nose out in front. Johnnie's legs, still white from winter, pumped faster and faster to cover ground and her short ponytail swung behind her. A half block later, the jet disappeared over the tree line and her lungs gave out.

Gulping air, she told herself that last night's pasta episode was behind her. She vowed to stay vigilant. As she and Brother walked, she recalled her early twenties, when she'd been a runner. She'd adjust her sweatband, put one foot in front of the other, and head down the streets of Portion. It could be 101 in the shade, the heat bouncing off the black asphalt, but she did her time. She ran for her mind as much as her body. She ran to stay alive. To gain some kind of inner strength that would keep her from killing herself with food. She never wanted to die alone in a bathroom, her esophagus ruptured, or choke to death on a spoon.

But even now, as she and Brother Dog worked their muscles, a shadow tagged along—a fourteen-year-old with reddish brown hair parted straight down the middle, hanging limp past her shoulders. Ruddy-cheeked and bashful, a scarlet rash between her thighs. Her pudgy legs had to pump to keep up. Johnnie wanted to backhand her, trip her, tell her to go away. After all these years, she thought she'd ditched the lonely girl who wanted to shed fifteen pounds, to have a boyfriend. The girl who would do whatever it took to get there, even if it meant declaring war on her body.

Brother pulled on the leash, lunging at a squirrel that

darted across their path. Johnnie reined him in as the squirrel scampered up the nearest tree. Craning her neck, she caught sight of the chattering rodent on the lowest limb, flipping its fluffy tail in a tease. Brother barked, and Johnnie tried to calm him down.

Then, one after another, the canine chorus began. Up and down the street, dogs barked in a symphony of yelps and yaps. "See what we've done, handsome man. We've got the whole neighborhood riled up."

Back on the sidewalk, she ordered Brother to heel. He flashed his brown eyes and obeyed. A black and white cop car drove past, going in the opposite direction. For a second her heart stopped; she almost turned to follow the cop, to make sure he didn't pull up in front of her house. Glancing back, she was relieved to see that the car kept heading south on Dooley instead of turning on Merriweather. Then Cade's words charged through her mind: "You've had all of us dying since the day we were born."

She sighed. And now she'd have to add a green Army staff car to her list of vehicles to fear.

As they waited at the next intersection for the light to turn green, she checked her watch. They'd only been gone ten minutes. Brother panted and she reached down and patted the top of his head. "Good boy." The light turned and they started across Red Bud Lane as a garbage truck squeaked to a stop in front of the crosswalk. The stink hit her head on.

"Whew. The smell could knock a buzzard off a shit wagon at fifty paces." She hadn't heard this saying in years—it was one of Aunt Beryl's favorites, the old biddy—and yet it had floated to the top of Johnnie's memory like fresh cream. She waved at the dark-skinned driver and hoped he couldn't read her lips. He tipped his hat and grinned.

As she stepped up on the curb, Portion Cemetery loomed before her in one long stretch of weathered tombstones, scruffy post oaks, and a black wrought-iron fence that ran the length of Dooley Street as far as the eye could see. Her plan was to loop around the cemetery and head home.

Half a block away, a woman walked out of the big arched gate that served as the cemetery's main entrance. Russet-haired and frail, she glided along in a calico dress and flats as she headed north on Dooley. Johnnie caught her breath, squinting to get a closer look. Even from this distance, she could see that the woman's long hair was gathered at the nape of her neck in an elegant ponytail, tied with a ribbon. The same way Mama used to wear her hair when going out.

Mama would be fifty-eight now, about the same age as the woman ahead of her on the sidewalk. Johnnie let her imagination run wild ….

Yesterday Dale had seen Mama at the war memorial. Could she still be in the area? Had she stopped by the cemetery this morning, maybe on her way to see Granny Opal to surprise her right before Mother's Day? Granny's house was half a mile west. Johnnie had been searching for Mama all these years, and now she was right in front of her and headed to Granny Opal's.

"Come on, boy. Let's follow her." Putting one foot and paw in front of the other, they picked up their pace.

Every cell in Johnnie's body sprang to life. Her skin prickled as she and Brother worked to close the gap between them and Mama. But as Johnnie tried to control her breathing, to keep her heart from bursting out of her chest, the past twenty-three years flashed before her eyes. She thought about all her mama had missed: Grandpa Grubbs' death, the births of her three children, Dale's climb up the ladder in the construction business. Her recovery from what Aunt Beryl called her "little gluttony problem." Granny Opal's too-tight smile as she tried to hold it all together, year after year.

Suddenly, Johnnie couldn't hold back.

The fury over being abandoned shook her. She didn't recognize the frantic scream that exploded from her mouth.

"Mama! It's me. Johnnie!" Her voiced pierced the morning air.

The woman appeared startled at first, but instead of stopping to look back, she kept going. Her stride turned into a half-walk half-jog as she tried to get away.

Johnnie punched her fist in the air. "Mama, goddamn you! It's me. Your daughter." She took off running, Brother panting at her heels. They had just passed the big arched gate.

The woman kept moving. Johnnie and Brother were gaining on her. They were close enough to see her ghostly calves, the streaks of gray that threaded her hair.

"Mama. For God's sake, stop. You've got a grandson about to enlist in the—" The word *Army* formed in her mind but strangled in her throat. Her mouth opened but nothing came out.

The woman slowed down for a second and glanced back. They'd closed the gap. A few more yards, and Johnnie could have reached out and touched her.

Then Brother let out a bloodcurdling yelp. He began to limp. Blood spurted from his right paw. In one quick flash, Johnnie saw the shards of glass from what remained of a broken beer bottle and her mama fleeing away. Brother pushed against her, crying with pain.

She crouched down and tried to coax him away from the broken glass. She cursed whoever had tossed it. There was no way Brother could make it home on foot. With one arm around his trembling barrel-like body, she fumbled to unzip her fanny pack. If she could just get to her cell phone, she could call for help.

Her hand was shaking so badly, she had trouble with the zipper. Then her throat closed up, swollen shut like she'd been stung by a thousand bees. She couldn't swallow. She couldn't breathe.

From the corner of her eye, she saw a faded red VW Bus come out of the cemetery gate and sputter to a halt.

"Mrs. Kitchen?"

Whipping her head around, she clutched at her throat and watched in slow motion as Mr. Marvel cut the engine, dislodged his girth from the driver's seat, and wobbled over to where she and Brother were huddled on the sidewalk. He wore a pair of garden gloves.

Brother growled and his hackles stood up. She still couldn't breathe … felt faint.

Before she realized what was happening, Mr. Marvel placed something over her face. She was dying, and now he was going to smother her, finish her off. She prayed he didn't hurt Brother.

Through her terror, she heard him say, "Blow into the bag, Mrs. Kitchen. You're hyperventilating."

* * *

Johnnie's Journal
4:00 a.m.
Up From a Dream
May 10, 2007

Dear Mama,

I am running, with Brother Dog beside me. He's off leash. Heading into a neighborhood of shotgun houses and cracked sidewalks, I hope to catch a glimpse of you crouched against the blistered side of a house, a hovel that passes for someone's home. It's the middle of the night and we are bathed in darkness, saturated in black air. A few blocks away, towering over the gnarled limbs of ancient trees, the skyscrapers have dimmed and emptied out. Even the janitors have gone home.

I've been here before, in broad daylight, passing out flyers with your picture, ignorance and youth my only protection. But now I feel afraid and Brother senses it. Our eyes meet.

The next thing I know, I am running on four legs, only inches above the sidewalk. My muscles work like they've never worked before, and I can see things I've never seen before. I am

Brother. I've slipped into his skin, hiding behind his rich dark coat, and he is carrying me away.

No one would dare harm a big dog running in the night.

Johnnie

CHAPTER 18

~ও

May 18

THE FOLLOWING FRIDAY, JOHNNIE HEARD a soft knock at the front door. Peeking out the kitchen window, she half-expected to see a frail woman in a cotton dress standing on the porch. Instead, she spotted Dale's truck parked at the bend in the driveway. What was he doing here this time of morning? Maybe he'd stopped by to pick up a few things. Or maybe he'd come to pick a fight. Either way she was embarrassed. The last time he'd come home she had punched him in the chest.

She took a deep breath and opened the door. Her eyes were drawn to his faded Levis and short-sleeved plaid shirt. The hair on his tanned forearms shimmered like spun gold.

He rubbed his palms together. "You got any sweet tea?"

Gripping the doorknob, she tried to calm her sprinting heart. "No, but I can make some."

She held the door wide open and stepped aside to let him pass. "How come you're not at work?"

"Actually, I'm just down the street at the Dooley Mansion. We start on it next week. Thought I'd drop by since I'm in the neighborhood."

Her teeth started to chatter and her body to shake.

His hand brushed against her arm. She was barefoot, wearing only shorts and a sports bra. "Are you cold? Looks like you just got back from walking Brother."

She shook her head and shut the door, avoiding his blue eyes, the same eyes that had pulled her across a crowded patio at a frat house in Denton.

His callused thumb grazed her cheek. "You know what today is, don't you?"

She stared at his steel-toed work boots worn at the tips, afraid to look at him. "It's our twenty-third wedding anniversary, Dale."

He leaned down and nuzzled her neck, reaching to free her ponytail. "I'm real thirsty, Johnnie Girl."

The tenderness in his voice invited her to join him. As he twined his fingers in her hair, she warmed under his touch.

Lifting her face to his, she gazed into his eyes … searching, searching for her way back.

Her lips parted, meeting his.

"Drink," she whispered, and they moved together as one down the hallway toward the bedroom.

That evening, at dusk, they walked hand in hand up Merriweather, the western sky ablaze in reds and yellows. A slight breeze had chased away the heat of the day, and the smells of other people's suppers cooking floated through the air.

Johnnie couldn't remember the last time she and Dale had gone on a date, a date where they strolled along like young lovers without the kids or dog in tow.

"Glad you got off work early." She leaned into his shoulder then glanced up in time to see his eyes crinkle in a grin.

"Hey, being the boss has its perks." He reached down and patted her on the behind.

She giggled, still basking in the afterglow of their morning together. After they'd made love, she fixed his sweet tea and sent him back to work, fully quenched, with a smile she hadn't seen in weeks. They hadn't talked much, but it was a start.

Rounding the corner onto Main Street, she spotted Mr. Marvel's VW Bus parked in front of Farrow & Sons, a canary yellow two-story structure with large white columns that gave the impression the whole place was trying too hard to look inviting. *At least they'd stopped spray-painting the lawn green every winter*, Johnnie thought. That was like putting makeup on dead people.

A chill sped up her spine.

Last week, after Brother cut his foot at the cemetery, Mr. Marvel gave them a lift. On the ride home, he tapped his stubby fingers against the steering wheel and said, "Sometimes the dead feel more alive than the people right in front of you." At the time, Johnnie had been inhaling exhaust fumes—the bus reeked of gasoline and sweat—and her mind was on Brother's injured paw, the blood-smeared floorboard, and the woman who got away.

But now, seeing the red bus in front of the mortuary brought Mr. Marvel's words back into focus.

"What's he doing there on a Friday night? The parking lot's empty."

Dale looked around. "There doesn't appear to be a visitation."

"One minute I feel sorry for him and the next, well …. Did I tell you I saw him kissing a box of kids' cereal in the grocery store?"

Dale chuckled. "Maybe he's on a diet and he was kissing his favorite cereal goodbye."

She glanced back in time to see Mr. Marvel come out of the mortuary. Just then, a large jetliner came low over South Main on its final approach into DFW Airport. After a few steps, he halted and craned his neck skyward, watching the jet's flickering lights until they disappeared from view on the other side of the freeway a half-mile away.

Even in the fading light, Johnnie could see that Mr. Marvel wore his pilot uniform.

She tugged on Dale's arm and whispered for him to slow down. "Yesterday, around this same time, I saw him step off his porch and throw what appeared to be a child's balsa wood glider. The glider sailed through the air and landed a few feet from the curb."

"Yeah, so? Lots of men still play with toys. Some just cost more than others."

"No, Dale. It's what he did when he went to pick it up." Her throat ached at the memory and she shivered.

By now they'd stopped walking and Dale was frowning with impatience. "Come on, honey. I could sure use a beer."

Johnnie swallowed. Dale had no idea. "He stroked the tiny wings as if it were a small bird in his hand. The whole time he was crying softly, 'Edwin, Edwin.' And then he broke that little glider in half."

Dale's jaw twitched and he rubbed a nervous hand across her back. "He's an odd fellow, Johnnie Girl. You need to keep an eye on him. Don't let him in the house when you're home alone. He seems a bit unpredictable."

No sooner had Dale finished talking than the VW Bus sputtered past and headed up Main, the red taillights blending in with the northbound traffic. Millions of tiny white lights twinkled up and down the street, making the trees sparkle and outlining the tops of buildings. Every night looked like Christmas in historic downtown Portion—a town whose century-old brick storefronts greeted visitors with deep bay windows and beveled glass doors.

Johnnie looped her arm through Dale's and they headed up Main, looking for a place to eat. A jazz band played for a small crowd flocked around the gazebo by city hall, but in the back of her mind, she heard a grown man crying, *Edwin, Edwin* ....

A SHORT TIME LATER, THEY strolled past The Grapevine,

Portion's premier winery and tasting room. Johnnie tossed her hair back and laughed. "Did I ever tell you about the time Whit and I almost got kicked out of that place?"

Dale cocked his head and gave her a mock frown. "I'm almost afraid to ask. No telling with you and Whit."

She knuckled him playfully on the arm. "They were having a free wine tasting. Let's just say we got our money's worth."

Dale stopped to peek in the window. "Looks pretty hoity-toity, if you ask me. What happened? Y'all get schnockered?"

"Boy howdy." She felt tipsy from the night air, the music, the parade of Friday night traffic filing up and down Main Street.

Dale moved for the door. "Come on, honey. Let's go see if they remember you."

"Oh, heck no." She grabbed him and pulled him down the sidewalk. "Keep walking, cowboy."

When they got to the intersection of Worth and Main, her eyes were drawn to a new neon sign high over the grand corner entrance of the stately old bank building across the street.

The sign over the large transom window said: THE PREACHER'S HOUSE—*a tavern and emporium of good eats.* Above the sign, the date 1900 was etched in black on a white limestone block. On a marquee beside the ornate leaded glass doors flashed the welcome: Happy Hour 5-7 p.m.

Right then and there, Johnnie made up her mind that's where she wanted to eat. For once, she didn't care what was on the menu. Fried, grilled, blackened … they were all the same at this moment. It was the building that called to her—a place that enchanted her as a child—and the light shining through the massive glass doors. Squeezing Dale's hand, she wondered how she'd passed by the former bank all these years, barely giving it a thought until now.

"Oh, Dale, I haven't been through those doors in years. Let's go in."

He glanced at his watch then back up at the sign. "The Preacher's House, huh? Looks like we just missed happy hour."

High overhead, the light turned green and they stepped off the curb to cross the street.

Suddenly, she was eight years old, holding Grandpa's hand and skipping along beside him as they headed toward the bank. "I just *love* those *fancy* doors," she chattered, pulling him along.

Grandpa laughed and let her lead the way. "Not to mention those sweets they give you, right, young lady?"

Dale held the door open for her, and as she stepped across the brass-plated threshold with the word BANK embossed in the metal, some of the magic faded. Gone was the pretty young teller with the bright red lipstick and bouffant hair, smiling down at Johnnie behind the brass bars and marble counter. The space seemed smaller now, the hardwood floors less shiny, the dark brick walls less formidable. But the ceiling still soared, and the antique fans still whirred.

"Howdy, folks. Welcome to The Preacher's House."

Lost in thought, Johnnie flinched at the sound of a man's voice. She hadn't seen him approach.

He was trim and slightly balding, with a clipped salt and pepper beard and a bar towel draped over his shoulder. Smiling, he said, "My name's Chick. I'm the proprietor."

Dale pressed his hand gently against her back. "Hey, Chick. Dale Kitchen. Nice to meet you. This is my wife, Johnnie."

Chick gave her a cordial nod. "Is this your first time here?"

She glanced around the room, eyeing the cozy cluster of tables and a long antique bar to the left. People were having dinner and a young couple sat at the bar watching the Rangers on a flat screen TV. "No, but it's our first time for dinner."

Dale's fingers played at the curve of her back, and she wondered if he was horny again. Or was it a signal for her to move along, not go into some long-winded spiel about her childhood in Portion?

She gave him a slight smile, then wiggled free from his touch.

As Chick grabbed two menus and showed them to their

table, Johnnie remembered the day she and Grandpa opened up her first savings account. The teller had just given her a sucker when Grandpa bent down and handed her a passbook. "This is *seed* money for college," he said, "and we're going to watch it grow." But she'd dropped out after two semesters and married Dale. And all that seed money had gone into her growing family.

Her eyes misted over and her vision blurred. When Dale pulled out a chair for her to sit down, she realized what she needed to say to him over dinner.

Once they were seated, Chick clapped his hands and said, "What can I get you folks to drink?"

Johnnie ordered a glass of Chardonnay and fiddled with the edge of the tablecloth.

Dale leaned back in his chair. "Normally, I'd have a Bud Lite. But tonight," he paused, grinning at Johnnie, "I feel like something special. What do you recommend?"

Chick crossed his arms. "How about a Texas Beer? Brewed right here in Fort Worth?"

Dale nodded. "Sounds good to me."

"We've got a new one called Storm Cloud. It's an IPA. Real popular right now."

"Storm Cloud it is," Dale said, tapping the table.

"What's an IPA?" Johnnie asked after Chick left.

"India Pale Ale. It's a type of beer." Dale glanced around, taking in the architecture. "Didn't Bonnie and Clyde rob this place back in the day?"

"That's what Grandpa used to say. He said they robbed the bank on Good Friday then killed those two state troopers out on 114 on Easter Sunday."

Dale shifted in his chair, and Johnnie wondered if he was nervous about being alone with her, making small talk and acting like nothing had happened. Until they dealt with the affair, Jeral's ghost would always be sleeping in their bed, inviting himself to dinner, and nudging his way into every family conversation. The only way to get rid of him was to talk about what had happened, but Dale didn't want to. He told Johnnie that morning he just wanted to get past it. Move on. Forget it ever happened.

Chick returned with their drinks then excused himself to wait on another customer.

After he left, she stared at the label on Dale's beer—a picture of an old sailing ship being tossed about in a gale. *That's us,* she thought, fingering the stem of her wine glass. We're that boat out on open water, caught in the middle of a storm. All we can do is ride it out and hope there's something left over when we hit dry land.

It was now or never, she realized. She wouldn't push Dale to talk about the affair and why she strayed, but she would no longer stay silent about her desire to go back to school.

"Dale, you know how you said earlier that you didn't know what to get me for our anniversary …?"

Dale thumbed through the menu, barely glancing at her. "Yeah."

She sipped her wine. "I know what I want. What I've been wanting for a long time."

He looked up from the menu, his eyes cautious but caring. "Yeah, what's that?"

Resting her chin on her steepled fingers, she began, "I want to go back to college. I've been trying to tell you for years."

Dale put the menu down and took a swig of beer. She noted how his jaw flexed, how he turned away at the mention of college. "Johnnie, we've been over this. You know we don't have the money."

The smile slid right off her face, and her eyes stung with the old hurt. He was dredging up the same worn-out excuse even though it no longer applied.

Taking a deep breath, she clasped her hands on the table and kept her voice low. "It's not the money, is it? Not really, especially now that Cade's joining the Army. That frees up some funds."

She studied the way Dale's tongue probed against the inside of his cheek. The way he tried so hard not to show emotion.

And then she knew.

She knew why he'd been holding her back all these years. Why he blew her off every time she tried to discuss school. How could she have missed it? The answer was sitting right in front of her. In the powerful chest muscles and scattering of blond hair peeking out the V of his button-down chambray shirt, opened at the collar. In the bronzed hands, callused from years of hard work, that opened and closed over each other as he quietly cracked his knuckles.

"Dale, is it because you didn't finish? Is it because you were only one year away from getting your degree? This isn't about me at all, is it? It's about *you*."

He turned his soft gaze toward her and let out a heavy sigh. "You know what my old man told me when I dropped out and went into construction? He told me I was his biggest disappointment. That I'd never amount to anything without a college degree."

She took his hands in hers, bringing them up to her lips. "And look at you now. These hands built me a beautiful life. You've worked so hard to build your business. The kids and I have never wanted for anything."

Dale looked away, then back at Johnnie. His eyes said it all. "Go take your classes. As many as you want. Happy anniversary."

Closing her eyes, she rested her cheek on his hands. She couldn't bear to see the look that passed over his face ... the look that said *I give in.*

Later, after they'd finished dinner and Dale had paid the tab, Chick walked them to the door and thanked them for stopping by.

Johnnie had downed two glasses of wine throughout the

evening, one over a plate of grilled salmon and asparagus, and she was feeling rather frisky. "So, Chick, why The Preacher's House? Why not Chick's Place?"

"Or the *Chick*-en Coop?" Dale threw in, smiling at his own joke.

Clamping a hand over her mouth, Johnnie giggled and kicked Dale in the shin.

Chick laughed and slapped the door with his bar towel. "I knew this old preacher once. He told me he mended more broken souls sitting around his kitchen table over a pint than he ever did in church. So after I lost my job in telecommunications, I decided to follow his example." He gestured around the place with his towel. "I hope you folks felt at home here. Come back any time."

Out on the sidewalk, a car horn honked and someone gunned an engine.

Dale stuck his hands in his pockets and rocked back on his heels. "I got a call from my old man this afternoon. He's coming for Cade's graduation. Wants to stay through Memorial Day. You okay with that?"

Johnnie stared at a NO PARKING sign by the curb. The last thing she wanted to do was play hostess to her father-in-law, especially now, with so much going on in her family. She breathed in the night air and tried to find the humor in the situation.

"Well, on the bright side, this will give me a good excuse to clean the house. Don't want the colonel running his white gloves under my toilet rims."

Dale laughed. "Don't worry. He reserved a hotel room." Then he hugged her close and whispered, "Let's go home."

They headed down Main Street, arm in arm, past The Palace Theatre where D.J. got hassled by a cop. Past the place on the curb where a young Callie Ann bolted from the crowd and almost got trampled by a horse during the annual Christmas parade. Past the recruiting station where Cade and Dale had visited last week ... and signed Cade's life away.

CHAPTER 19

❧

Monday, May 21, 2007

Around noon, Johnnie and Callie Ann loaded up Brother to take him to the vet to get his paw checked. Dark clouds had rolled in, and it was sprinkling when they left the house.

"Probably just a tease. It's been over a month since the last rain." Johnnie glanced sideways at her daughter and kept talking. "I can just hear your dad now. He's probably standing out in front of the Dooley Mansion, begging the clouds to blow away. We need the rain, but your dad and his crew need the work."

Callie Ann stared out the passenger window and said nothing. Johnnie might as well have been talking to herself. Maybe her daughter was thinking: *Why do adults always yap about the weather when kids could care less?*

"How did your final this morning go?" Johnnie tried again then glanced at Brother in the rear view mirror. He sat on his haunches directly behind the front bucket seats and stared straight ahead.

Callie Ann shrugged. "Okay, I guess. One down and four to go." She wore her hair pulled to one side. Her profile reminded

Johnnie of old school photos of her mama when she was a girl. Other times—like now, when her daughter turned her head a certain way—she looked like Dale's mom. How was it, Johnnie thought, that her three children had grown up without knowing their two grandmothers? One had been lost to cancer; the other was missing in action.

A big fat raindrop plopped on the windshield. Then another.

"When do you leave for drill team camp?" At the stop sign she hung a right and they headed up Main Street.

Without looking, Johnnie could feel her daughter's smoky eyes burn a hole in her.

"Gosh, Mom, don't you ever stop talking? Why do you ask so many questions?"

Callie Ann's words stung all over her body; it was as if a nest of invisible wasps had attacked her. Just like the time years ago when Johnnie had simply asked, "Hi, baby, how did dance practice go?" Callie Ann had flounced her tutu in the car and snapped, "Sometimes I wish I had a different mother."

Johnnie swallowed the hurt and reminded herself that Callie Ann had her moods, that sometimes out of nowhere she could say hateful things and not mean them.

In no time the rain started coming down in sheets, the street now wet.

Up ahead, the light turned yellow and she slowed as the car in front of her ran a red light. That's when she saw him out of the corner of her eye. Caught in the downpour, an elderly man in a wheelchair rolled toward the crosswalk. She thought of pulling over to help him, but all the parking slots were taken. Besides, she hated to parallel park.

She switched on her wipers as the man in the wheelchair sat getting drenched. He seemed so helpless, his only protection an old-fashioned fedora to shield his face from the driving rain.

About this time, she spotted Dale's truck coming toward them on the other side of the street. He must have abandoned the job and headed out on an errand.

"Oh, look, there's Dad," Callie Ann pointed.

Dale swerved his truck to the curb and started flashing his emergency lights; then he hopped out and made a mad dash toward the man in the wheelchair. From under his arm, he whipped out an umbrella, held it over the man, and pushed him across the street to the other side. A bolt of lightning zigzagged right down the middle of Main Street.

Her eyes fixed on the windshield wipers swishing back and forth, Johnnie felt a memory crash in on her as Dale got the man situated under the awning of the corner drugstore ....

SHE HAD JUST POPPED A handful of laxatives when Dale came home from work, all lovey-dovey and in the mood. She was on top when her bowels cut loose. They both froze as Dale tried to comprehend what had happened. Without saying a word, he stripped the bed, carried her to the shower, and cradled her under the warm spray of water for what seemed like hours. They never talked about it again.

CALLIE ANN PRESSED FORWARD IN her seat, one hand on the dashboard. "Dad is such a good person." She glanced up at the light. "Mom, you can go now. It's green."

Johnnie wiped her eyes. They proceeded through the intersection, her vision blurry.

"Mom, why are you crying?"

How could she tell her daughter what had just gone through her mind?

"You ask too many questions," she blubbered, but it came out a laugh. With her left hand on the steering wheel and her eyes straight ahead, she fumbled for her purse and plopped it in Callie Ann's lap. "Can you hunt through there and find me a tissue?"

In her head, she heard Karen Carpenter and Mama belting out about how rainy days and Mondays always get them down.

* * *

Johnnie's Journal
May 21, 2007
Dripping wet and waiting to see the vet

Dear Mama,

   Sometimes, in the middle of a storm, you can't hear the thunder.

                    Johnnie

CHAPTER 20

❧

Saturday, May 26, 2007
Graduation Day

"**Y**OU DUMB JOCK!" D.J.'s VOICE thundered as Johnnie entered the side door, a grocery bag in each arm. "You pissed away your scholarship. Now you wanna play G.I. Joe? This isn't a game, bro."

She winced as D.J. flung his words through the air like machetes.

In his yellow cap and gown, Cade puffed up like a horned toad. "I want to serve my country."

Johnnie set the bags on the kitchen island and stared at her sons, who had yet to see her.

D.J. had his back to her. "What, so you can be a big war hero like Pat Tillman? If you get killed in that insane war, you'll be just another dead body processed through Dover."

D.J.'s words hacked into her heart. The one trait she could always count on: he didn't mince words.

Cade paced back and forth between the den and kitchen, the hem of his gown billowing at his sides, the tassel on his mortarboard swinging in his face. "Dude, somebody's gotta fight those ragheads."

Johnnie flicked the light switch on and off to get their

attention. "Do I need to haul the boxing gloves out of Dad's closet so y'all can duke it out?" When the boys were young, Dale got tired of them fighting so he bought a set of boxing gloves and made them punch each other until they wore themselves out.

D.J. swiveled around. "Uh, hey, Mom." He ambled toward her, a sheepish grin on his whiskered face. A summer blazer topped off his slim black jeans. "Cade and I were just talking."

"You look nice. You cut your hair." She reached up to hug him and let her fingers brush the waves that fell right below his collar.

"I figured I'd better clean up for the occasion. Where's Dad?"

"He went to pick up your grandpa from the airport."

"So ... Dad's moved back home then?" He held her at arm's length. "Not *shacking up* at Granny Opal's?" He tilted his head and chuckled. "That was a little weird, Mom."

"Tell me about it."

Cade glanced at his watch. "Mama, I don't have time to wait on the whole fam-damily. I have to be at the convention center in an hour. We'll have to take pictures later."

Even as she stared at him in his cap and gown, she saw a gap-toothed, cotton-top little boy with stubby legs pumping hard as he rounded the bases at T-Ball, sliding in for his umpteenth homerun. In a few weeks, he would head off to basic training. Then what? War?

Her eyes darted to D.J., all decked out for his brother's graduation. But her mind slipped back to the Christmas break when the boys ran away from home ....

AT NINE AND FOUR, THEY loaded up their red wagon with a sleeping bag and juice boxes and got as far as Soldiers Park. They set up camp at the base of the war memorial, D.J. armed with his brand new BB gun. That's how a frantic Johnnie found them: Cade snuggled in a sleeping bag, D.J. standing guard. When Johnnie lashed out at them about how they could have been kidnapped, D.J. lifted his BB gun and said, "No way, Mom. I would have shot them in the nuts."

A WHIMPER CAME FROM THE hallway. Johnnie glanced in that direction, expecting to see Brother upset by the boys' raised voices. Instead, Callie Ann appeared, wrapped squaw-like in a blanket. Brother Dog came up beside her, sat on his haunches, and stared out at all of them as if he were Callie Ann's own personal bodyguard.

How long has she been standing there? Johnnie wondered. What did she hear?

"Sis, you okay? You need to go get dressed. We're leaving as soon as Dad and Grandpa get back from the airport."

Callie Ann didn't move.

Cade pivoted. "Oh Lord, Callie Ann. You're not even ready." He glanced at Johnnie. "Mama, I got to go."

Johnnie went to put the groceries away. She still had to change clothes and put on makeup. "Go. Be careful driving."

And with that Cade was out the side door in a swirl of yellow. "Somebody send me a text so I can find y'all in the crowd."

D.J. hollered, "I got it!" Then he called to Brother, "Come give me a kiss, ya big lazy mutt."

Johnnie stashed the milk in the fridge and was about to ask D.J. to put the dry goods away when Callie Ann let out a gut-wrenching cry.

"Mother, make him stop," she wailed, flinging off the blanket and throwing herself on the couch. "Please don't let Cade join the Army."

* * *

Johnnie's Journal
Memorial Day
May 28, 2007

Dear Father "Unknown":

At least that's what my birth certificate says about you. Mama's name appears as a statement next to the word Mother: Victoria Grubbs. No question about it. But not *Father*. You appear as one eyebrow-raising word: UNKNOWN. But I guess *unknown* is better than nothing at all. Better than a flatline _____ after the word "father." As if you've always been dead.

Until Dale found those two photos, you'd been like an unknown soldier to me: a vague recollection of a man in uniform. Today, on a day set aside to remember our war dead, my kids—your grandkids—finally have a face to go with your name and rank.

I hope you didn't suffer,

Johnnie

CHAPTER 21

~

Memorial Day—Late Afternoon

D.J. LIFTED THE LID TO the cake box and let out a quiet chuckle. "Where are the little green Army men? Don't tell me Granny's lost her touch."

Johnnie elbowed her son. "Shush, she might hear you." She gestured at the back door where Granny had stuck her head out to apologize to Cade for missing his graduation on Saturday.

Breathing in the aroma of buttercream frosting, Johnnie stared at the yellow sheet cake decorated with a plastic tank in one corner and a miniature diploma in the other. Johnnie read the message scrawled in green icing across the center of the cake: *Congratulations Cade, Portion High '07, Go Army.*

"She does love her theme cakes," D.J. added, peeking over his shoulder at Johnnie. "Remember mine?"

Johnnie smiled and patted him on the arm. "How could I forget? Yours was a giant electric guitar, complete with strings made out of dental floss. You know Granny was ahead of her time. She ran a bakery out of her home long before any of us ever heard the term *cottage industry*."

"How's she doing? She seems to have slowed down a bit since the last time I was home."

No sooner had D.J. spoken than Granny appeared. "D.J., you get taller every time I see you." She slapped him on the back, but it seemed to Johnnie that some of the pep had gone out of her grandmother over the last few weeks.

Johnnie grabbed the stack of paper plates and plastic forks and handed them to D.J. "Son, would you mind taking these out back?"

After D.J. left, Johnnie placed her hand on Granny's shoulder. "Have you had any more dizzy spells since Saturday?"

Granny pulled at one of her earrings. "No, but I did bump my head on the cupboard door yesterday as I was baking Cade's cake. Good thing I'm hardheaded." She rapped her fist against the side of her head to make light of the situation.

"Here, give me a hand with the cake." Johnnie lifted it from the box and placed it in the center of the kitchen table. It might have been her imagination, but Granny's hands seemed to tremble a bit more than usual as she fussed with a corner of the icing that smudged in the transfer from box to table.

Granny stepped back to admire her handiwork. "I hate that you postponed the graduation party just for me."

"Nonsense. Cade wouldn't think of having the party without you," Johnnie lied, eyeing new liver spots on the backs of Granny's hands. Or were those fresh bruises? In truth, Cade was thrilled that they'd waited until today to celebrate. The last thing he had wanted to do Saturday night was hang out with the "old folks" back at the house.

As Johnnie went to grab the tossed salad and deviled eggs, Callie Ann breezed past with an empty glass in her hand. She headed straight for the colonel's bottle of Johnny Walker Red.

"What are you, his barmaid?" Johnnie frowned at her daughter's yellow booty shorts, which barely covered her rear. Wearing them to drill team practice was one thing. Parading around in them in front of her brothers and her grandfather was another. She could just imagine the colonel calling Callie Ann over, asking her to sit on his lap, and then sweet-talking his granddaughter into fixing him another drink.

Callie Ann tossed her hair back. "Oh, Mother. He just asked me to refresh it. It's not like I'm going to start drinking or anything. That would be my dumb brother, Cade. Now … what do I add first? The Scotch or the ice?"

"The ice," Granny cackled, glancing up and down at Callie Ann's long slender legs. "Then the booze and a splash of water. And make me one, too, while you're at it."

Johnnie blinked. "Since when did you start drinking hard liquor, Granny?"

Granny chuckled and opened the door for Johnnie. The tang of barbequed chicken filled the air. "Longer than you've been alive, my dear." Her eyes seemed to light up when she saw Dale at the far end of the deck, standing over the hot grill. She leaned toward Johnnie and whispered, "I sure do miss having Dale around. He's quite the handyman."

As Johnnie went to set the food on the rectangular patio table shaded by a large umbrella, she couldn't help but overhear the ongoing conversation between D.J. and his grandfather.

"You thought about a career in the Air Force, son?" Dale's dad hitched up his trousers and sniffed.

Slouched in a lawn chair on the deck, D.J. fiddled with his plastic cigarette lighter. "Nope, Colonel. I want to work with my hands."

"Hell, you can do that flying airplanes," the colonel grumped, "or working on them."

D.J. kept a straight face. "I'm not exactly *military material*, Colonel." Then D.J. lit up a cigarette right in front of his grandfather. He might as well have blown smoke in the old man's face.

"When the hell did you start smoking?"

"Back in high school, Grand-*paw*. You know that."

"You still in that hippie rock band?"

D.J. chuckled and puffed on his cigarette. "You mean War-4-Money? We broke up right after high school."

The colonel glanced in the direction of the back door where Callie Ann had disappeared with his glass. "How's your friend? Smuts, Klutz …?" He snapped his fingers as if it would help him remember. "Oh, you know, what's his name? The kid in your band."

"You mean Tutts? He's over in Iraq."

Dale's dad pulled up a lawn chair and sat down. "Iraq? What the hell's he doing there?"

D.J. flicked his ashes over the side of the deck. "Hopefully not getting killed."

"Steven Tuttle's in the National Guard," Johnnie offered, hoping to deflect some of the colonel's verbal flak away from her son.

Les Kitchen seemed at a loss for words … as if he couldn't fathom that one of his grandson's friends had gone to war. He stuck his hands in his pockets and glanced sideways at D.J. "Well, you tell him I said to keep his head down."

D.J. nodded and puffed on his smoke.

Callie Ann bustled out and handed the colonel his drink. "I hope I didn't make it too strong, Grandpa."

"Or too weak," Johnnie heard Granny chuckle under her breath.

The colonel took a sip, gave Callie Ann a thumbs-up, and turned toward D.J. "So I take it you're still studying art?" He rolled his eyes skyward.

D.J. smirked. "Is that a problem?"

Les Kitchen took another sip of his drink. "How the hell you expect to make a living doing that?"

Dale put the lid on the grill. "He'll find his way, Dad. Just like we all do."

Dale's dad set his drink down and pressed his lips together. Finally, he nodded with his chin back toward the house. "You've done real well for yourself, son. There's no denying that."

Dale turned and gazed in the same direction as his dad. But Johnnie knew Dale's thoughts weren't on his home as much as they were the business he'd built over the years. Starting from scratch. All the old buildings he'd restored instead of watching them get torn down. The jobs he'd created for others. Hiring men no one else would take a look at, teaching them how to show up on time, get their work done, and take a good paycheck home to their families, along with their self-respect.

She wrapped her arms around the back of Dale's waist, resting her forehead between his shoulder blades. She was proud of him for standing up for himself … and for D.J.

Cade moseyed up and gripped his grandpa by the shoulder. "So, Colonel, what do you think about me joining the Army?"

"A grunt, huh? You gotta be shitting me? Isn't the Air Force good enough?"

Cade tugged at his grandfather's ears. "Look, everybody, it's Dumbo. He's got his wings out and he's ready for takeoff."

Only Cade could get away with such shenanigans. The colonel chuckled, his face turning red.

Brother walked up and dropped his toy at the colonel's feet. Johnnie couldn't help but laugh. "I think he wants you to play."

Dale's dad huffed as he bent over to pick up the doggie toy to toss it. Johnnie tried to envision her father-in-law in his younger days when the only spare tire he had rested in the trunk of his classic convertible instead of around his belly. She couldn't imagine Dale letting himself go all soft and slack like his dad. She wondered if Les was happy in retirement. His life revolved around golf, car shows, and the occasional date.

"When do you ship out?" she heard him ask Cade.

Cade grabbed a bottled water from the ice chest. "Not sure yet. Maybe October. I go for my first Army physical sometime in June."

As Johnnie listened to their conversation, her eyes followed Brother, scrambling down the steps of the deck and out into the yard. Retrieving the toy, he raced back for more.

Out of the corner of her eye, she saw Callie Ann sneak up behind Cade and drop an ice cube down the back of his shorts.

Cade yelped and danced around the deck, trying to shake the ice loose.

"Some soldier you'll make," Callie Ann laughed, taking refuge behind Granny Opal, who was sipping her drink at the table. "That could have been a grenade for all you know."

Everybody laughed but Johnnie.

After a moment, Dale patted her hand. "Honey, can you grab the platter? The chicken's ready."

As she headed for the back door, she could have sworn she saw Callie Ann wipe a tear from her eye.

Later, as they were seated around the patio table having dinner, Johnnie watched Callie Ann pinch a deviled egg between her fingers and scoop the yoke part out with her tongue. Johnnie looked away. Sometimes it bothered her to watch other people eat, even her children.

Cade heaped on a second helping of salad, and D.J. asked for another roll. The colonel returned from another trip to the bathroom after announcing that he was recycling his Scotch. Granny Opal complimented Dale on the chicken, and Johnnie was about to rave on Granny's baked beans when Callie Ann piped up, "Hey, D.J., tell everybody what happened this morning when you went to buy cigarettes."

D.J. looked up from his plate. He put his fork down and cleared his throat.

"So, I'm standing in line at the 7-Eleven. The guy in front of me pays for his stuff and says to this young female cashier, 'Happy Memorial Day.' Man, I thought that chick was going to come over the counter. She shoves the guy's change at him and snarls, 'What's so *fucking happy* about Memorial Day?'"

Johnnie cringed.

Before anyone could say something, D.J. picked up his plastic fork and stabbed at a pile of baked beans. "Sorry about the F-bomb," he apologized. "I'm just reporting what I heard."

Johnnie took a deep breath and reached for Brother's head. As usual, he was at her side, waiting for a scrap to fall. She needed to hold onto the one member of the family who wouldn't judge her. Wouldn't judge any of them.

Running her fingers through his soft fur, she said what needed to be said.

"Well, considering that my father died in war, I have to agree with that young lady at the 7-Eleven. There's absolutely *nothing* happy about Memorial Day. It's a day set aside to honor the war dead."

Granny looked away in an attempt to ignore the comment. After a moment, she picked up the Scotch and water Callie Ann had made for her and downed the rest of her drink.

Then she rattled the ice in her glass as if it was her gavel and she now had the floor.

"Today our family has gathered to celebrate Cade's graduation from high school. That is something to be happy about." She slammed down her glass and glared at Johnnie.

Johnnie couldn't remember the last time she'd seen her grandmother look so defiant.

After a moment, Granny Opal turned her attention to Cade. "Well, graduate, are you ready to cut your cake?"

CHAPTER 22

❧

The Painting

AFTER THE FAMILY POLISHED OFF Cade's graduation cake, Johnnie busied herself in the kitchen and had just cranked up the dishwasher when she heard the side door open and close. D.J. appeared with something brown and rectangular under his arm.

"I couldn't finish it in time for Mother's Day. It's not my usual style, but my professor liked it."

"Oh?" She wiped her hands on a dishtowel, curious what was hidden beneath the wrapping.

D.J. laid the flat package on the island and slit open the butcher paper with a pocketknife. "Okay, close your eyes."

She squeezed them shut. "Don't you want the others to come inside first before you open it?"

"No. They'll see it soon enough."

Clasping her hands, she bowed her head and listened to the rustle of paper sliding off an object.

"Okay, you can look now."

Lifting her head, she caught her breath then burst into tears. She looked past D.J. standing there, his long fingers acting as an easel to prop up the painting. In faded hues of red, gray, green, and yellow, a middle-aged woman in a simple dress was walking away from the field of view, her long tresses tied back with a ribbon. She appeared to be glancing over her shoulder as if startled. Jagged tombstones and blades of grass peeked through an iron fence to her left.

D.J.'s voice cut through the quiet. "Mom, did you notice the title?"

Holding her face in both hands, Johnnie blinked at her son then let her gaze drop to the bottom of the painting. She choked up when she saw the title and his signature:

The Lady Walks
—D.J. Kitchen

She read it silently at first, then out loud.

"The Lady Walks." She looked at him and shook her head. "How did you do that? You painted it as if you were there."

D.J.'s intelligent eyes crinkled into a grin. "I started it right after you called me that morning and told me you'd seen her. You were pretty upset. I decided to have a little fun with the queen."

Johnnie reached for her son. "Your Grandfather Kitchen was out of line earlier. You know that, right?"

D.J. wrapped a strong arm around her. "It's okay, Mom. The colonel's just frustrated. He's old and fat and misses his flying days."

Her eyes went back to the painting ... then up at her son. She could smell the hint of cigarette smoke on his T-shirt, but for once she didn't mind.

At times like now, the scent reminded her of Mama.

Later, after Granny Opal had gone home and Colonel Kitchen had gone back to his hotel, Johnnie decided it was time to show D.J. the photos. They stood in the entryway, the painting propped on a slim table next to the door. A large mirror hung over the table. She removed the photos from a drawer and handed them to him.

"Your dad found these hidden in the nightstand in Uncle Johnny's old bedroom."

About then, Cade walked up and peeked over D.J.'s shoulder. "Dude, you look just like him, except for your long hair and that fuzz on your face."

Johnnie observed how D.J. stared at the two photos then up at his reflection in the mirror.

"Damn. I've always felt like the black sheep of the family 'cuz I don't look like any of you." He turned his head from side to side then raked a hand through his dark hair, exposing the strong jaw line Johnnie loved.

Cade slapped his brother on the back. "That's freaking scary, man."

D.J. grinned. "Don't take this the wrong way, Mom. But now I know it wasn't the milkman." The boys laughed.

Dale walked up behind them. Johnnie saw him before the boys did and wondered if he'd heard the joke.

"Son, you could be Francis Murphy's twin." Dale nodded toward the photo of Johnnie's dad in uniform.

Cade turned to his brother. "Dude? Do you believe in reincarnation?"

The room got very quiet. D.J. rubbed his whiskered chin as a slight smirk spread across his face. "Nah, I don't believe in that bullshit," he chuckled, his dark eyes glancing from Johnnie back to his little brother. "But if I did, I'd say I'm here to warn you," he laid a hand on Cade's shoulder, "war can be fatal, bro."

He passed Johnnie the photos then slipped out the front door to have a smoke. Before he closed the door, he glanced back at her. "Mom, you need to get that framed."

She assumed he meant the painting.

She caught Cade's blue eyes staring at her in the mirror. He looked wounded.

"Your brother's just worried about you," she told him. *We all are*, she added silently.

Cade shrugged and walked off. "Yeah, he sure has a funny way of showing it sometimes."

Dale gestured toward the painting. "D.J.'s good. I don't know where he gets his artistic bent."

Johnnie turned and gazed at her husband. "Are you kidding me? Take a long hard look at this place. This *house* is your canvas."

Dale reached for her hand. "What did Granny Opal say? About D.J.'s painting?"

Johnnie stared at the ghostly image of her mama captured in oil. "She hasn't seen it yet. Or the two photos, for that matter." She handed Dale the photo of her dad with his arm slung over her uncle's shoulder.

Without his specs, Dale held the photo at arm's length. "What I can't figure out is why your family never told you they'd been friends."

Johnnie gazed at her uncle on crutches. "I never heard about any broken leg, either."

THE NEXT MORNING, AFTER DALE left for work, Johnnie went to pour a cup of coffee. The words *Proud Army Mom* stared back at her from the cupboard above the coffee maker. Lifting the hefty mug—she'd been shoving it aside every morning for weeks—she read the words out loud to Brother Dog. He wagged his tail, happy for the attention.

"So you approve of this, do you? Of our boy joining the military?"

Brother's mouth hung half open, his teeth exposed in a doggy grin.

They were the only ones up. All three kids were still asleep. D.J. had a couple of days off before he had to head back to Denton for summer school and work.

With a sigh of resignation, she poured coffee into the new

mug and held it with both hands. Breathing in the steamy aroma, she took a sip.

Your son is a grown man. The quicker you accept that, the better. Dale's words volleyed through her head like incoming mortar rounds.

Brother nudged her leg, wanting to play.

"Let's go sit on the porch. Before it gets too hot. We'll go for our you-know-what tonight when it cools off."

He grabbed a toy and headed for the front door.

As she passed by the painting still propped on the entry table, something caught her eye. Something she hadn't seen the night before.

Clinging to her mug, she bent and stared at a tiny string of pearls slung over the speared tip of one of the iron fence posts in the painting. It appeared as if the pearls had been flung through the air as the woman passed by the cemetery.

A floorboard squeaked behind her. She turned to find D.J. coming up the hallway, his long hair tumbled from sleep.

"Hi, honey. Did you sleep okay on that new air mattress?" She wondered if it bothered him that Cade had completely taken over the bedroom they once shared.

"Sure. Any coffee left?"

At that moment, in the still of the quiet house, she remembered her father's voice: low, deep, just like D.J.'s. *Be good for your mama. I'll see you when I get back.*

She smiled and watched him walk toward her. "I see the pearls. How come you didn't point them out last night?"

He stuck his hands in the pockets of his jeans, rumpled and in need of a wash. "Yeah, I was wondering when you would find them."

"Grab some coffee. Let's go sit on the porch."

Brother dropped his toy and stared straight ahead, waiting patiently for Johnnie to open the door.

D.J. stooped down and peered at her new mug. "Proud Army Mom, huh?" He cocked an eyebrow. "Next thing ya know, you'll be slapping a bumper sticker on your Suburban."

CHAPTER 23

❧

The Talk

"So ... TELL ME STRAIGHT UP ...." D.J. sat in the rocker, his long legs stretched out before him, his bare feet crossed at the ankles. He took a sip of coffee and rubbed Brother's side with his foot. Brother sat on his haunches, his ears perked up as if he were hanging onto D.J.'s every word. "How are you and Dad *really* getting along?"

Johnnie swayed to and fro in the porch swing, careful not to spill coffee all over her lap. She gazed at her son. She was hypnotized by his dark pensive eyes, eyes that searched for the truth and would accept nothing less. "We're working on it. Your dad just needs some time."

"So this whole thing's not for show then? You know, Dad moving home 'cuz his old man's in town?"

Two pairs of eyes were on her now. Brother gazed at her from across the porch as if he too were hungry for the truth. *Either that or a treat*, Johnnie thought.

"I promise you, son. Your dad and I are committed to each other." She paused, rubbed at an old coffee stain on her cotton robe. "It's just that, well, things got a bit complicated."

D.J. set his cup down and pulled a pack of cigarettes from

his pocket. "You mean the affair." It was a statement, not a question.

Hearing him say it caused her to gulp. She focused on how neat and trim the lawn looked after Dale had edged and mowed it right before the colonel arrived. "It happened a long time ago. I was young. And stupid."

He must have noticed how her hands shook, how her teeth chattered when she finally answered him. He craned his neck as if studying the porch ceiling.

After a moment he spoke. "Mom, I'm not judging you, okay?" Stroking Brother's head, he added, "Are you and Dad in counseling?"

"No. I offered. You know your dad. He refuses to ask for help."

"Dad's old school. I'm not surprised."

"Part of him blames Mama for leaving right after our wedding. That and all the stuff she kept from me over the years. But like I told your dad, I have to take responsibility for what happened. I'm the one who was unfaithful to him. Not her."

D.J. fished a plastic lighter from his pocket. "Speaking of family secrets, when are you going to confront Granny Opal about those photos?"

Her eyes met his. "It's not that easy, son. She's eighty-four years old. I've tried to confront her my whole life. There's no changing that old woman. Anytime you try and talk to her, she clams up and puts up a wall."

Pulling a cigarette from the pack, D.J. scissored it between his fingers and gestured across the street. "So, how long's that shovel been sticking out of the ground?"

She sipped her coffee, remembering how she'd worried about Callie Ann catching a ride home in the rain. "About two months. It hasn't moved since Mr. Marvel stuck it there after he threw it in front of dipshit's Jeep."

"Good thing I wasn't home. I'd have grabbed that shovel and beat the crap out of that cocky little bastard." Flicking the lighter, he lit his cigarette and took a long drag.

Watching him, she remembered how Mama would hold smoke in her lungs for what seemed like forever before releasing it in one long, drawn-out breath.

"Well, you may get your chance yet, if your sister keeps sneaking around with that guy. Your dad already had a talk with her. A lot of good that's done."

"Baby sis's boyfriend and I may need to have a chat." He waggled his brow and puffed on his cigarette.

About then they heard the VW Bus sputter up the street and pull into the driveway next to the cottage. Mr. Marvel dislodged himself, went around to the back of the bus, and hefted a bag onto the ground.

"Looks like potting soil."

"Or cat litter," Johnnie noted, spotting the two cats sunbathing in the window.

"So what was he digging for? You ever ask him?" He flicked his ashes over the side of the porch.

"No. Once he threw that shovel, I was afraid to."

D.J. shot her a glance. "Cade says he's a pilot. Who does he fly for?"

Johnnie rose from her swing. "Why don't you ask him? Looks like he's headed over here now."

They watched as he wobbled over. He was wearing a large pair of khaki shorts, round black shoes with thick rubber soles, black socks, and a faded blue T-shirt.

"Good morning, Mrs. Kitchen. I see you have a visitor."

Brother rose on all fours and let out a low growl.

D.J. ground his cigarette out on top of an empty Coke can and came down the steps. He gestured toward Mr. Marvel's driveway. "That's a sweet old bus you've got there. Back in high school, me and my buddy Tutts could've hauled our band gear around in it."

Johnnie pictured D.J. and Steven cruising down Main Street in that beat-up old bus, psychedelic flowers and the name of their band painted on the side. Grandpa would've rolled over in his grave. *Bunch of longhaired hippie freaks. Must be from California.*

Mr. Marvel tipped his gimme cap and wiped a thick paw across his sweaty brow. "Son, has anyone ever told you that you look like Jesus?"

D.J. smirked and rubbed his scruffy beard. "Yeah, but my ex-girlfriend thought I looked more like Charles Manson." He shot a dark glance at Johnnie then twitched his brow.

Mr. Marvel chuckled nervously and took a step back. "Well, I don't suppose that relationship lasted long."

D.J. threw his head back and laughed. "Yep, I've been through a few since then."

Johnnie saw the glint in D.J.'s eye.

Brother growled again, this time louder.

Mr. Marvel seemed to lose his footing for a moment. "Oh dear, he smells my cats, Cleo and Otis." He backed up, a bit unsteady on his feet. "Sorry I haven't been too neighborly. Been taking care of business. I trust his paw is all healed?"

Johnnie glanced at D.J. "Mr. Marvel's the nice man who brought us home the day Brother stepped on a broken beer bottle."

Brother growled louder, his hackles up, his tail down. He looked like he might leap from the steps any moment and go straight for Mr. Marvel's throat.

D.J. ordered Brother to sit.

Mr. Marvel began to back away, his pudgy hands in a defensive position as if he could stop a ninety-pound dog from tackling him. "I just came to tell you I saw that woman again at the cemetery. The one you were hollering at. I tried to speak to her but she took off." He tipped his cap and waddled as fast as he could back across the street.

Johnnie's mouth went dry. She tried to form the word *Mama*, but nothing came out. Trembling, she reached for D.J.'s hand and felt his firm grasp.

She stumbled back against the steps, her butt colliding with the hard concrete.

D.J. told Brother to stay as he ran to get her a drink of water.

Breathing big gulps of air, Johnnie watched Mr. Marvel retrieve a new shovel from the back of his bus. He walked to the same spot as before and started digging.

That poor man, she thought. He had no idea the earthquake he'd just set off in her heart.

CHAPTER 24

~⌒~

Mr. Marvel's Plan

THE NEXT MORNING WHEN JOHNNIE went to get the paper, she spotted the tiny orange flag poking out of the ground by the hole.

Mug in hand, she stashed the paper under her arm and stepped off the curb to get a closer look. Halfway across the street, she could make out the name: Edwin.

"Good morning, Mrs. Kitchen."

Startled, she sloshed hot coffee on her wrist. Glancing up, she saw Mr. Marvel squeezed into an aluminum lawn chair on his porch, stroking the cat curled on his lap. She was thankful she'd changed out of her robe into shorts and a T-shirt before going outside that morning.

"You scared the daylights out of me," she scolded, more embarrassed than annoyed because he'd caught her snooping.

"I'm sorry. I didn't mean to. Come sit a spell and keep me and Otis company."

She hesitated. Hadn't Dale warned her that Mr. Marvel seemed a bit unpredictable? But it was broad daylight …. Besides, she'd ridden in his bus and he hadn't abducted her. If anything, the man looked lonely.

"Okay, but just for a minute. My dog's out back and he'll be scratching at the door wondering where I am."

"He's a handsome boy, that dog of yours. I'm sorry he doesn't like me. At first I thought it was Cleo and Otis. Then I realized it was the paper bag."

"The paper bag?" Climbing the rickety steps, she tried to catch a glimpse inside the cottage's interior. But the blinds were closed and all she could see was a second cat sunbathing in the windowsill.

"At the cemetery," Mr. Marvel said, cracking open a peanut, popping the morsel into his mouth, and tossing the husk. Peanut shells littered the porch's gray wooden floor, and they crunched under her feet as she made her way to the other lawn chair.

Was this breakfast? she wondered, as the scent of roasted peanuts filled the air. Sipping her coffee, she glanced around at the porch's peeling paint and tried to forget how she'd freaked out that day after seeing her mama at the cemetery.

Mr. Marvel offered her a peanut but she declined. Even resting, he seemed out of breath, wheezing and coughing as he continued to shovel nuts in his mouth. He shifted his girth, and the nylon slats strained under his weight.

She gazed out across the patchwork of weeds and grass to the flag staked out by the hole.

Setting her coffee mug on the splintered porch rail, she avoided his eyes. "Mr. Marvel ... who's Edwin?"

He took a deep breath then exhaled as if he'd been holding his breath his whole life. He set the bag of peanuts down and dusted off his hands. "Edwin was my baby brother."

"What happened to him?"

"He was five. I was eight. He wanted to be an Army man and jump out of airplanes. I wanted to fly them. It was right before dusk. The sun was still glaring above the trees. Mother was out back hanging clothes on the line. She had just hollered at us to put the glider away and go wash up for supper.

"Edwin begged, 'Throw it one more time, bubby.' I released the glider, and it went sailing straight for Edwin. But that day something went wrong. Maybe I threw it too hard. That balsa glider sailed right over the top of Edwin's head. He ran backward, trying to catch it in his fingers. He was a wiry little fellow. The next thing I knew I heard screeching tires, and I hit the ground. When I looked up, Edwin was lying in the street, his legs all wrong, his tongue twisted out of his mouth." Mr. Marvel's voice cracked and he stopped to swipe at something in his eye. He gave Otis a gentle pat, then continued, "He died right there in the street, bleeding out like a deer. By then Mother had come around the corner of the house. She took one look at Edwin's broken body, threw her apron over her face, and took off screaming down the street. She got as far as Dooley. It took three men to subdue her."

Johnnie massaged a spot over her left eye. "Who hit him?"

"Some vacuum salesman late for an appointment. He claimed the sun was in his eyes."

As she took in the story, the truth began to sink in; she'd lived at 420 Merriweather for over twenty years, and yet she never knew that a little boy had died right in front of her house. Right in the same spot in the road where the kids had learned to ride their bikes, rollerblade, and play Frisbee.

No roadside memorial, no hastily constructed cross or lonely teddy bear to mark the spot. Not even an X in the road like the one at the foot of the grassy knoll where President Kennedy got shot. Nothing. Only black asphalt and an empty curb. To the casual observer, time had erased all memory of the mishap. But for Johnnie, it was as if it had just happened. She could see Edwin's lifeless body broken in the road, his big brother heaving and blubbering and wiping his nose, while a beautiful young mother went screaming down the street, trying to get as far away from the point of impact as possible.

"Maybe she should have kept running," Mr. Marvel said, picking up the bag of peanuts. Every few seconds he cracked open a shell, tossed it, started chewing a nut, then brushed his fingers together like a huge praying mantis.

She stared at the rolled up newspaper in her lap and didn't say anything for a long time. Finally, she said, "So your mother blamed you for Edwin's death?"

He didn't answer. He didn't have to. The cracking open of nut after nut was answer enough.

Johnnie leaned toward him. "Why did you move back here if this place causes you so much pain?"

His silence only provoked more questions.

"So what's with the hole out by the curb?"

He stopped chewing. "I was hoping to get a tree planted in Edwin's memory by early spring. Then that jackass in the Jeep came flying down Merriweather going the speed of heat. Took something out of me that day. Now it's too hot. Maybe this fall … if I'm still around."

Brother's high-pitched yelp ricocheted across the street.

She grabbed her mug from the rail. "So you're leaving then? Selling this place?"

"Arrivals and departures, Mrs. Kitchen. That's the nature of the business."

As she stepped off the porch, Otis purred for attention.

* * *

Johnnie's Journal
June 5, 2007
11 p.m.
420 Merriweather

Dear Millicent,

I hope you don't think I'm being forward calling you by your first name. Things have changed a lot since your day. People are less formal. And hardly anyone hangs laundry on a clothesline anymore. We all use dryers. Had you been using a dryer that day it wouldn't have changed things. Like all busy mothers with young children, you were preoccupied with housework.

It's been a week since your son, Eugene, told me what happened to Edwin. Although I never met you, I can't seem to stop thinking about you.

Sometimes late at night when the wind blows through the trees, I think I hear you crying for your lost son. But it's the son who lived that suffers now…

Maybe you can reach out through time and space and wrap your merciful arms around him.

Your "almost" neighbor,

Johnnie Kitchen

CHAPTER 25

～

June 6, 2007

"WHO'S THAT LADY IN D.J.'s painting?" Granny's voice quivered over the phone.

It was 7:30 in the morning, and Johnnie had just poured her first cup of coffee. Granny's question caught her off guard, jolted her system stronger than any caffeine. "Which painting, Granny?"

"You know which painting. The new one hanging in your entryway." Granny sounded more irritated than tired.

"Oh … *that* painting. So you've seen it then." Johnnie had put off showing Granny the painting since the night D.J. unveiled it.

"Yes. I stopped by to pick up my bean pan yesterday afternoon but no one was home. So I let myself in."

This was one of those times Johnnie regretted giving Granny a key.

"I'm sorry I missed you. I was still working my shift at the pantry."

Granny coughed. "I asked Brother Dog about the painting when he met me at the door, but he just wagged his tail and brought me his toy."

Well, at least she had a sense of humor.

"Granny, I'd rather not talk about this over the phone. Can you meet me at the cemetery before it gets too hot?"

"The cemetery? Why there?"

Because that's the last place I saw Mama, she almost blurted.

Instead, she took a deep breath and said, "Something happened there a few weeks ago and—"

"Meet me at *The Last Supper*," Granny cut in before the line went dead.

WHILE SHE WAITED FOR GRANNY to arrive, Johnnie spotted a young soldier in uniform, walking among the graves. Perhaps he'd lost a buddy in Iraq. After a while, the soldier's dark form disappeared into the ocean of gray markers and leafy trees. She shivered, thinking of her dad. Then of Cade, hell-bent on following in his footsteps.

Glancing around, she recalled the exact location where her first boyfriend, Clovis Franks, was buried. Her eyes followed the back fence line until she found the statue of the Virgin Mary. *The Catholic section*, her mama had stressed that day as they trailed along behind the funeral procession. And somewhere nearby, possibly in the children's section, rested young Edwin Marvel. She vowed that on her next visit she would find his grave and bring flowers.

Leaning against the Suburban, she was overcome with gratitude. Here among the dead, she'd never felt so alive. All around her were reminders of past lives used up and gone forever, except in the memories of the loved ones they'd left behind. Despite her many setbacks, she was still here; she'd been given a second chance to do something with her life.

Next week she was going to apply for college.

As she brought her hands together in prayer, she heard Granny's Lincoln lumber through the arched entryway and circle the cemetery. The car came to rest behind a large monument engraved with a relief of *The Last Supper*.

Pushing away from the Suburban, Johnnie fought back the idea that this was a setup. An ambush to attack Granny with a barrage of questions once everything was revealed. First, she'd explain the story behind D.J.'s painting. Then she'd tell Granny how Dale had seen Mama at the war memorial. Once Granny digested this news, Johnnie would present the photos. But first they would visit the family plots.

"Some guy in a Hummer nearly ran me off the road." Granny flashed her crooked smile, showing off her new set of dentures. "I'd like to have given him the high sign." Shifting a clay pot in her arms, she reached to kiss Johnnie. "I thought I might as well bring some lilies. They were on sale at a new nursery on Red Bud Lane."

Although it was the middle of June, Granny wore a royal blue sweater and matching sparkly cap pulled down over her ears. A wedge of silver hair poked out one side.

"Granny, you're dressed like Old Man Winter just blew into town."

"I can't seem to get warm these days."

"I see you've got on your shit-kickers. You going dancing?" Johnnie teased, hoping to keep the conversation light for now.

"I always wear my lucky red cowboy boots to the cemetery. In case of snakes and haints."

They moved toward the family plots.

"Granny, I'm going back to college this fall."

"I always knew you were smart." Granny handed Johnnie one of the flowerpots. "You just weren't focused."

So much for keeping the conversation light.

"I was *sick*," Johnnie reminded her, inhaling the lilies' sweet fragrance to keep from going on the defensive. After all these years, Granny still refused to accept how debilitating Johnnie's eating disorder had been.

At her grandfather's grave, Johnnie stooped to place the flowers on his side of the double headstone.

Granny patted her shoulder. "Grandpa had such dreams for

you. He was disappointed when you dropped out. But he sure liked Dale."

Everybody liked Dale, Johnnie thought. Everybody but Jeral Cagle.

Johnnie straightened and for a second she lingered, staring at her grandmother's name and date of birth engraved on the opposite side of the marker. Sadly, she wondered how long it would be until the final date was added.

At her uncle's grave, she fixed her gaze on the inscription:

> Jonathon "Johnny" Grubbs
> March 25, 1945–August 8, 1963
> Beloved son, brother, uncle

The word "uncle" appeared to have been added at a later date. The lettering style didn't match the rest of the engraving.

Granny hovered nearby, silent except for the sound of her stomach growling. "Oh my! The older I get, the more my stomach talks back," she joked, patting her midsection.

Johnnie sensed Granny would do anything to avoid talking about the real issue at hand: that she'd given her only son back to the earth, and his death had caused some kind of rift between Grandpa and her mama.

"Granny," Johnnie hesitated, setting down the other pot of lilies, "how did you do it? How did you go on after Uncle Johnny died?"

Her grandmother looked at her and shrugged. "I didn't have a choice. You either go on, or you die, too. Besides, I had to think about you once you came along."

Johnnie reached for Granny's hand. "How come you never talk about Uncle Johnny?"

Granny's hand felt cold and bony, but her grip was firm as ever.

"Talking about him won't bring him back. Besides, three months after he died, President Kennedy got shot … and nobody wanted to hear about my Johnny Boy anymore. All folks wanted to talk about was what happened in Dallas."

Just then something seemed to catch Granny's eye. Johnnie watched in amazement as her elderly grandmother bent over with all the agility of a schoolgirl and plucked an ugly weed from Uncle Johnny's grave.

Brushing dirt off her hands, she looked Johnnie square in the eye. "Now, why don't you tell me about the lady and those pearls in D.J.'s painting?"

Johnnie took hold of Granny's elbow and steered the two of them toward a bench under a big oak.

Granny eyed the bench before she sat down. "I don't see any bird crap. Do you?"

Johnnie stifled a giggle. Her grandmother didn't normally use such language. "Nope. It's all clear."

Granny pulled off her cap and fussed with her hair. "Did you know I gave your mama my long string of pearls right after you were born? The ones I wore at my wedding."

Johnnie swallowed. This was going to be harder than she imagined.

"Are those the same pearls Mama's wearing in that photo taken on Main Street?"

Granny nodded. "They belonged to my mother, Hannah Rose. Your mama wanted to name you after her. But your grandpa insisted on naming you Johnnie. Victoria didn't get a vote."

Hannah Rose? Would her life have turned out differently had she been given such a feminine name?

She stared at the gold stitching on Granny's boots as Mama's words floated by once again, this time with new meaning: *I never should've let Poppy name you after my dead brother.* Her mama hadn't meant to hurt her that day. She'd meant to send her a message before she vanished.

Granny's ruby lips parted and she seemed to hold her breath.

"About the painting," she began, "I need you to tell me what it's about."

Johnnie turned to her grandmother, avoiding her eyes. "D.J. based it on something I saw. About three weeks ago as Brother and I were out for a stroll—"

"You saw her, didn't you?" Granny cut in, her voice rising in excitement. "You saw Victoria."

Nodding, Johnnie pointed in the direction of the entrance. "She walked out of the cemetery gate and headed north on Dooley. I couldn't believe it. She was right there in front of me."

Granny clutched Johnnie's forearm in a vice grip. "Did you talk to her?"

Johnnie forced herself to look into her grandmother's eyes, wide with hope. "I tried to, Granny, but Mama got away before I could catch up." She explained how Brother stepped on the broken beer bottle. How Mama kept walking. How she called after her.

"And you're sure it was her?"

Again, Johnnie nodded. "She's a little older is all, a little thinner. Dale saw her the day before at the war memorial. We think she saw him and got spooked. Why doesn't she just come home?"

Granny loosened her grip on Johnnie's arm, but she kept looking around, her head jerking this way and that, birdlike, as if she half-expected to see her daughter appear from behind every tombstone, every tree. "Maybe too much time has passed," she said at last. "Maybe she's afraid to come home."

"Why would Mama be afraid to come home?"

At that exact moment, as a long silence stretched between them, a mourning dove answered with his lamenting coo-OO-oo, coo-OO-oo.

Granny's face twitched, and her hands trembled. She balled them up and stuffed them inside her cap, using it like an old-fashioned hand warmer.

Surely the dove has been cooing all morning, Johnnie thought. But only now had they noticed.

Twirling a nervous finger around her ponytail, Johnnie knew it was time to show her grandmother the photos. "Granny, remember when you asked Dale to fix the top drawer in Uncle Johnny's nightstand?" She reached into her purse and pulled out the tattered envelope. "Dale found this taped to the bottom of the drawer. That's why it was jammed."

Granny's head jerked back. "Why ... that's Johnny's letter from West Point." Her lipstick bled into the weathered crevices above her upper lip. Spittle formed at the corners of her mouth. Her breathing grew labored as she stared at the envelope. "I thought your grandpa destroyed it. Along with the acceptance letters from all those other colleges."

Johnnie tried to pass her the letter but Granny refused it. "I don't need to see it. I know what it says." Her voice cracked and she stared off into the distance.

Without asking Granny's permission, Johnnie handed her the faded photograph taken at Fort Hood.

Breathing deeply, Granny fingered the picture. She stared at it a long time then shook her head and chuckled. "I always suspected that's where you girls went. Victoria tried to convince me you took a bus to Salt Flat, but I knew otherwise. I just played along and tried to keep your grandpa from finding out."

Hunched over her purse, Johnnie shifted on the bench. She recalled the dirty look her grandmother had given her on Memorial Day. At the time, she dismissed it because Granny had downed too much Scotch. But today was about taking risks, getting answers. "Why did you and Grandpa keep his identity from me all those years?"

Granny picked at something on her sleeve. "It wasn't our business to tell. It was your mama's. We tried to stay out of it as much as possible. Our job was to raise you."

There was so much Johnnie wanted to ask her, but she knew she was pushing it. She took a deep breath and pulled out the second photo. Her heart tumbled in her stomach and did somersaults as she handed it over.

She felt her grandmother's body stiffen. Heard her catch her breath. When she glanced over, Granny looked like she'd been electrocuted. After all these years the pain was still raw, hidden just below the surface. Then something stirred in her grandmother's eyes, something dark and frightening.

Granny dropped the photo and it fluttered to the ground, face up. Johnny Grubbs on crutches and a smiling Francis Murphy stared back at them.

Johnnie gaped at the photo and sighed, afraid to look at her grandmother. Finally, she bent over and retrieved it. "Why didn't anyone tell me they were friends? What happened, Granny? How did Uncle Johnny drown?"

The old woman's mouth hung open, but nothing came out. It was as if speaking simply required too much effort.

For the first time in her life, Johnnie saw Opal Grubbs for who she really was: a grief-stricken mother who'd lost a child.

After a moment, her grandmother patted her on the knee and hoisted herself up from the bench. "There's only one person alive who knows what happened. And she skipped town."

The roar from a backhoe ripped through the serene morning, its big metal teeth eating into the earth. Granny put on her cap and took off. Johnnie studied the gravedigger for a moment, then grabbed her purse and followed after Granny.

Helping Granny into her car, Johnnie remembered the time Dale broke his leg after falling off a ladder. Granny had rushed over to babysit while Johnnie drove him to the doctor. Later, when Dale hobbled into the house on crutches, his leg in a cast, Granny's face turned ashen. She'd kept her distance for weeks … until the cast came off.

Why had seeing Dale on crutches bothered Granny so much?

Inside the Suburban, Johnnie stared at the photo of her uncle and dad one more time before she started the engine and pulled out of the cemetery.

CHAPTER 26

❧

June 10, 2007

A RRIVING AT CHURCH LATE, JOHNNIE slipped into the back of the sanctuary and turned her phone on vibrate. Today was kickoff Sunday for Vacation Bible School, and unlike in past years, she had not signed up to volunteer. A giant cardboard whale dominated the center of the altar.

Reverend Parchman opened his Bible and read, "And the Lord commanded the fish, and it vomited Jonah onto dry land."

This verse always grabbed her attention, and she usually chuckled at the memory of her first attempts at reading it. Back in kindergarten, she thought the story they studied in Sunday School said the fish had vomited *Johnnie* onto dry land. It was her turn to read that day, and even before she finished the sentence, she impulsively raised her hand and announced, "But a fish didn't eat me." Everyone laughed, including the teacher. As far back as she could remember, she was always trying to place herself in somebody else's story.

But today, as she heard those familiar words, a heat rose up from the middle of her core and spread to all four limbs. Hands shaking and throat clenched, she plucked a pen from the back of the pew and scribbled into the margin of her bulletin:

> And the Beast commanded me, and I vomited Mama
> right up.

Clutching the pen, she stared hard at the words that had formed in her mind, now captured on paper. For a split second, she swore she heard Grandpa Grubb's disapproving tone: *You got some nerve rewriting the Bible, young lady.* She ignored him and kept writing.

> I spewed you out, Mama, along with gallons of ice
> cream, bags of potato chips, leftovers I'd rescued from
> the back of the fridge. Cast you out like a bad demon.
> All your lies. All your excuses. All the times you left me
> high and dry.

Anger welled up in her but she vowed not to cry. Not here. Not now. Not in the middle of church. The pen dug deeper into the paper.

> Every time I stood over the toilet puking my guts out,
> Mama, I thought of you.

Glancing up, she half-expected God to strike her dead.

While the preacher droned on, her old enemy rose up to taunt her. *You're no better than your mama was—all that sneaking around.* In the old days, Johnnie would have given in to the temptation to rush out of church, go home, and tear into a cupboard of food like a wild animal.

But she was in charge now. And she put the tired old voice in its place with the stroke of her pen.

CHAPTER 27

❧

Monday, June 25, 2007

WIND CHIMES JANGLED IN THE morning breeze as Johnnie approached Tarrant Hall on the sprawling campus of Portion Community College. The size of the building intimidated her. Several students milled around outside— mostly young people in their late teens or early twenties. Their voices and the stink of cigarette smoke formed an invisible barrier that reminded her of D.J.'s warning: "Whatever you do, Mom, don't try to act like everybody's mother. Just go to class and try to blend in."

An older gentleman hurried past, probably a professor on his way to teach.

How the hell was she going to blend in? She was a 43-year-old mother and a college dropout. The old dread of failure swirled around her like a heckling ghost.

She peeked at her transcripts from North Texas State. The big fat D in math and the F in American history glared back. Who was she kidding? She had no business going back to college. What if she failed and wasted Dale's hard-earned money? They'd need every penny to pay for Callie Ann's tuition. Johnnie felt selfish.

Taking a deep breath, she turned to leave.

A flash of color caught her eye. A red bird swooped down from a nearby mulberry tree and flew right in front of her, almost smacking her in the face. She flinched.

"John-neee … John-neee …."

Every hair on her body stood on end. Her scalp tingled. She glanced around, hoping to spot the cardinal again. But he was gone.

Then the skeptic in her kicked in. No, it couldn't be. Maybe once in a lifetime as a child but …. Surely what she'd heard must have come from a set of wind chimes clinking in the wind.

Car keys in hand, she took one last look at the building and made up her mind to leave.

Then a voice, gruff and prodding as ever, charged through her mind. *That's not just any bird, young lady. That's an angel bird, flown straight down from heaven. Now get your tail through those doors before I push you.*

Grandpa and Uncle Johnny! Even in death they showed up for her.

Slinging her purse over her shoulder, she took a deep breath and breezed into the foyer in search of the counseling center. A blast of cold air made her shiver. She wished she'd brought a sweater, worn something more than a summer shift that hit just above the knees. She hoped she didn't look lost or out of place as she glanced around, trying to get her bearings.

When her children were young and Dale was at work, she found it easier to go into unfamiliar or congested places if her kids tagged along. She used to joke that the kids were her seeing-eye dogs, helping her navigate the busy freeways of the Metroplex, the dark aisles of a movie theatre, or the crowded corridors at the mall. Somehow their chattering presence made her feel brave.

On this June morning, she'd have given anything to have them along, but they were far too old and busy with their own lives to escort their anxious mother. D.J. was back at summer school, Callie Ann had a babysitting job, and Cade had driven to the Federal Building in downtown Dallas for his first Army physical. *Army physical.* She couldn't even wrap her mind around it. Part of her hoped he'd fail, the other part prayed he'd pass. This was what he wanted.

After stopping to scan the building directory, she headed for the elevator. With each step, her pulse raced ahead. At that moment, a pregnant woman and three rambunctious toddlers bustled up to catch the elevator.

In spite of her nerves, Johnnie managed a smile. "Looks like you've got your hands full."

The young woman let out a throaty laugh. "We're like a herd of buffaloes." She had dark rings under her eyes but an engaging smile.

Even as Johnnie tried not to stare at the expectant mother's protruding belly, she felt the kick from a phantom foot deep within her own womb. She couldn't remember the pain of childbirth, yet she could still feel the sensation of tiny feet punting against the sides of her uterus. Lately these memories seemed to come with greater frequency. She could be anywhere, doing anything, and boom, she'd be zapped back to the past. It was as if she were living in two different dimensions: then and now. She was startled by the speed of her children's lives. They'd zoomed past her, leaving her on the sidelines with maternal whiplash.

She glanced at the three little kids then back at the woman. "Are you a student?" She couldn't imagine how anybody with young children and one on the way could possibly find time for college.

"Actually, I just graduated." The woman cupped one hand protectively under her belly. "I'm here to pick up my transcripts."

Johnnie fingered her purse strap. "My goodness. You

certainly are an inspiration. I haven't been to school in years. I'm just hoping my credits transfer."

The woman started to say something, but the elevator doors slid open, and two of the toddlers scrambled into the elevator ahead of their mother. "You guys wait up," she scolded, a hint of panic in her voice as she grabbed the other child and rushed forward.

Johnnie followed them onto the elevator. As the heavy steel doors sealed shut, her mind raced back to the slow, cranky elevator in the old medical building where she used to take the kids for their appointments with the pediatrician.

Cade had just turned four and was due for a checkup. As Johnnie pushed Callie Ann in the stroller, nine-year-old D.J. shot past her and beat Cade to the elevator. Cade threw a fit and charged after D.J. because he wanted to push the button first. A shoving match ensued, and D.J. slammed Cade against the front of the closed elevator.

Fear rocketed to her heart. "Freeze!" she yelled, and both boys pivoted. Then she lectured them, using as illustration a gruesome elevator accident she'd heard about on the news. A little boy had been playing on an elevator when it malfunctioned and shot straight up, trapping the boy between the doors.

"Mama, did the boy get hurt?" Cade scrunched up his chubby face in worry.

She peered down at him then over at D.J. "Yes, Cade, he died. It chopped his head off." The truth had just flown out of her mouth. She hated resorting to fear tactics to protect her kids, but sometimes she couldn't help herself.

D.J. let out a ghoulish howl and poked Cade in the stomach. "That's gross."

Cade sidled up to Johnnie. "Mama, was there a headstone on the elevator?"

She reached down and patted his back. "No, honey, but I'm sure there's a headstone in the graveyard where the little boy is buried." With that, the elevator doors sprung open and she herded her brood on board, prodding the boys with a gentle nudge from the stroller.

THE ELEVATOR IN TARRANT HALL dinged. She broke out in a cold sweat. For a moment she couldn't swallow. A quick swig of water from a bottle she kept in her purse staved off a wave of panic.

Cade's words from a few weeks ago marched across her heart. "After I serve, I can use the GI Bill … and Mama, I know you've been wanting to go back to school."

As Johnnie stepped off the elevator onto the third floor, she heard the expectant mother call out "good luck" before the doors closed. Spurred on by this stranger's reassuring smile, Johnnie put Cade out of her mind, smoothed her hair back, and strode down the hall in search of the counseling center.

Thirty minutes later, she found herself in the cluttered office of Mr. Paul Peoples, a student advisor. Was it her imagination, or were authority figures getting younger these days? Mr. Peoples didn't seem much older than D.J. Short and stubby with curly hair and a round face, he looked like he might have played the tuba in high school.

He folded his hands on his desk and grinned. "So, you want to go back to college? Any idea what you want to study?"

Seated primly in a wingback chair across from him, Johnnie clutched her purse on her lap and tried to appear confident. "Well, I've always been interested in writing. But my counselor in high school laughed at me when I told her that. She said there was no money in it. That I should pick something more *practical*."

Mr. Peoples bobbed his head as if in agreement. "Yes, well, she had a point. Very few writers and artists make a living at it. You know the old saying, 'Don't quit your day job.'"

She thought of D.J. and the uphill battle he would face once he graduated. Then Dale came to mind. Despite what his old man said, Dale had made a decent living working with his hands.

Squeezing her legs together, she wished she'd worn a longer dress. When the advisor didn't say any more, she felt the need to fill the silence. "I've always regretted that I dropped out of college." Her voice trembled and vibrated in her head.

Mr. Peoples gave her a hasty nod. "Sure. Sure. I hear that a lot." He glanced down at her transcripts. "Let's see what we have here."

She cleared her throat and waited.

Rocking back and forth in his chair, he hummed to himself as he looked over her paperwork. Finally he stopped rocking.

"Ouch. An F in American history." He looked up at her, his bushy brows twitching like caterpillars. "What gives? You made a B the first semester."

She reached for her water bottle. "It was a night class, middle of winter. I had to walk across campus in the dark. After two weeks I quit going."

"Why didn't you drop the course?"

It was easier to stay in the dorm and binge. Not face the professor who stared at her tits the first night of class. Or was that her imagination? Either way, she would've had to confront him and ask him to sign her drop slip.

She unscrewed the cap and chugged the rest of her water. "Because I was young … and stupid. And then Karen Carpenter died." She twisted the empty bottle in her hands. The plastic popped and crinkled before she set it down.

"Karen Carpenter?" He studied her for a moment.

"You know, the singer."

"Ah, yes. She was before my time."

"Did you know she had an eating disorder? Like to have killed my mama when she passed. And then I got married and Mama went missing. And well—"

This seemed to get his attention. "Wait, missing? You mean like … like she just disappeared off the face of the earth?"

"Yeah, I think she was abducted by aliens." Johnnie kept a straight face. "But they must've reprogrammed her before they brought her back, because when I spotted her out by the cemetery last month, she acted like she didn't know me." Her joke almost backfired on her. Something caught in her throat and she looked away.

Mr. Peoples cleared his throat. "So … she's back now?"

Glancing around his office, she realized she was making a fool of herself. "Look, I apologize. I'm just nervous. The only reason I'm here is because my youngest son is joining the Army and …." She suddenly ran out of air.

Mr. Peoples looked confused. "I'm sorry. I'm not following you."

She folded her hands on her lap. "The GI Bill will pay for Cade's college when he gets out of the Army. In the meantime, I can take some classes without straining the family budget."

"The Army's a very honorable profession, Mrs. Kitchen."

She scratched the back of her neck and realized she'd gotten him off track. This was not a therapy session, a place to dump her problems.

He glanced back down at her transcripts. "Lots of Bs, a few As, a C in speech." He paused. "Hmmm … D in math for general education. Was that a night class, too?" He blinked at her.

She took a deep breath, held it for a second, then let out a heavy sigh. "No. It was a morning class, twice a week. I went every day and never understood a damn thing. Numbers elude me. When I was a little girl, I prayed to God to make me smarter in math. But the harder I prayed the dumber I got. Any time I tried to work with numbers, it felt like the top of my head split open and an eggbeater scrambled my brain. All the numbers scattered. Grandpa tried to help, though."

Her mind flashed to when she was nine, hunched over the kitchen table late at night. Grandpa was drilling her with flashcards and she was trying to count on her fingers. Suddenly he pushed away from the table and stood up, his hands jammed in his slacks. "Good thing you're pretty like your mama. She isn't good at math either. Now take your Uncle Johnny. That boy could do calculus standing on his head." After Grandpa went to bed, Granny slid a warm cookie into Johnnie's hand, but she could hardly swallow it.

She flicked away a tear as she met Mr. Peoples' curious gaze.

He shoved a box of tissues in her direction then continued his spiel. "I'm afraid that D won't transfer," he added. "You'll have to retake math. I usually tell students it's best to plunge right in. Get your math credits out of the way first."

She leaned forward. "I barely know my multiplication tables."

He gave her a blank stare.

"You know what I did when I got that final grade in math? I wolfed down a gallon of Rocky Road, half a pizza, and a bag of Doritos I stole from my roommate. Then I walked down the hall to the community bathroom and puked my guts out."

Mr. Peoples' jaw dropped. She stared at his shocked expression. This wasn't going to work. Going back to college was scary enough without having to sign up for math right away.

"All righty then." Mr. Peoples swiveled around in his chair to face his computer screen. He started punching in something on his keyboard. "We'll get you signed up for the math placement test. You'll most likely have to take one of the developmental courses first before you can take college algebra."

Johnnie kept a straight face. "You mean math for retards, don't you?"

Mr. Peoples looked over at her. "Now, Mrs. Kitchen, I wouldn't go that far. I like to refer to it as brushing up on your math skills."

"But Mr. Peoples, you don't understand. I have no math skills. That's the problem."

He shrugged. "There are always tutors."

She leaned forward in her chair. "You didn't hear me the first time." Her anger spurred her on. "I have no math skills. Zero. Zilch. Nada. Zip."

"It can't be that bad," he said.

Johnnie threw her hands up in the air. "You haven't been listening to me."

Mr. Peoples looked shocked.

She stood up, snatched her transcripts off his desk, and turned to go. "I certainly hope this isn't how you treat young kids fresh out of high school." She slung her purse over her shoulder and marched out of his office.

Once she was in the lobby, she advanced to the reception desk. The woman looked up with a concerned smile.

Mr. Peoples came out of his office. "Johnnie?"

He called her *Johnnie*. Not Mrs. Kitchen. Not somebody's wife. Not somebody's mama. Just Johnnie.

She tilted her head in his direction. For the first time she noticed he leaned on a cane.

"Come on back. Let's see if we can't get you enrolled in at least one class this fall. And I assure you, it won't be math."

Squaring her shoulders, she apologized for her outburst and went back into his office.

Mr. Peoples stashed his cane under his desk and turned to his computer. "Now let's see here. You say you've always been interested in writing. Then let's get you signed up for a writing class."

She bowed her head and tried not to shake.

She was a little late to the party. But to the party she would come.

* * *

Johnnie's Journal
August 28, 2007
Demolition Day

Dear Granny,

On my last day to volunteer at the food pantry before the first day of classes, I drove past the old elementary school one last time and watched a bulldozer demolish what was left of the cafeteria. They finally tore down the tall slide, that one piece of playground equipment that reigns supreme in my memory. Remember what happened on that slide when I was in third grade? I was at the top of the ladder, waiting my turn to go down, when Willie Slaughter poked his head under my dress and howled, "I see London, I see France, I see Grubb-worm's underpants."

I shoved Willie so hard he fell off the ladder and cracked his head open. Then I got sent to the principal's office, where I promptly pooped my pants.

After you picked me up and brought me home, I hid in the bathroom, embarrassed and confused because I was both a victim and a criminal all at once. I was trying to clean my underwear in the toilet when you barged in, unlocking the door without my permission. My shame and the smell filled that small space.

When I tried to tell you what that bully had done to me, all you talked about was how upset Grandpa was going to be when he got the hospital bill for Willie's injuries.

Yep, I damn near slaughtered Willie, but that boy never did bother me again.

Johnnie

CHAPTER 28

～

First Tuesday in September 2007
Portion Community College

IT WAS 9:40 A.M., TEN minutes into her class. She glared at
the chalkboard and squeezed the pencil in her fist. Today's
writing prompt for Creative Writing 101:

> In-class assignment. You have 30 minutes to compose
> a letter to a person who changed the course of history.
> Good luck.

The instructor, a balding grad student in his mid-thirties,
dropped the chalk in the metal tray and left the room.

Johnnie's belly flip-flopped; she swallowed hard. This wasn't
in the syllabus. She broke out in a cold sweat and tried to block
the annoying sounds of rustling paper, someone humming,
and a young woman having a sneezing fit.

Johnnie needed privacy, time to collect her thoughts. Her
brain froze, shut off under the pressure. She couldn't think. It
was only the second day of class, and they were expected to
write about a person who'd changed the course of history? And
do this in thirty minutes?

Mr. Peoples' voice trumpeted through her mind: "An F in

American history? What gives?"

Calm down, calm down, she coached herself. This is not a history course. You can do this. Concentrate. She erased the mental images of stodgy statesmen in wigs and generals on horseback at famous battlefields. Let some other student write about them.

But who? Who could she write about?

She closed her eyes and waited. Waited for the message that told her to breathe in, breathe out, the idea would come. Her grip loosened on her pencil. Her breathing slowed.

Then her subject appeared, crouched at the edge of a clearing: the most beautiful woman she'd ever seen, naked but for some leaves. She looked like she wanted to make a run for it.

Johnnie glanced at the wall clock. Only twenty minutes left. She smiled to herself, bent over her paper, and let the words flow from her sometimes-irreverent heart:

Dear Eve,

Too bad it wasn't the snake you were after. You and Adam could've eaten on him for a week. Gathered up some twigs and cooked him over a spit. Snake-on-a-stick: the original shish kabob.

Instead, you went for that crafty little bauble … that red fruit, and look where it got you?

Guess we've all been suffering since.

Had I been in your bare feet, I'd have yanked that serpent out of that tree and bit his head off before he could tempt somebody else.

You poor woman. Grandpa always said it was *your* fault we were born into sin. He called you the *original sinner*. Mama and him got into it once right after church when I was about five. He told Mama, "You're no better than Eve." Granny just stood there, clutching her purse in one hand and me in the other. Grandpa was a good man, but he had a way of blaming things on women.

You know, Eve, you've been credited for every ill since the Fall of Man—from the pain of childbirth to death itself. Unlike Grandpa, I'm letting you off the hook.

You weren't there when a teenage Victoria Grubbs fooled around and got knocked up. And you weren't there when I had my own fall from grace.

Nope, Mama and I messed up purely on our own.

Historically speaking, I think you got a bad rap. Come to think of it, I never heard of a talking snake either.

CHAPTER 29

~⁀ි

September 11, 2007

THE NIGHT AIR SMELLED OF dryer sheets and cut grass, a sharp contrast from the skunk odor that had permeated the neighborhood the night before. The skunk was probably long gone, but Johnnie couldn't take any chances that Brother might get sprayed. He'd been skunked when he was a puppy, and the house stunk for weeks. So she sat out back on the deck, waiting for him to do his business. Floodlights from each corner of the house lit up the yard. His nose to the ground, she watched him track something along the fence line.

"That better not be Mr. Skunk you're sniffing," she called, glancing at her watch.

It was nine o'clock, and Cade should be back any minute. She'd sent him to the store for bread and milk. Dale was already in bed, and Callie Ann was glued to the TV, watching 9/11 coverage.

"I can only watch planes fly into buildings so many times," Cade had grumbled earlier on his way out the door. "And *that*, baby sis," he jabbed his finger at the TV, "is why I'm joining the Army."

Callie Ann twisted around on the couch, glared at him from

across the room, and fired back, "I don't care. I don't want you getting killed in some stupid war." But he'd already left the room.

That's when Johnnie had gone out back with the dog. Like Cade, she was tired of seeing the images over and over. Yet she felt guilty for not wanting to watch. She wanted to forget how she'd bitten down on a pencil that terrifying morning to keep from going into shock.

The day of the attacks, the kids had come home from school and huddled around the TV. Dale sent his crew home early and dropped by to check on Granny. Johnnie had worked to steady her hands as she made a pot of potato soup to comfort her family. After dark, they gathered out in the backyard, craning their necks at the star-speckled sky, overwhelmed by the eerie absence of jet noise. "There's not a plane in the sky," D.J. declared. His voice seemed to travel out of the backyard, floating over the rooftops of Portion, mixing in with the hum of the freeway.

Tonight, six years after that horrific event, a large jetliner streaked overhead as it lifted off from DFW Airport and headed north. Johnnie watched until the lights went out of sight. Then her eyes found Brother in a back corner. He turned his head, squatted, then kicked his back legs and walked off. He started to head toward the deck then something alerted him and he charged out across the yard, disappearing around the west corner of the house.

His barking ricocheted off the side of the vacant home next door and bounced back into the yard.

"Cade must be home." She clapped her hands to get the dog's attention. "Time to go inside, boy."

But Brother ignored her and barked at something on the other side of the short section of fence that faced north toward the street. "What is it, boy? What do you hear? It better not be that skunk rooting around in the bushes."

He glanced at her then started barking again.

She took him inside and went to investigate. Cade's pickup was not under the portico. Callie Ann had turned off the TV, and Johnnie could hear the shower running.

In the entryway, Brother danced at her heels, butting his nose against her. She flipped on the outside lights and peeked out. "You stay here. I'll be right back."

Out on the porch, she squinted beyond the glow of the floodlights. She homed in on a blob in the middle of the street, a large trash bag that had fallen off the back of a truck. But as her eyes adjusted to the light, the bag took shape. The shape of a person weeping near the spot in the road where young Edwin Marvel had died.

Fear clutched the back of her throat, and she got the heebie-jeebies. Was this person hurt? Did he need help?

Putting her own safety aside, she stepped off the porch and crept across the lawn. Her heart drummed in her ears. In the limited light, she could see a fat man sitting in the middle of the street, blubbering like a baby.

Mr. Marvel! She should have guessed.

She ran to his side. "What are you doing out here in the middle of the street? Are you hurt?"

"Mrs. Kit–cheen …?" he slurred, his voice choked with tears. "Leeb me alone."

He looked like Humpty Dumpty with a whiskey bottle wedged between his knees.

"You could get killed!" Fighting back panic, she glanced up and down the darkened street, checking for headlights. "We've got to get you out of the street."

His head lolled from side to side. "The hijackers ruined everything," he moaned.

Reaching behind him, she put her hands under his damp armpits and tried to lift him. But he was dead weight. She figured he outweighed her by at least a hundred fifty pounds.

The stench of whiskey and beef from his foul breath polluted the night air around her. She almost gagged.

In the dim light, she could see his tear-streaked face. She took pity on him.

"Mr. Marvel. You're too heavy for me to pick up. I need you to help me. I don't want anything bad to happen to you."

"It should've been me, not Edwin!" he wailed.

You can't reason with a drunk, Grandpa used to say.

"Mr. Marvel, don't say that," she scolded, her voice shrill.

"And now I'm grounded," he sobbed. "Doc says I'm too sick to fly."

"You're gonna be dead if you don't get out of the street."

"It doesn't matter. I'm dying anyway. Might as well get it over with."

"What do you mean, you're dying?"

"I've got a bad heart. Doc only gives me a few months—"

"Is that why you were at the mortuary back in the spring?"

He threw his head back and laughed. "Were you spying on me?" he roared, spitting his words like a crazy man. "Mother always spied on me. She didn't trust me after Edwin died."

Impatient and scared, Johnnie played along with his game, hoping he would get up and move any second. "No, I wasn't spying on you. I was out on a date with my husband."

"I was hoping you had a crush on me," he giggled, his head bobbing around as a line of drool hung from his bottom lip.

"Mr. Marvel, you know I'm a married woman," she chided playfully.

"All the good ones are," he sighed.

Taking a deep breath, she looked up at the night sky then back at her neighbor. "If we don't get you moved, you're going to end up like Edwin. How do you think that would make your mother in heaven feel?"

"Happy," he cried, as great tears of grief poured down his wet cheeks.

"No! She would be *sad*. Seeing you coming through the pearly gates flatter than you are wide. Knowing you killed yourself in the very spot where Edwin died? Why, that's almost blasphemous."

"But I'll never fly again," he blubbered.

Squatting in front of him, she grabbed his pudgy face in her hands. "Look at me. Even birds can't fly around forever. What goes up must come down."

Was that a nod? Hard to tell in the dark. For a second she thought she'd reached him. But then he seemed to sink deeper into himself. His head fell forward, and his chin rested on his wide chest. "Flying is all I have. Besides my cats."

She swallowed. Until this moment, she never realized how lonely he must be. No wife. No children that she knew of. Not even friends.

"But if you kill yourself, who will take care of Otis and Cleo?"

"I've made arrangements," he mumbled, tightening his grip on the bottle. "Don't worry about it."

A pair of headlights came toward them from the west. Even from this distance, she could tell the lights sat high, like the lights on a pickup.

She pushed and pulled against his massive weight, but he didn't budge. The lights drew closer and closer. She could hear country music blaring from the truck's radio.

She pummeled his shoulders with her fists, yelling, "Mr. Marvel, move your *ass!*"

The headlights bore down on them. She could hear the truck's motor, the music blaring louder and louder from the driver's open window.

Save yourself, she thought, but she couldn't leave him. She couldn't leave this sad and lonely man who'd been dying a little each day since his brother died.

From deep within her, some primal rage roared up.

The approaching lights lit up the street, blinding her from seeing most of the vehicle except the massive grille and shiny steel bumper.

Without another thought, she grabbed the half-empty bottle

from between his legs and flung it toward the yard.

Adrenaline pumping, she wrapped her arms around his smelly body and pushed.

Tires squealed against asphalt as the driver slammed on the brakes, and their bodies rolled to the curb.

She couldn't breathe, her chest crushed under a weight that felt like an elephant.

The pickup screeched to a halt inches from her head. Headlights illuminated the area.

With the wind knocked out of her, she beat her fists against the large man's sides. "Mr. Marvel, get off me," she gasped. "I can't breathe."

She heard the thud of footsteps, someone running toward her, breathing heavily, lifting and tossing aside the lung-crushing load.

"Mama!" Cade cried, the terror in his voice ripping into the night.

From somewhere nearby, Mr. Marvel whimpered like a wounded animal.

Rising up on her elbows, she looked into her son's terrified face.

"Oh Jesus, Mama! I almost killed you."

Cade stood and grabbed his head, walking in circles in front of his pickup. He doubled over like he was going to be sick.

THE NEXT AFTERNOON WHEN JOHNNIE stepped out on the porch to check the mail, she found a note and a pot of store-bought chrysanthemums by the front door.

The note read:

9/12/07

Dear Mrs. Kitchen,

Otis and Cleo aren't speaking to me. They are so embarrassed about my momentary lapse of judgment. Remind me to steer clear of watching too much news, especially on the anniversary of a tragic event. I am forever in your debt that you would risk your life to save a sorry sack of a fellow like myself. My deepest apologies to you and your son. I shudder to think what would have happened if you hadn't come along.

Please accept these chrysanthemums as my gift to you. They were my mother's favorite flower.

Respectfully yours,
Eugene Marvel

CHAPTER 30

∿

War Hits Home

"**M**OM, I GOT SOME BAD news."

With her cellphone jammed to her ear, Johnnie felt her heart plummet as she stopped midstride between buildings, unable to carry the weight of D.J.'s words along with her backpack. The heat of Indian summer bounced off the brick as she dropped the bag to the ground and tried to prepare herself for the worst.

"What's wrong?" A flurry of students rushed past but she barely noticed them.

"Tutts' patrol got hit by an IED. The blast hit the Humvee's left side." D.J. paused, his breathing labored. "Tutts was driving."

Her phone almost slipped from her hand. Every muscle in her body went limp. Only her heart, squeezed tight inside her chest, still seemed to be working.

"Oh, Jesus." The buildings closed in on her. She couldn't think straight. Dizzy, she groped her way to the nearest bench, leaving her backpack in the middle of the sidewalk.

"Two of his buddies were killed outright."

Her brain scrambled to process the news. The war in Iraq had just invaded the peaceful campus of Portion Community

College, yet Johnnie seemed to be the only one aware of it.

"Wait … you mean he's not dead?"

She heard D.J. light up a cigarette.

"Mom …. There are some things worse than death."

The grill from the student union filled the air with the odor of fried onions and burnt meat. Her mouth watered, but not from hunger.

"Oh, God. Did he lose an arm? A leg? What?"

"Mom, the blast hit the driver's side." D.J. exhaled. "The left half of his face is pretty much gone."

A flame of bile shot up her throat, searing her windpipe. Looking around, she wanted to scream. She doubled over, sucking big gulps of air.

All at once her fears zoomed in on Cade. "Have you talked to your brother?"

"He's out playing ironman. The kid hasn't even been to basic training yet, but all he talks about is *Special Forces*."

D.J. was right. Cade was on overdrive in the workout department. Lately, he'd taken to running all the way out to the lake, diving in for a long swim, then running home. If he wasn't doing pull-ups from a bar over his bedroom doorframe, he was flat on his back on the den's braided rug, calling Callie Ann to come hold down his feet while he did sit-ups. Brother Dog would stretch out nearby and yawn.

"What did Cade say when you told him?" Johnnie wondered if Steven's injury would blunt Cade's enthusiasm.

"He said it *sucks*. But don't get your hopes up, Mom. The kid's not backing down. He never worked this hard at baseball."

Johnnie sighed. D.J. had a point. She'd never seen Cade so focused.

"Hey, I gotta run. I'm late for class. I'll catch ya later."

Class. She'd completely forgotten. Biology started in two minutes. She went to get up, but gravity pulled her down.

Steven's face loomed into view, whole and unshattered. His

black beret set at a jaunty angle, he waved and smiled. *Her name is Beth. Give her a call.*

"I think this belongs to you."

Dazed, Johnnie glanced up at the middle-aged woman with frizzy black hair and sallow skin. The woman dumped Johnnie's backpack on the ground next to the bench.

Johnnie didn't know how long the woman had been standing there. She was still trying to absorb the impact of Steven's injury. Every time she thought about it, a bomb detonated in her heart.

"My son's best friend from high school just got blown up in Iraq." Her words came out flat but lethal.

The woman plopped down on the bench beside Johnnie and patted her leg. "Whoa, I'm really sorry. Was it an IUD?"

Any other time, Johnnie might have laughed.

"IED," she corrected, not bothering to hide her irritation.

"Sorry, that's what I meant. So he's dead then? From this roadside bomb?"

Johnnie blinked. "No, he's disfigured."

The woman hugged a three-ring binder to her chest. With a flourish, she shook her disheveled hair and pointed her chin at Johnnie. "*Well*, that should give you a buttload of material to write about."

Johnnie stared at her. This was the woman from writing class. The one who always came in late. The one she'd seen jogging in street clothes out in the parking lot. The one she'd heard retching in the bathroom stall that morning.

"You're Beverly Hills, right? I recognize you from class."

The woman bobbed her head and giggled. "Yeah. That's me ... Miss Hollywood."

You don't exactly look like a movie star, Johnnie thought, eyeing the woman's wrinkled capris, baggy T-shirt, and worn-out running shoes.

"So ... is Beverly Hills a pen name?" She'd lost all decorum in the wake of D.J.'s call.

"My *nom de plume.*" Beverly twirled her hand in the air. She grinned at Johnnie. "You like it?"

"It certainly grabs your attention," Johnnie deadpanned. "I hope you don't mind me asking, but what's your real name?"

Beverly dropped her head like a ragdoll. "It's Beverly Pickleworth." Pushing her bottom lip out in a faux pout, she burst out laughing. "Now do you see why I changed it?"

Johnnie's gaze drifted to her classmate's hands. Sure enough, she found what she was looking for. On Beverly's right hand, the knuckles were red and raw, gnarled bumps covered with years of scar tissue. Her own scars were barely visible compared to Beverly's. A mixture of revulsion and compassion powered her next question. She could not, would not stay silent.

She reached for Beverly's hand. "How long have you been fighting this?"

Beverly jerked her hand away like she'd been stung. She crossed her feet and stared at the ground.

Johnnie took a deep breath and looked away. After a moment, she turned toward Beverly.

"I heard you in the bathroom this morning. It's not just a young woman's illness, is it?"

Beverly tapped her fingers against her leg and didn't say a word.

Johnnie continued to pressure her. "Listen, Beverly. You can't bullshit an old bullshit artist. I battled bulimia and won. But it's the hardest thing I've ever done."

Beverly stood up slowly, still clutching her binder. "I have to get to work. I'm sorry about your son's friend. I'll see you in class." And with that she jogged off.

JOHNNIE HOISTED HER BACKPACK OVER her shoulder and headed for biology. Some wars were fought on foreign battlefields, like the one that ruined Steven's face. Others raged in the minds of people like her classmate, Beverly.

Which wars are the hardest to win? she wondered.

As she pulled open the heavy glass door and entered the science building, the images of Steven Tuttle and Beverly Hills rode along beside her in a mental sidecar she couldn't unhitch.

CHAPTER 31

∽

Creative Writing 101
Portion Community College

Writing Prompt: On Being Ten

IT WAS A FEW DAYS after my tenth birthday, March 1974. Grandpa and I sat on the dock after church. His pant legs were rolled up to his knees, long white calves exposed, his large feet immersed in the water. I was still in my Sunday best, my lacy socks and Mary Janes tossed aside. My legs were too short for my feet to touch the water, so I swung them in the air and watched a dozen dragonflies skim the surface. Beyond the cove, we heard the putt-putt of a small motorboat.

"Grandpa," I started, "Aunt Beryl says I'm a *ligament* child."

Grandpa's smile slipped away like the afternoon sun behind a cloud. "When did she tell you that?"

"Directly after church, before she packed up and headed back to Salt Flat. We were sitting on her suitcase, trying to get it to close." I turned and squinted at him. "What does 'lig-a-ment' mean?"

Grandpa's mouth twisted funny and a look came over him that scared me. "It means nothing," he spat, but I knew it did. "Pay no attention to that sister of mine. She's been living too long under that West Texas sun. Her brain's fried."

"Mama says Aunt Beryl's about as friendly as a cactus."

"Or a rattlesnake," Grandpa groused.

From somewhere deep inside me, something broke free. "Aunt Beryl says I was born at the Denton School for Unwed Mothers." The tattle flew out of my mouth so fast, like a trapped bird seeking air. I clamped my hand over my mouth. "Oops, she told me not to tell."

Grandpa studied me. "That old busybody." He looked angry, but not at me.

Before I could ask another question, we heard Granny's shrill voice cutting straight through the tree line, down the embankment. "Yoo-hoo! Lunch is ready."

If we cocked our heads just right, we could see her standing out back by the clothesline, not too far from the drop-off.

"Grandpa, Aunt Beryl says Mama's not married 'cuz she cats around and drinks like a fish."

Grandpa shook his head, then stared out at the water. "Young lady, I've lived by this lake most of my life, and I've yet to see a fish take a drink."

I made fish lips then started to meow. "Grandpa. Look at me. What kind of fish am I? I'm a *catfish*."

Grandpa laughed, and said, "You're a silly one at that," and we gathered our things and headed up to the house.

Later that day, I told Mama what Aunt Beryl had said. About me being a *ligament* child.

Mama balled up her fist and fumed. "That old woman never did learn to keep her trap shut." She scowled at me and warned, "Next time Aunt Beryl comes to town, we're gonna have us a *come to Jesus*."

Somehow I knew this did not involve church.

CHAPTER 32

❦

Late September, 2007

Her backpack buzzed. She tried to ignore it as Dr. Lambert's lecture on mitochondria and cell division went right over her head. Scribbling the information into her notebook, Johnnie reminded herself that anything was better than math. Even college biology. And whoever was trying to reach her could wait.

Her phone vibrated a few more seconds then stopped. Relieved, she squinted at Dr. Lambert, thankful for a female professor who sometimes got off topic and talked about her grown children during lecture. Johnnie found this comforting. Shifting in her seat, she hoped no one heard her phone.

But then it vibrated again, and this time fear squeezed her heart. Someone was determined to reach her.

Being the oldest student in class, she tried not to draw any unwanted attention. She fixed her eyes on her professor, reached into her backpack, and lifted her phone to her lap. With a slight tilt of her head, she glanced at the words *missed call* displayed on the screen. Then the voicemail icon appeared and her stomach did a barrel roll.

Something was wrong. Without giving it another thought,

she picked up her backpack and bolted for the door.

"I'm sorry," she called over her shoulder, interrupting Dr. Lambert's lecture. "I need to take this call."

Out in the hallway, she took a deep breath and stopped to listen to Dale's voicemail.

"The school nurse just called. Callie Ann fainted this morning. I'm taking her to the ER."

The emergency room? A tornado twisted through her gut.

But even as she pressed speed dial to call Dale, one thought kept tugging at her heart, *What is wrong with my baby girl?*

Then another thought crept in, dark and petty. Why did the school nurse call Dale first and not her?

Shifting her backpack, she quickened her pace and pushed open the heavy steel door just as Dale's voice came on the line.

"So you got my message?"

"I'm on my way," she told him.

Outside, the cold air slapped her in the face. She breathed in deeply then exhaled, trying to expel her fear.

At Portion Regional Hospital, she spotted Dale's truck near the ER, the cab empty. Grabbing her purse, she rushed into the emergency room's waiting area. The antiseptic smell lit up her sinuses. A friendly nurse directed her to the examining room.

Peeking in the door, she felt her knees go wobbly at the sight of her daughter lying in a hospital bed and wearing a gown, her hair gathered in a messy ponytail. Dark circles rimmed her eyes.

Callie Ann gave her a sleepy grin. "Hi, Mom. Sorry to get you out of class. Don't you have a test today?"

Johnnie rushed to her side. "Not till next week. What's going on, sis?" She felt her forehead, cool to the touch. "You don't feel like you're running a fever."

Callie Ann sighed, her eyes more gray today than blue. *Grandpa Grubbs' eyes,* Johnnie thought. *Warm and tender one moment, cold and distant the next.* "I told Dad I didn't need to go to the ER, but he insisted. I just got a little dizzy. And then I threw up."

"And passed out and hit your head on a locker," Dale said, talking to Callie Ann but staring at Johnnie across the hospital bed where he stood, his large hands clasped together. He was wearing a flannel jacket, and his eyes conveyed worry.

"You threw up?" Johnnie searched her daughter's face.

Callie Ann stared up at the ceiling, looking annoyed. "And no, Mom. I didn't make myself sick if that's what you're thinking. You always ask us that."

Callie Ann was right and Johnnie knew it. Because of her past, she planted suspicion where none was warranted.

"Has the doctor been in yet?" she finally asked, looking around the cold, sterile room. A plastic bag containing Callie Ann's clothes hung from a hook near the bed.

Dale shook his head. "All they've done is take her vitals."

She turned back to Callie Ann. "Sis, when you say you felt dizzy ... dizzy like how?"

Callie Ann bunched the hospital sheet up under her chin and yawned. "Like when I was a little kid, and I'd go out into the yard and spin and spin and spin ... just to watch the world go round. Only I wasn't spinning. I was changing classes."

Johnnie touched her daughter's cheek. "Do you still feel dizzy?"

Callie Ann shook her head. "No, just tired."

"Does your head hurt? Where you hit the locker?" She reached up and felt a knot on the side of her head.

Callie Ann flinched. "Only when you touch it."

Dale strode across the room and stuck his head out the door. "Wish that doctor would hurry up and get here."

Callie Ann gestured for Johnnie to come closer. "Mom, can we talk when Dad's not around?"

Johnnie kissed her daughter on the forehead then held her at arm's length. "Sure, sis. But first you need to see the doctor."

After the physician on call examined Callie Ann and couldn't find anything wrong, he suggested she see her family doctor if she had any more fainting episodes. Suspecting she might have suffered a mild concussion from the fall, he wanted her to stick around a couple of hours for observation. Johnnie and Dale slipped out to let Callie Ann rest.

Out in the waiting room, they bought coffee from a vending machine and milled around, neither one ready to sit down.

Sipping her coffee, Johnnie noticed an attractive woman seated nearby, staring at Dale. At first, Johnnie thought the woman might be one of Dale's former clients. With long blonde hair, a country club tan, and a short tennis skirt to go with it, she had that moneyed look of someone who lunched with friends and indulged in salon and shopping excursions. Perhaps Dale had remodeled her home, or at least given her an estimate on a job. But Dale seemed oblivious to the woman as he sipped his coffee and checked his phone messages.

All at once, Johnnie realized the woman was checking him out. For the first time in years, she saw her husband through the eyes of another woman. Before her stood a sandy-haired man in his mid-forties, with a ruggedly handsome face and an extremely nice build.

To her chagrin, it dawned on her that women had been paying Dale this kind of attention for years. And she had been asleep. More, he'd never taken advantage of it. *I've never been unfaithful to you. I've never screwed around on you.*

She tucked a loose tendril of hair behind her ear, blew on her coffee, and suggested they find a seat, preferably away from the blonde.

They sat side-by-side, holding their coffee cups, two wounded creatures with a new set of rules. Before Dale found out about her affair, they'd been comfortable in their silences. But now, as a hush fell between them, Johnnie wondered what Dale was thinking. Although things seemed back to normal in the bedroom, sometimes Dale would stare off into space afterward. Or he seemed distracted when she asked him a question.

Even with hot coffee, she started to shiver. Dale set his coffee down, took off his flannel jacket, and draped it over her shoulders. She breathed in his masculine scent, a mixture of warm skin, perspiration, and aftershave.

She offered him a weak smile. "Thanks."

Dale took a long sip of coffee then cleared his throat. "She didn't want me to call you when I went to pick her up."

Johnnie shifted uncomfortably in her seat. "Is that why the school nurse called you instead of me?"

Dale nodded. "She didn't want to bother you. She said you have enough to worry about. What with Cade leaving soon for basic and your classes."

Johnnie stared at the dark liquid in her cup. "But I'm her mother. That's my job."

Setting his coffee down, Dale massaged the spot above the bridge of his nose. "Do you think she's sexually active?"

Johnnie took a nervous sip of coffee. "I don't know. I hope not. I mean …. We've had the talk. We've had many talks."

He folded his hands, crossed his legs, and looked down at the floor. "Two things crossed my mind when the nurse called. She's either pregnant or into drugs."

Johnnie sighed in frustration. "She is not into drugs. I know my daughter. She gets dizzy one time at school and you jump to conclusions."

Dale drained the last of his coffee and started tearing at the top of the empty Styrofoam cup. "Okay, but what would we do if she got pregnant?"

Leaning back in the chair, Johnnie rested her head against the wall. "I don't know, Dale. I don't like to think about it."

Dale got up and tossed his empty cup into a nearby trash bin. He turned to look at her, keeping his voice down. "I don't like to think about it either. But she's the same age your mother was when she got pregnant with you."

Johnnie felt as if she'd been punched. It took her a second to get up out of the chair. "I need to stretch my legs. I'm stiff from sitting in class all morning."

Dale was one step behind her. He caught her by the elbow, his jaws clenched as if he was afraid to say too much. "Look, I'm sorry. That was a cheap shot."

Turning, she headed up the hallway to check on Callie Ann. She still had on Dale's jacket.

Callie Ann hit the mute button on the remote, silencing the corner TV. "Did Dad leave?"

Johnnie dropped her purse in a chair by the bed and rested her arms on the rails. "No, he's still out in the waiting room. You must be feeling better. The color's returned to your cheeks."

Propping herself on the pillow, Callie Ann leaned on one elbow then pulled the sheet back, flexing her leg and pointing her toes. "Since I'm going to miss drill team practice, I can at least stay limber."

Johnnie admired her daughter's long slender legs, her coral-painted toenails. "You have Mama's legs, you know … and the same delicate feet. I always wanted pretty legs like you."

Callie Ann studied her. "You have nice legs, Mom."

Johnnie crossed her arms and chuckled. "Not like you and Mama."

Turning slightly, Callie Ann flexed her other leg. "I keep waiting for her to show up on our doorstep. It kind of freaks me out, too. I mean, what would I say to her? 'Hi, my name's Callie Ann. You must be Queen Victoria, my long-lost grandmother.'"

She tucked both legs in and burrowed under the sheets. "Then I'd invite her in, and if she tried to run, I'd lock her in a closet and hold her captive until Granny Opal got there." Squeezing her eyes shut, she bared her teeth in a snarly grin.

"You look like the Big Bad Wolf," Johnnie teased.

Callie Ann's eyes flew open. "The better to eat you with, my dear," she laughed, playing along. For they'd both loved the story of "Little Red Riding Hood" when Callie Ann was young, and Johnnie took pleasure in knowing that her daughter remembered.

Fussing with the blanket, she gazed at Callie Ann's long eyelashes enhanced with mascara, her lips pink from a fresh coat of lip gloss. She looked like the picture of health, not the same pale-faced girl she'd encountered only an hour ago. But then a tear slid down Callie Ann's creamy cheek, and Johnnie suspected that whatever brought Callie Ann to the emergency room might have more to do with her emotions and less to do with her physical health.

"What's going on, sis? What did you want to talk to me about?"

Callie Ann hesitated then sniffled. "Mom, how old were you when you lost your virginity?"

Her virginity?

The question set off alarms, but Johnnie tried to appear calm. She propped her elbows on the rail, cupping her face in her hands. She recognized within her the constant tug-of-war between telling too much or not enough in any situation. This was one of those times when she decided there was no right or wrong answer. "Let's just say I was older than most."

"Like how old?" Callie Ann pressed.

Johnnie peered into her daughter's eyes. They'd gone from gray to blue then back to gray. "Why do you want to know?"

Callie Ann shrugged. "I'm just curious."

"Umm … I was nineteen."

Callie Ann's eye widened. "Nineteen? That's kind of old, isn't it?"

Johnnie straightened, stretching her neck from side to side. "I held out as long as I could. I was petrified of two things. Looking like a slut and getting pregnant."

"Was Dad your first?"

Johnnie took a deep breath. "I dated a few guys before I met your Dad, but yeah, he was my first."

Callie Ann nodded thoughtfully, biting the inside of her mouth. "And your second?"

Johnnie rubbed her left temple, avoiding her daughter's trap. "I'm not going to answer that."

Outside, a siren pierced the air, and they both looked toward the doorway. Johnnie couldn't see the ambulance as it pulled into the emergency entrance, but her stomach dropped as that old sensation of fear twisted through her gut.

After the siren stopped, they avoided each other's eyes for a moment.

Finally, Callie Ann spoke. "Mom, did you have a boyfriend when you were my age?"

It took Johnnie a second to collect her thoughts. She remembered her first kiss, the first time a boy stuck his hand down her pants. "He was three years older than me. His name was Clovis Franks."

Callie Ann pulled absentmindedly at her hair, working the ponytail loose from the elastic band. "Did he pressure you to go all the way?"

"Yeah, a little I guess. But he wasn't a jerk about it. Then he was killed and—"

Callie Ann sat up in bed. "Killed? How?"

"A bus crash."

"Oh, Mom. How awful. I'm sorry." She lay back against the pillow and fidgeted with her hair, concern etched on her face.

Johnnie narrowed her eyes on her daughter. "So who's pressuring *you* to have sex?" *The creep in the jeep*, she wanted to say. "That guy Alex?"

Callie Ann unleashed her ponytail and combed her fingers through her tangled hair, avoiding the knot on the side of her head, "You mean Jerkwad! We broke up two months ago because I wouldn't put out."

Thank God, Johnnie thought, relieved for now. She couldn't wait to tell Dale.

"Why didn't you say something?"

Twisting her hair back in a tight ponytail, she said, "I didn't want you to make a big fuss over it. I know you don't like him." With those high cheekbones, she looked more like a blonde Victoria Grubbs every day.

"I hardly know the boy," Johnnie said, thinking back over the past few weeks, recalling Callie Ann's mood swings, how ugly her temperament could get at times.

"I was okay until this morning when Alex bumped me in the hall. He couldn't wait to tell me about all the girls he's slept with since we broke up. He called me a prudish little bitch … said it in front of all my friends."

Johnnie wanted to wring that black-haired rooster's neck. "Good thing I wasn't there."

"And that's when it happened …. One second he was making fun of me, the next I turned to get away. Then a bunch of ROTC guys came down the hall toward me …. I saw their uniforms and freaked out. I thought about poor Tutts and what happened to his face … about Cade going off to war. Then the world started spinning, and the next thing I knew, all these people were standing over me and I couldn't breathe. I thought I was dying."

Wiping tears from her eyes, Johnnie leaned over the bedrails and cradled her daughter in her arms. "Oh, sweetheart. I'm no shrink, but I think you had an anxiety attack."

Callie Ann rested her head against Johnnie's breast. "Have you ever had one, Mom?"

Johnnie rocked her, breathing in her daughter's scent of fruity lip gloss and clean hair. "Yes, baby, I have."

"Did you have one when your boyfriend died?"

Swallowing, Johnnie kissed the top of Callie Ann's head.

It was time to write about Clovis.

* * *

Johnnie's Journal
September 2007
Portion Regional Hospital

Dear Clovis:

I don't grieve for you anymore, but I feel your mother's grief. Twenty-eight years later, the headline still makes me sad: "Church Bus Slams into Narrow Bridge, Portion Teen Killed." Bits and pieces of the story fly around in my head, black and white newsprint, words dismembered from whole sentences: Former altar boy, Clovis Franks. Seventeen. Killed coming home from youth mission trip. Mass of Christian Burial at Church of the Blessed Virgin.

At the funeral, the priest said your mother named you Clovis after some French king. I guess she had a thing for nobility. Your brother recalled how you loved to stride into a room and tease, "Hello, peons, the King of the Franks is here," especially when your dad's relatives came to visit. And the spell you cast over the nuns, even prim little Sister Jean. Who can forget the parish social when you asked her to dance—the hint of a giggle that broke free as she reached from her starched habit to accept your hand?

You told me once how you went to confession every time we made out. Oh, sweet boy, all you did was grope and grind, then wipe yourself with a towel. Fifteen and pudgy, I craved your affection. Not to have your baby. Behind the gym after lunch, you smothered me with kisses, the taste of Red Hots burning my mouth.

Your death plunged me into a dark hole. A hole I couldn't climb out of for years.

It all started with a box of donuts after Mama and I returned from the cemetery.

Johnnie

CHAPTER 33

❧

First week in October, 2007

"Was he better in bed? Did he have a bigger dick? Was it his money? What was it, Johnnie?"

Dale's questions sent her scrambling to her feet. She slammed her biology book shut and fled for the nearest exit. "I'm at the library," she whispered. "Can we talk about this tonight?"

God, she hoped the other students in her study group hadn't heard his voice boom from the tiny speaker when she flipped open her phone. In her mind, the whole library heard what he said.

Once outside, she huddled near the door and stared at her brown clogs, crossing her arms to stay warm. All she had on was a pair of jeans and a ribbed sweater designed for fashion, not warmth. Her jacket and purse were still inside. Panic mounted as she kept looking back, trying to concentrate on Dale's questions while making sure no one walked out of the building with her purse.

Dale sighed. "Sorry to interrupt you. Look, you're obviously busy …."

After months of not wanting "to go there," he was suddenly in the mood to talk about her affair. Right now, in the middle of the day, in a week when she had a test coming up. She glanced at her watch: 11:15. Her group had only been in session ten minutes.

"Are you still at work?"

"I'm letting the crew take an early lunch. I'm gonna stay here and eat my pimento cheese sandwich and guard the tools."

She needed to study but Dale needed to talk. Flinging the door open, she went to get her things. "I'll meet you there in fifteen minutes. You want anything from Sonic?"

There was a long pause. "You know what I like."

THE TWO-STORY PRAIRIE-STYLE HOUSE WASN'T a mansion by Hollywood or Highland Park standards, Johnnie thought, but everyone in Portion referred to it as the Dooley Mansion. One of the oldest homes in town, built by a pioneer doctor at the turn of the century, the 4,000-square-foot brick structure commanded attention with its towering chimneys, wide overhanging eaves, grand front porch topped by a balcony, and gabled dormer window—the home's crowning glory.

Even now as she pulled into the narrow driveway to meet Dale, Johnnie imagined ghost children peeking out from the attic's third-floor window. This is where the "witch lady" had lived when Johnnie was a kid. Every Halloween—when Mama was around—she and Johnnie stopped by here for popcorn balls and candied apples. In her pointy black hat and flowing cape, the witch served hot apple cider from a black cauldron and regaled young visitors with tales that sent them screaming into the night. Mama always lingered, chatting with the witch like they were best friends. Years later, while reading the obits, Johnnie learned that Mrs. Delthia Overby was an eccentric widow who never had children, drove a Cadillac, and wore red fox stoles long after they went out of fashion. She donated her body to science and her wealth to charity.

Over the years, the home fell into disrepair and sat vacant until some investors from Dallas decided to cash in on the growing popularity of historic Portion. And Dale was the lucky contractor chosen to bring the home back to its original splendor.

At the top of the driveway, Dale glanced up from a sawhorse where he was cutting a board. He set the saw down and came toward her.

She took a deep breath and pushed the door open with her left side. Grabbing the two drinks, she tried to avoid his probing eyes. "Here's your cherry limeade. With a double shot of cherry syrup and an extra lime."

Dale took the drink and motioned toward the house. "You know I had my eye on this place years ago, but we couldn't afford it."

Quit trying to give me things then make me feel bad about the money, she thought. But what she said was: "Who needs all that space? I've got all the house I need."

And suddenly, in her mind, they weren't talking about the house anymore. They were talking about her affair with Jeral Cagle.

Did he have a bigger dick? Was it his money?

They walked over and sat on the tailgate of Dale's pickup, sipping their limeades.

The noon sun felt good against her back as she watched two squirrels chasing each other from tree to tree. Somewhere in the distance, she heard the warning *beep, beep, beep* of a truck backing up.

"You warm enough in that jacket?" he asked, rolling up the sleeves of his flannel shirt.

She nodded and played with her straw. Dale peeled the lid off his drink. He scooped out a lime wedge and started sucking on it. The clean scent of citrus lingered in the air.

Neither of them spoke.

Finally, Dale removed the shriveled lime wedge from his mouth. He studied it a moment then tossed it into a large dumpster full of rubbish.

Johnnie glanced at her lap. She struggled to keep her voice even, but it came out all jittery. "Dale, I never meant to hurt you."

He looked away, chewed his lip, then hopped off the tailgate to stretch his legs. "I'm sorry I sounded so crude on the phone, but …. Well, I need to know why you had to go elsewhere. Did I not satisfy you? Was I not good looking enough? I know all the ladies thought Cagle was a stud muffin."

Johnnie stared at her drink, her fingers pinched around her straw. "Oh God, Dale. It was such a long time ago."

Dale shoved his hands in his pockets. "Johnnie, I need to know what I'm dealing with. You owe me that much."

She set her drink down and leaned against the end of a ladder in the bed of Dale's truck. The ladder poked her in the back and she welcomed the pain.

"Do you really want to know this?"

Dale frowned. "I've had months to think about it. It's what I don't know that's driving me crazy."

With a heavy sigh, she began. "You were always gone."

Her stomach knotted up as she watched him struggle to understand.

Cracking his knuckles, he raised an eyebrow. "So it was the sex then."

Tears welled up in her eyes. She had no right to cry. If anybody should cry, it was Dale. She didn't want to hurt him any more than he'd already been hurt, but he wanted the truth; it was time to come clean. "He didn't know I was sick," she replied. "He didn't know about the bulimia."

Wiping her eyes, she saw Dale gulp. He looked stunned … as if this was the last thing he expected to hear.

She pressed ahead, trying not to trip over her words. "I was so lonely back then. I hated being alone. You were always out of town at one job or another."

Dale began to pace in front of her. "I was exhausted," he said, shaking his head at the ground. "All I wanted was to give you a good life."

"Sometimes I felt like one of your old houses. That all you wanted to do was *fix me* and grow your business." The words tumbled out, fast and furious, and hung there between them in the open.

He twisted around and scowled at her. "So you're saying it was *my* fault?"

Shoulders sagging, she tried to explain, "No, Dale! That's not what I said."

He went back to cracking his knuckles.

Shielding her eyes from the sun, she rushed on, "I was so needy back then. And sick. I was looking for anything to make me feel better."

Dale shot her a look. "Were you still going to therapy?"

Slowly, she shook her head and lowered her gaze. "It got too expensive, remember? We didn't have health insurance back then."

He halted midstride and closed his eyes, running a hand through his wavy hair.

She started to wiggle her foot. "It doesn't excuse what I did."

He scratched the back of his neck. "How long did it last?"

"About a month. By then, I was so eaten up with guilt I couldn't stand myself."

Dale gazed up at the sky as if remembering something from a long time ago. "Is that why you used to cry so much after we made love?"

She looked away, unable to speak.

More silence.

Finally, Dale cleared his throat. "Something else has been bothering me for months."

She waited, dreading the question.

"Why did you tell our son about your affair? What made you blurt it out?"

She remembered that night back in March when Cade said he

hated himself. "He was consumed with guilt over the drinking incident. I was worried he might kill himself." She paused. "This happened right after the Cooper kid shot himself."

Dale took a deep breath and picked at a scab on his hand. "I once saw a GI blow his head off. I was riding my moped behind base housing when I came upon this airman sitting in a ditch with a gun to his head."

Johnnie's whole body jerked up, her back flat as a board. She'd been with this man since she was nineteen years old, and she'd never heard about this.

"He was a young kid," Dale went on. "Not much older than me. Maybe eighteen. He looked me square in the eye then pulled the trigger. I left before the sky cops showed up. I never told my old man. I thought it would hurt his career."

She was afraid to look too deep into Dale's eyes, for fear the young airman might stare back. "I can't believe you never told me."

He shrugged. "I never told anyone. I just tried to forget about it. Hey, I was a colonel's kid. We suck everything up."

Suddenly, she had the urge to run. She jumped off the tailgate and rushed toward a rusty iron gate, half off its hinges. The gate led to a large, unkempt backyard and what had once been a garden. A climbing rosebush clung to an old trellis, a few coral buds about to burst open.

She felt like that rosebush, blooming out of season, clinging for dear life. She slowed to a jog and stopped in front of an old birdbath full of rotting leaves and muck. The stench made her gag. She doubled over, trying to block the image of the young man shooting himself in the head. And then out of nowhere, Steven Tuttle's face came swimming into view.

From behind her, she could feel Dale wrap his strong arms around her, encircling her with his warmth. With one move, Dale turned her around and cupped her wet face in his hands.

When she finally spoke, her voice was thick from crying. "I'm so ashamed."

Dale slid his arm around her back. "Come on. I have something I need to show you."

She felt too weak to walk, but Dale propelled her forward across the lawn and through the iron gate. She swiped at her eyes with the sleeve of her jacket. They were moving toward the porch, up the steps she'd climbed as a little girl to collect treats from the witch.

She caught her breath at the enormity of the entryway, the high ceilings, the hand-scraped wood floors, the white crown molding, and the wide staircase that called to her.

"We had to bring most of this place down to the studs. All new sheetrock. Plumbing and electricity. We knocked down a couple of closets to make bathrooms. We're waiting on the marble and granite and most of the fixtures."

Johnnie turned this way and that, admiring the clean lines of the house.

Dale glanced at his watch. "The guys will be back any second. I'll give you the grand tour next time. Come on. We're going up to the attic."

"The attic?"

Up the stairs they went, past the landing on the second floor. "The owners want to turn it into a honeymoon suite."

"I used to think ghosts lived up here. Little kids cooked and eaten by the witch."

Dale chuckled. "Okay, when I open this door I want you to close your eyes."

"Should I be scared or excited?"

"That depends."

She heard him open a door, and he led her several steps into what appeared to be a large space. Their footsteps echoed across new hardwood floors. The air felt cold and she could smell fresh paint.

"Okay, you can open your eyes."

After she adjusted to the light, she glanced around at the spacious room that ran the length of the house. One whole wall contained built-in shelves and cabinets. But her eyes were drawn to the only window in the former attic: the dormer window she'd admired from the street.

He jutted his chin toward it. "Check out the view."

His voice echoed off the empty walls as her clogs clopped across the barren floor to the window.

"The colors are magnificent from up here," she sighed, looking out over the town of Portion. The treetops were mottled in harvest gold and autumn red, and the rooftops of Main Street were outlined against the blue sky.

Dale moved back to give her space. "Do you see it?"

Her eyes scanned the horizon from left to right. "See what?" she said. And then she saw it ... the shoreline just below the bluff. The place she'd been drawn to her whole life.

Fingers of electricity skated up her back.

"Oh my God," she started to cry. "You can see the cove from here."

"Johnnie, I think your mama's been here, too. Up in this attic. Maybe as recently as last spring."

She twisted around, squinting into every corner of the room. "Why do you say that?"

"Because one of the owners stopped by here this morning and we got to talking. He said that back in the spring, when they first came to look at the property, somebody in their group saw a woman looking out this window. By the time they got upstairs, she was gone. They found tin cans full of cigarette butts with lipstick on them."

Johnnie leaned her forehead against the cool glass. Somewhere below, Mama was strolling the streets, hiding out in some bathroom, hunched over a booth in some fast food joint. Portion was part of the greater Dallas/Fort Worth area, and in a metroplex of six million people, it was easy to get lost, easy to hide.

"Oh, Mama," she said aloud. "We can't keep putting our lives on hold, waiting for you to come home."

Dale put his arm around her, and they leaned into each other for support.

A couple of pickup trucks with toolboxes mounted behind the cabs pulled up and parked next to the curb.

He patted her on the rump. "We better head downstairs. Can't have my men thinking the boss and his wife are trying out the new honeymoon suite. Besides, you've got a test to study for."

As they turned to leave, she glanced one more time at the dormer window that overlooked the cove and most of Portion. She pictured her mama standing there, chain-smoking one cigarette after another, and gazing out … into the past.

CHAPTER 34

~⌇~

Creative Writing 101
Portion Community College

Assignment: A Turning Point in my Life
"Donuts, Coffee, and Salt: Fun for the Whole Family"

"MAYBE WE SHOULD GET HER stomach pumped."
Granny placed a cool hand on my forehead and smoothed back my hair. When I was a child, she'd always known how to comfort me, but no amount of love or kind gestures could help me now. I needed relief and I needed it fast. I could barely breathe.

Mama paced back and forth in front of the davenport where I was curled up, my new seersucker skirt unzipped at my waist. I'd already removed the matching vest, buttoned over a summer T-shirt I'd worn to my boyfriend's funeral. Mama was still dressed in the hot pink number she'd grabbed at a secondhand shop the day before. She looked more like a junior bridesmaid than a mama. It was June, 1979. The summer I learned that a boy could be sliced in half by a jagged piece of glass.

"She inhaled *donuts*, not pills." Mama's voice had an angry edge to it.

"Yes, and you've already made that trip to the ER once now,

haven't you?" Aunt Beryl mumbled at the back of Mama's head.

I didn't know what she was talking about, but a look came over Mama's face like I'd never seen. She spun around and hissed at Aunt Beryl, "Maybe it's time you headed back to Salt Flat."

Grandpa stepped from the shadows and glared at Aunt Beryl. She glared back. His eyes seemed to cast a warning. Hers flared with defiance.

I hated that everybody was fighting because I'd gobbled a dozen donuts in the parish hall while Mama was off flirting with the handsome priest who drank beer at the parish picnic. You'd never see that at the Methodist Church. Each time I crammed down a donut, I pictured poor Clovis sewn back together, pickled in formaldehyde, and lying in a velveteen coffin. I saw him lowered into the ground, his grave smothered with flowers that would be dead the next day. Standing by the punch bowl, I'd overheard how he'd been riding up front, keeping the bus driver company while the others slept. When the front bumper hit the bridge abutment, he'd been thrown through the windshield. Half of him ended up down in the creek, while the other landed on the bridge. His Saint Christopher medal still dangled around his bloody neck.

With each bite of donut, I numbed myself, concentrating on the moist texture, the rush of sugar hitting my bloodstream. After a while, I stopped feeling. Blocked the image of Clovis's battered body. The good Catholic boy who went to confession every time he copped a feel. The sweet boy helping to keep the bus driver awake through the night.

Granny Opal turned her head as another putrid belch escaped my lips. The air reeked with the stench of sulfur.

Aunt Beryl swatted her hand over her face. "Whew, child. What in God's name did you swallow? A dead 'possum?"

"Just a few donuts, then supper." My words were short and rapid, like my breathing. Supper consisted of two helpings of pot roast, potatoes, carrots, and onions, topped off by two slices of Granny's coconut cream pie. Moments after the meal, my gut began to rumble as the stew fermented and the pressure built. I'd never been so miserable.

I thought I might suffocate. My windpipe felt swollen shut.

Mama stared at me like I was stupid.

An invisible band tightened around my middle. It was as if a cement truck had backed up and dumped wet concrete down my gullet, and now it was hardening in my stomach.

"I'm going to split wide open, I'm so full," I moaned. "Somebody help me. I can't breathe."

"You look six months pregnant," Aunt Beryl muttered, and all the air went out of the room. Mama's face turned ashen. Grandpa jammed his hands in his pockets.

I wanted to cry but my tears were trapped at the back of my throat.

"Can it, Aunt Beryl!"

Mama's eyes stared cold and hard at Grandpa's sister.

Aunt Beryl hoisted herself out of the chair and departed in a huff.

Granny rose and went into the kitchen, followed by Grandpa. Mama stopped in front of the piano, the fingers of her right hand tapping out some nameless tune. A few moments later Granny and the others returned.

Granny held out a tall glass of black liquid. "I want you to down this as fast as you can. It's a mixture of coffee and salt. Supposed to induce vomiting." She placed the glass in my sweaty paw.

"Down the hatch." Grandpa hovered nearby, his eyes the color of steel wool.

Shuddering, I chugged the salty concoction all at once. Within seconds, the witch's brew bubbled inside my gut, followed by a churning sensation.

"She's white as a ghost," Grandpa said, his gruff voice masking his concern.

Mama steered me down the darkened hallway to the

commode, my skirt riding my curvy hips. She grabbed me from behind and thrust her fist into my sternum. "One, two, three, urp. One, two, three, urp," she commanded, as if counting would actually help.

Where she learned this I had no idea, but within seconds, I doubled over and black sewage gushed from my body. Somebody flushed the toilet a couple of times as I kept heaving.

The wretched stench and Mama's sickly sweet perfume lingered in the hall bathroom long after everyone but me had cleared the room.

"That smell could knock a buzzard off a shit wagon," Aunt Beryl barked in her crotchety voice from somewhere down the hall.

I didn't eat for two days following that stunt. Then something clicked in my brain. *I could eat as much as I wanted then get rid of it*. Sort of like an unwanted baby. All I had to do was abort the food. Instead of drinking coffee and salt, I learned to stick my finger down my throat.

CHAPTER 35

∿

Mid-October

A FEW DAYS BEFORE CADE left for basic training, Johnnie leashed up Brother Dog for a brisk stroll before class. Bundled in one of D.J.'s old hoodies to ward off the crisp morning chill, she led Brother west on Merriweather and hung a left on Main Street. Then they jaywalked over to Soldiers Park.

With Brother panting at her side, Johnnie stood at the base of the war memorial and stared into the face of the old soldier. "Talk to me, Mr. Statue. I know you're not real. But still … tell me your secrets."

A sudden gust picked up and a few fallen leaves scuttled by, the dryer ones scraping the sidewalk. She glanced over her shoulder a few times, always on the lookout for a lone woman.

Brother whined and sat on his haunches. Johnnie gazed into the soldier's dark eyes. When she had stared for a good long time, a strange thing happened. With leaves swirling around her, she saw what her mama saw. Heard what her mama heard. Hundreds of thousands of young men in battle, calling across the waves of time, crying out in pain and anguish, "Mama, Mama," before they took their last breath.

Then a thousand faces turned into one: the face of a handsome lieutenant with deep-set eyes and a knowing smile.

She shuddered and yanked a little too hard on the leash. "Come on, Brother. Time to head home."

Glancing one last time at the soldier, she pleaded with him as if he could hear: "Don't ever let me see my Cade's face in your eyes."

CHAPTER 36

≈

Cade's Departure

THE SUN LIT UP THE eastern horizon, casting a bloody orange glow over Portion. Frost covered the ground and leaves piled up against the fence.

Dale was wearing his puffy vest, flannel shirt, and work jeans. After stashing his lunch cooler on the seat of his truck, he turned to wrap Johnnie in his arms. "Try not to worry. He said he'd call us when he got there."

The night before, she and Dale had dropped Cade off at the Crown Plaza Hotel near downtown Dallas, the overnight hotel for all North Texas enlistees processing into the military the next day.

They would not see him again for nine weeks—until he graduated from basic training. Except for church camp and baseball tournaments, he'd never been away from home this long.

Dale pecked her on the cheek and crawled in behind the steering wheel. "Have a good day in class. I'll see you tonight." Then he backed down the driveway and headed east on Merriweather.

Her chin propped on her fist, she watched Dale's taillights

until they disappeared around the corner onto Dooley. She pictured him headed north, past the cemetery on his left, his mind and hands ready for work. How many times would he stop today and think about their son? Think about the day he co-signed Cade's enlistment papers. Even if Dale had refused to sign, Cade would have joined in July, the minute he turned eighteen. Had that been the case, Cade might still be at home, tucked away in his warm bed. But that would have only postponed the inevitable. Dale had just helped make it happen a few months sooner.

Hugging her robe close, she made her way back up the driveway and stopped at the side door under the portico. Cade's pickup sat silent at the top of the drive, the front bumper facing the street where he'd backed it in yesterday afternoon. She stared at the huge bumper, the grille that always reminded her of a giant nutcracker's mouth with too many teeth.

How different things would have turned out had she not pushed Mr. Marvel out of the way seconds before Cade barreled down on top of them.

At one hundred twenty pounds, she had no upper body strength. She could barely lift the boys' smallest dumbbells. So where had that kind of strength come from? She'd wondered for days. A week later, Cade was still grabbing her biceps and teasing, "Show me your muscles, Super Mom." But she knew the near miss really freaked him out. Made him feel weird sometimes when he was around her.

Had she not rolled Mr. Marvel into the curb, three lives would have been ruined that night. She and Mr. Marvel would have been killed outright, and Cade, well …. She closed her eyes, thinking of the hell he'd have to live with, the agony of having killed his own mother who was trying to save a neighbor from killing himself.

She opened the door and went inside the house. Pouring coffee into her *Army Mom* mug, she ventured into the entryway and stood in front of the slim table she now referred to as her "home altar."

"Let him be okay," she whispered, her eyes sweeping over a few treasured objects she'd placed with care. Cade's silver cross, removed hastily last night, dangled over the white Bible she received in third grade. The two photos Dale found were framed and placed on either side of a large yellow candle. *The Lady Walks* hung on one side of the mirror, the handwritten Mother's Day poem on the other.

She set down her coffee and picked up the cross. Fingering the chunky chain like a string of rosary beads, she thought about last night, when Cade slipped through her fingers like water.

"MAMA, PLEASE DON'T CRY," CADE had begged her on the drive out. He rode shotgun up front with Dale.

Johnnie sat behind Cade and squeezed his shoulder, a silent promise that she would abide by his wishes.

It was already dark out when Dale pulled the Suburban into the hotel parking lot.

No one spoke for a moment.

"Well, this is it," Dale said, breaking the silence.

Cade got out first and slung his Army camo backpack over his shoulder. All he had on was a polo shirt, jeans, and running shoes. Inside the backpack was a change of underwear, his temporary Army ID, and recruitment papers. He jammed his phone in the front pocket of his jeans and reached to hug Johnnie.

"I love you, Mama. I'll call when I can." They embraced only seconds. She pulled away first.

She'd already said goodbye to him days ago when Cade started disengaging from the family. He didn't hug her as much. Seemed aloof. Distant. But she'd catch him sneaking hugs with Brother. Somehow it was okay to hug the dog, but hugging his mama was off-limits.

"Daddy …." He towered over Dale. They started to shake hands. "Thanks for everything."

Dale gripped him hard, patting him on the back with the heel of his hand, then his fist. As if he couldn't quite relax, couldn't quite let go.

Under the overhead light in the parking lot, Johnnie noticed something shiny in the V of Cade's collar.

"I thought you couldn't wear any jewelry to basic." She eyed the silver cross they'd given him for his birthday.

Cade looked down. "Oh, good catch, Mama. They would've taken that away from me. Considered it contraband." He removed the chain and handed it to her. "Take care of this for me until I graduate."

He turned and hiked across the parking lot. At the revolving door, he pushed his way through, not even bothering to look back. She expected him to turn once, stick his hand in the air and wave, but when the door did not spit him back out to them, she knew he'd passed the point of no return.

She was out of breath for a moment.

Dale threw both hands high into the air, waving as if in surrender as tears streamed down his ruddy cheeks, past his chapped lips.

They gathered themselves up and got into the Suburban.

Dale could hardly talk. When he did try to say something he sounded like he had a cold. Johnnie stared at the traffic and the tiny pin lights on the dashboard. As they flew down the freeway toward Portion, a lump the size of a baseball lodged in her throat.

LOUD MUSIC BLARED FROM A clock radio at the back of the house. Draping the cross on her Bible, Johnnie picked up her coffee and padded down the hall toward Callie Ann's room. It was 7:30 and they both needed to get ready for school.

The music stopped and a bedside lamp switched on.

Johnnie poked her head in the door. "Morning, sis. Where's Brother? Didn't he sleep with you?"

Callie Ann sat halfway up in bed, stretching. "I thought

he was with you." She rubbed her eyes, her voice crusty from sleep. "He jumped off the bed hours ago."

Johnnie gripped her mug, trying to overlook piles of dirty clothes strewn about, mismatched shoes scattered on the floor, a towel draped over a chair, and a gym bag dropped a few feet from the door. Now wasn't the time to nag Callie Ann about her room.

"We need to get a move on it. I'll go find Brother. He's probably back on my bed."

She peeked in her room, dappled with sunlight, but Brother was not there.

"Where are you, silly boy?" she called, heading back up the hall, thinking he was at the back door, waiting to be let out.

Cade's bedroom door was ajar. She thought he'd shut it when they left yesterday evening for Dallas. Light came through the open blinds when she walked into the room the boys had once shared. Gone were the bunk beds, replaced by a single twin where Brother was curled up on Cade's pillow. His tail thumped against the rumpled sheets, but the rest of him didn't budge.

She set her mug down and rubbed the top of his head. "What are you doing in here, big dog? Don't you need to go out?"

Brother sighed, and it sounded more like a whistle. He glanced at her and then burrowed his chin deeper into his paws.

"You miss him, too, don't you, boy?" She crawled next to him, wrapping her body around his warmth. Except for the unmade bed, Cade had left the room spotless. *I don't want you picking up after me, Mama*, he told her one morning when she caught him dusting his trophies and rearranging his shelves. Military-themed posters now mingled with images of professional baseball players and team photos of Cade, dating all the way back to T-Ball.

Callie Ann appeared at the door. When she saw Brother, she ran to him, jumped on the bed, and buried her face in his side.

"You smell like Fritos and brownies and everything good in the world." Her voice cracked. "Better than Cade's stinky sheets."

Johnnie breathed in the scent of gym socks and sports deodorant. "They smell like *boy* to me."

"I miss him," Callie Ann whispered.

"Me, too," Johnnie choked, stroking her daughter's hair.

They both collapsed on Brother, their tears seeping into his fur. He remained still, head erect, offering his body as a giant sponge.

CHAPTER 37

∾◡∽

They Hate Us

TWO NIGHTS LATER AS JOHNNIE was cleaning up the kitchen, Cade's phone number lit up the Caller ID on her cellphone.

"It's Cade," she hollered, shutting the dishwasher with her knee. Dale tossed aside the newspaper, sending pages flying over the leather chair as he made his way across the den to join her. She flipped open her phone and put it on speaker.

"Cade? Honey?" She held the phone in the air, waiting for him to speak. Dale fidgeted with loose change in his pocket, bending his head to listen.

"Mama! I got less than a minute to talk," his voice blared from the tiny speaker.

"Your dad's here, too," she said. She and Dale huddled around the phone, as if they could wrap their whole bodies around his voice.

"They're taking our phones away tonight. We don't know when we'll get them back." He sounded shaken.

Dale removed his reading glasses, biting on one stem. "How ya doing, son?"

"They hate us," Cade cried. "They fucking hate us."

Johnnie bit her lip and reached for Dale. "Who hates you, baby?"

"The drill sergeants, Mama. It's not like The Military Channel on TV."

"You can't take it personal," Dale said. "Their job is to strip you down and build you back up."

Cade sighed. "I know that, Daddy. I love y'all. I'll call when I can." *Click.*

The phone went silent in her hand. She stared at Dale, knowing she couldn't rescue her son.

Dale looked at her and shrugged. "Cade's a good man. He'll do fine."

After a moment, she closed her phone. Her son was over five hundred miles away, but his voice still thundered in her ears.

They hate us. They fucking hate us.

THE NEXT MORNING, BROTHER DOG trotted to the back door and rattled his tags. Pulling her bathrobe tighter, Johnnie let him out and made a bowl of instant oatmeal.

After taking Brother for a walk, she settled down to study. She sipped her coffee while she flipped on the TV to get the latest news.

A middle-age father from a small farming community in Iowa was telling a reporter how he'd just returned from the post office after mailing a letter to his soldier son. The moment he turned down his street, he saw a dark-colored sedan parked by the curb in front of his house. Two uniformed men waited on his front porch. The father said he gunned the engine and kept driving. He got as far as the cornfields on the edge of town before he turned around and headed back.

Johnnie picked up the remote and aimed it at the TV. Right before she hit *off*, the man said, "I wished I'd kept driving."

* * *

Johnnie's Journal
(hardcopy sent snail mail)

October 2007
420 Merriweather
Portion, TX (home base)
Private Cade Kitchen
Fort Leonard Wood, MO 65473

Dear Cade,

It's cold here and most of the trees have changed colors. Whit stopped by yesterday with two giant pumpkins from the farmers market. We set them on the top step of the porch, and the orange really stands out against the red brick of the house. She stayed and helped Callie Ann and me make a soldier scarecrow. We dressed him in a camouflage uniform we found at the army surplus store in Euless. A squadron of geese flew over about the time we'd finished, and their honking sent Brother on a "wild goose chase" around the yard. He was still yapping and running circles long after those geese were out of sight.

Son, I can't possibly imagine what your days are like, even though I've watched videos about basic training. I keep thinking about what you said the other night on that thirty-second phone call. How it wasn't like The Military Channel. When things get rough, remember that the spirit of Lieutenant Murphy walks with you, beside you. Yes, I believe in these things. You come from sturdy stock, Cade Kitchen. Don't ever forget it. You've always been a hard worker like your dad. I am proud of you.

Brother misses you. Callie Ann and I took your truck to the store the other day and when we got home, he came running out and ran straight to the driver's side. While Sis and I unloaded groceries, that dog stood there, wagging his tail like he was waiting for you to get out of the cab. We hug him a lot these days.

My classes are going well. Biology is tough, but I'm really enjoying my writing class. The colonel called the other day and asked for your address. Be on the lookout for a letter from him. He's commissioned your brother to do a painting of him from his flying days. I expect he'll pay top dollar, too. I'll close for now.

Soldier On, Son—

Love, Mama

CHAPTER 38

❧

Late October, 2007
Cottonbelt Café

"I WAS GOING TO SUGGEST we meet up at the war memorial after I got out of class." Johnnie twisted the paper napkin in her fingers. White particles littered her lap, and she brushed them from her black jeans onto the floor beneath the lacquered table. She hoped the woman seated across from her hadn't noticed.

Big boned and plain, Beth Tuttle leaned back in the padded booth, shielding her coffee cup with both hands. "Oh, I can't go near that place. Not since Stevie's patrol got attacked."

Johnnie looked away, squinting hard through the large plate glass window of the café. "And I can't seem to stay away," she whispered.

"Your son hasn't deployed yet, has he?" One second Beth Tuttle's face seemed almost flat, devoid of all emotion, the next, her upper lip trembled.

"No. He left for basic a week ago. We haven't talked since he got to Fort Leonard Wood and made that thirty-second phone call." She held her pinkie finger to her mouth, her thumb to her ear, mimicking Cade's call. "I got less than a minute to talk."

Beth nodded. "I remember that call. Stevie sounded like a robot."

"I check the weather for Missouri every day. They got their first snowfall this morning." Johnnie tried to block the image of Cade freezing his butt off in formation at dawn, while drill sergeants screamed obscenities down his throat. But she kept this thought to herself. Why fling her minor worries at a woman whose son had been maimed in battle? Nor did she blab about how her father had been killed in war. Why jab a stick in an open wound?

Steven's mother gazed up at an old photo of a steam locomotive chugging into the Portion Depot. The photo hung over the window above their booth. "No, the Cottonbelt was a good choice. Remember when our boys worked here? They both started out busing tables."

Johnnie grinned at the memory. "D.J. used to complain about the Sunday crowd. Said church-goers were the rudest customers." She sipped her orange spice tea and nibbled on a bran muffin—almost as good as the ones Aunt Beryl used to make.

Steven's mom tilted her head, as if remembering. "Stevie said the same thing. Said the preachers were the worst tippers," she chuckled. "That was his first real job, you know. Outside of mowing lawns."

"D.J.'s, too. I think they were only fifteen. Remember how they saved their money and bought guitars?"

"Oh, the music they played! I'm surprised no one ever called the cops. Aggressive metal. I think that's what they called it."

"Beth, why haven't we met until today? Our sons were best friends in high school. I'm sorry I never reached out to you before."

"Oh, heck. Not to worry." She gestured with her hand. "It's as much my fault as yours."

Johnnie took a deep breath. "D.J.'s agnostic now." She had no idea why she blurted this out. She gauged the other woman's face, looking for disapproval, even the slightest frown. But no frown came.

Beth nodded, picked up her coffee, and took a sip. "He's not the only one."

"Oh, no. Steven, too?"

Slowly Beth shook her head. "No. He got religion when he worked at the funeral home. It's me. I lost mine the day my son got half his face blown off."

Johnnie caught her breath, tried not to cringe. Of course, she knew how bad Steven's injuries were, but somehow they sounded even ghastlier when described by his mother. There was no nice way to discuss them, no way at all to soften the blow.

Johnnie looked at her lap, then at Beth. "I don't even know what to say."

Beth shrugged. "It's okay. You're here. That's what matters."

After a while, Beth set her cup down and stared at Johnnie. "Of course, with Stevie's injuries, getting his old job back at the mortuary is out of the question. Who wants Frankenstein driving a hearse?"

Johnnie was speechless. Her mouth went dry at the image of Steven pulling up next to her at the gas station last spring. How handsome he'd looked in his coat and tie! And the morning he dropped Cade off at the house. She jumped as the sound of dishes clattered to the floor somewhere in the café.

"That poor waiter," Beth said, not even bothering to turn around.

Johnnie watched as several busboys scurried about, picking up broken pottery. The manager bustled out of the shadows to apologize to his patrons and to help the staff clean up the mess.

Beth seemed unfazed by all of this.

After a long pause, she resumed speaking. "I mean really, can you imagine? People would mistake a funeral procession for a Halloween parade. They'd think the house of horrors had taken to the road." Beth's voice began to break up, to disintegrate as if her teeth and tongue could no longer form words, as if her whole mouth was crumbling in on itself like the ruins of an ancient city.

Johnnie felt helpless as she sat there in the booth, her emotions under siege.

Finally, she reached across the table for Beth's hand. But just as she moved to console her, a flash of movement outside the window caught her eye.

A thin woman in an Army surplus field jacket strolled by, her shoulders hunched against the crisp fall air. Her long tresses were tied back with a ribbon, her slender calves exposed below a plain cotton dress. She was headed north on Main toward Soldiers Park.

Johnnie froze. *Mama!*

Without hesitation, she bolted from the booth and ran outside, almost knocking over a cartful of pansies blooming in front of the café. Her eyes searched up and down the sidewalk in both directions, pausing in front of several old storefronts. No trace of the woman anywhere.

What if Mama had died the night she called from a payphone? And now she was nothing more than a restless spirit roaming the streets of Portion.

She shivered.

A hand touched her shoulder. "Johnnie, are you all right?"

Her legs wouldn't move; her feet were cemented to the sidewalk. Her hands were clamped over her mouth to stifle her silent scream.

But it was only Beth Tuttle by her side, concern swimming in her liquid eyes. She wrapped an arm around Johnnie's shoulder and led her back into the café.

"It's okay, dear. I had panic attacks, too, right after Stevie left for basic. One time I left a cartful of groceries I'd just paid for inside the store. I heard a siren then saw the EMTs running through the door. I don't know why, but I pushed my cart against a wall and fled."

The heavy smell of breakfast still hung in the air even as the lunch crowd began to arrive.

Johnnie couldn't bring herself to tell Beth why she ran outside.

* * *

Johnnie's Journal
(I'm PUBLISHED!)

Letter to the Editor
Portion Telegraph
November 2007

Another boy from our community has been killed in Iraq. As I stood by the war memorial at Soldiers Park and watched his procession come up Main Street on its way from the airport to the mortuary, I couldn't help but think of a young guardsman from Portion named Steven Tuttle.

Tutts, as my two sons call him, was terribly disfigured a few months ago—half of his face got blown off—when his Humvee crossed paths with an IED. Before he deployed, Steven worked part-time for Farrow & Sons, driving that very hearse that now carried the remains of a fellow soldier. Steven's mother, a single parent, had to quit her job so she could be with her only child as he recovers in a military hospital in San Antonio. To quote my oldest son: "Sometimes there are worse things than death."

Sometimes there's just death.

My dad died in Vietnam when I was six. The bomb that killed him wasn't called an IED. But a bomb's a bomb, and it blew him to bits just the same. Although I barely remember him, I can't forget him. His death was the great tragedy of my childhood. It sent my mama over the edge.

My youngest son just enlisted in the Army. He's still at basic training, but you can imagine what goes through my mind. Now Veterans Day is coming up on November 11th. Everywhere I go I hear people say, "Thank you for your 'sacrifice,'" when talking about the war dead or injured. The more I hear this, especially from folks who don't have a "dog in the fight," I want to scream, "Hey! I don't want my son sacrificed for anyone. Not for you. Not for the fat cats in Washington …."

And damn sure not for me!

Johnnie Kitchen,
one p.o.'d mama

CHAPTER 39

~⁓

9 November, 2007
Brooks Army Medical Center, San Antonio, TX

Dear Mrs. Kitchen,

MY MOM SENT ME A copy of your letter to the editor from the *Portion Telegraph*. Congrats on getting it published. D.J. mentioned one time that you like to write.

Don't worry about Cade. He's got "The Lieutenant" watching over him now, along with a couple of my buddies who already deployed to Heaven. When I first heard about my injury, I wished I'd gone with them. But then I heard my mom's voice by my bedside, and I decided I was being selfish. My dad split years ago, and I'm all she has left.

I've got some good news to share. I heard from my former employer the other day. Farrow & Sons wants to set up a foundation in my name. How do you like that? A mortuary honoring the living? Pretty sweet, huh? Mr. Farrow says it's the least he can do.

About my facial injury: not sure how much my mom or D.J. told you, but the impact destroyed much of my left side. (That was my best side, too.) When I look in the mirror, I see two people. On one side I see who I was. On the other side I see who I am now. At least I still have sight in my right eye. Maybe next Halloween I can dress up as a pirate. ☺

When I get out of here, I plan to go back to school to become a counselor. Maybe work with wounded warriors. The GI Bill will help me earn my master's degree, and my Purple Heart will give me credibility with the vets.

Got a text from D.J. the other day. He might come visit me over Thanksgiving break. I told him to bring a sketchpad. I want him to do a portrait of me so I can hang it in my new office one day.

Next time you're up at the war memorial, will you stop and say a prayer for all the guys who didn't come back?

WAR-4-$$$,

Steven

CHAPTER 40

✌

(Submitted for consideration to Portion
Community College Literary Magazine)

"Granny Opal's Cake Factory"

"CAKES NEED TO COME OUT of the oven," Granny fussed
at Mama, but her eyes were on me. "Don't let them sit
too long or they'll never lift out of the pan. Then I'll have to
feed them to the birds."

We sat in the breakfast area having tea. My plump fingers
were wrapped around a dainty teacup, and I was still wearing
my Brownie uniform and beanie. I dreaded that time back
at the table after supper when Grandpa would grill me with
flashcards.

Mama bustled into the room and went to work lifting cakes
out of the brown double oven and shoving buttered pans back
in. Cakes cooled on wax paper on the gold-speckled peninsula
that divided the breakfast room from the kitchen.

Granny leaned toward me. "When I first started out, I made
so many mistakes I threw half my creations in the yard. Poppy
claimed we had the fattest birds on the lake. He said, 'If those
jays and robins get any plumper, they'll never fly.'"

Giggling, I clinked my teacup against the flowered saucer

and then worried I might have chipped it.

Mama shut the oven door with a bang and set the timer. "And now we have the skinniest birds on the lake … right, Ma?" She licked her thumb and middle finger and picked at something on her eyelashes. " 'Cuz you don't make mistakes."

Granny rose from the table, her porcelain smile sliding into a grimace. "Let's hope those cakes don't fall. I'd hate to tell the mayor's wife that her daughter's wedding cake won't be ready in time."

Mama lit up a cigarette, and I went to change out of my uniform. As I made my way down the dark hallway toward the bedroom I shared with Mama, the tops of my thighs rubbed together, irritating the angry rash that had formed there. I ducked into the bathroom to smear petroleum jelly on my legs, praying for the burning to stop and for God to make Mama and Granny Opal get along.

When I got home from school the next day, Mama was gone. Again.

CHAPTER 41

∿

November 13, 2007

Beverly Hills had avoided Johnnie for weeks. Then today after class, the woman in jogging shoes and baggy pants cornered her in the hallway.

"Tell me, Johnnie Kitchen," she said, rolling a breath mint around on her tongue, "what's the magic pill that helped you get better?"

Johnnie took a deep breath and narrowed her eyes on her classmate. "Magic pill? There is no magic pill."

Beverly's bloodshot eyes bulged from her sallow face. *Probably from purging before class,* Johnnie thought, taking a step back.

"But how did you do it? How did you stop?"

Her question was a plea for help. Help Johnnie suddenly didn't feel qualified to give, even though she'd come on so strong back in September. But Beverly seemed desperate, and Johnnie knew that if nothing else, she could give her classmate hope, hope that one day she could get better, too.

She glanced at her watch. "I need to get to biology. Can you walk with me for a sec?"

Nodding, Beverly fell in step beside Johnnie, and they

headed outside. Both were clad in winter coats. Overhead, the bluish-gray clouds hung heavy like snow clouds, but no moisture fell.

Beverly flung one end of a fringed scarf over her shoulder, her neck wrapped in layers of dyed wool. "Okay, Johnnie Kitchen. Tell me the truth. How did you stop abusing food?"

Johnnie only had a couple of minutes to respond. Her brain scrambled to assemble words into a message that could possibly help this woman pushing sixty—a woman who'd clearly been suffering for decades.

Stuffing her hands into her coat pockets, Johnnie bent her head into the cold. "Keep in mind that I'm no shrink, just someone who's been there. This may sound odd, because we're talking about an eating disorder, but for me, food and weight weren't at the heart of my compulsive behavior." Her teeth chattered, but she pressed on. "But I didn't know that back then. Turns out bulimia was merely a *symptom* … a symptom of things like anger, rage, despair. Things I had no control over." She stole a quick glance at her new friend. "Are you following me?"

"Sure, sure." Beverly nodded at everything Johnnie said. "So if it's not about food and weight, what is it about?"

Johnnie burrowed her hands deeper into her pockets. "When I binged, I stuffed emotions down, not just food. And when I threw up, anger and rage spewed out, too. For years I internalized these normal human feelings—and I acted them out through bulimia."

Beverly slowed down for a second, as if this information had pushed her backward like a gust of wind.

The science building loomed before them. Johnnie had thirty seconds to get to class.

Tearing a sheet from her notebook, she scribbled her phone number and passed it to Beverly. "Give me a call sometime. I need to scoot. Maybe we can meet for coffee."

Beverly glanced at the number. "Thank you, Johnnie

Kitchen. Thank you." She smiled, clamping her lips shut to hide a mouthful of rotten teeth. Clutching the paper in her hand, she turned and jogged across campus, the tail of her scarf flying behind her.

Johnnie stood at the door a moment, watching her go. Her brief encounter with this woman had both drained her and pumped her up at the same time. This woman who spoke in singsong and ran Johnnie's first and last name together as one.

You've got to want it bad enough, she should have told Beverly. *No amount of wishing is going to make it go away. You've got to fight for it. And even when you think you've won the battle, you can never let your guard down.*

With a newfound confidence, Johnnie turned and headed toward class. If she could conquer bulimia, then she could damn well pass biology.

CHAPTER 42

༄

Later That Day, After Class

KEEPING HER EYES ON THE road, she reached for the radio to change stations. A male announcer's rich baritone voice boomed from the Suburban's speakers: "On this day in history, November 13, 1982, The Vietnam Veterans Memorial was dedicated in Washington D.C. Otherwise known as *The Wall*. Over 58,000 names of our nation's finest are etched into two black granite slabs rising out of the earth on the National Mall."

One of these days she would go there and find her dad's name, then visit Arlington. But not yet.

When the announcer added, "Folks, can you believe it's been twenty-five years?" Johnnie mumbled, "Oh yeah? And when are they going to erect a memorial for all the warriors who died in Iraq and Afghanistan?"

She reached for the off switch and settled back against her seat. *And what about the disfigured, the disabled, those suffering from PTSD?* Steven Tuttle's letter still weighed heavily on her heart. Plucking it from a stack of junk mail late yesterday afternoon, she'd slit it open with shaky hands. She'd waited two hours to call D.J., her voice strained as she read it to him. This morning before class, she read it one more time before she and Callie Ann left the house.

Leaving the highway, she headed north on Main. Flags still lined both sides of the street from the Veterans Day celebration on Sunday. Glancing to her left, she noticed where someone had put a spray of red flowers at the base of the old soldier. From here, they looked like poppies. At the next intersection, beds of pansies bloomed in front of Farrow & Sons.

Turning right, she headed east on Merriweather. Most of the pecans and oaks had dropped their leaves, but a few stragglers still clung to branches as gray as the sky. Pumpkins and scarecrows adorned many of the yards and porches. A pilgrim couple made out of plywood waved from the immaculate yard of a large two-story Victorian, one that Dale's company had restored years ago.

Up ahead, her red bungalow stood out, thanks to the soldier scarecrow standing guard. And directly across the street from him, a new Christmas tree rose from the place in the yard where Mr. Marvel had been digging his hole.

Christmas tree? Oh my goodness! While she'd been at school, Mr. Marvel had finally planted a tree in Edwin's memory. An evergreen about the same height as Mr. Marvel, who stood next to it in khakis and a T-shirt, leaning on a shovel. A water hose snaked across the lawn, soaking the ground at the base of the tree.

Her eyes misted up at the beautiful sight. She started to roll down the window, to holler at Mr. Marvel as she drove up. Wasn't he freezing without a coat? What kind of pine tree had he planted? Whatever it was, they would call it *Edwin's Tree.*

Then *TIMBER!* Mr. Marvel went down. One second he was standing there, leaning on the shovel. The next second he was flat on his back, his legs sprawled out in front of him like he was making snow angels. Only there wasn't any snow, and his legs weren't moving.

Lurching to a stop next to the curb, Johnnie threw the

Suburban into park, grabbed her cellphone, and rushed to his side. From the corner of her eye, she saw Otis and Cleo curled up in the living room window.

"Mr. Marvel, Mr. Marvel!"

His face was gray, his mouth open. He wasn't breathing.

Dropping to her knees, she fumbled with her phone, her hands shaking as she jabbed at the numbers 911.

The operator came on the line and Johnnie tried to steady her voice. "I think my neighbor's having a heart attack."

"What is your location?"

Her mind went blank for a second. "Uh, Portion. Portion, Texas. Four-twenty Merriweather. Across the street. Please hurry."

"Is he breathing?"

"I don't know. I don't think so."

"Do you know CPR?" the operator asked calmly.

Johnnie glanced at Mr. Marvel's open mouth and started to gag. "No! Oh God, oh God, oh God …."

"You need to pinch his nose and blow into his mouth. Do you think you can do that?"

Gulping, Johnnie swallowed the bile in her throat and fought the urge to vomit. Her own breathing came in rapid bursts. What if he was one of her kids? She had to do this. She *could* do this. Hadn't he helped her?

She dropped her phone in the grass and bent over Mr. Marvel's face, doing as the operator instructed. She took a deep breath and blew into his hammy mouth. She did it once. Then twice.

Mr. Marvel gasped a few times. She sat back on her knees, wiping her mouth with the sleeve of her coat. She felt both revulsion and utter terror.

She heard sirens in the distance. They were getting closer and closer.

"Please hurry. Please hurry," she whispered, biting back tears.

The firehouse was only blocks away.

Mr. Marvel sputtered, "Mother? Mother … is that you?"

Johnnie choked up, fighting her own urge to stop breathing. She swallowed, wanting to cradle his head on her lap, but afraid to move him. She didn't know what to say.

"Mother? Mother … is that you?" he asked again, his eyes wide and glistening.

Swiping back tears, she leaned toward him, willing herself to keep her voice smooth and soothing. "Yes, Eugene. It's me," she said, brushing her fingertips against his clammy forehead. "I'm here."

"Mother? Mother, I see Edwin," he whispered, taking his last breath.

Every hair on Johnnie's body stood on end.

Glancing up, she half-expected to see a little boy standing in the middle of the street, his hand outstretched, waiting to take his bubby home.

When the EMTs showed up seconds later, Mr. Marvel stared up at her, his eyes unblinking.

He had a smile on his face.

* * *

Portion Telegraph Obits
Captain Eugene S. Marvel

Captain Eugene Marvel, a retired commercial airline pilot, passed away November 13, 2007. Captain Marvel achieved his boyhood dream of becoming a pilot, but he was forced to hang up his wings early due to declining health and heart disease. At his request, his ashes will be buried with those of his mother and little brother in the family plot.

In his early years, Captain Marvel flew for Braniff International Airways and most recently for Express Cargo of Dallas. He graduated from Southeastern State Oklahoma University with a degree in aviation.

He is survived by his two cats, Cleo and Otis, his fifth grade teacher, Miss Freda Sinclair, and by a neighbor who befriended him in his final days, Mrs. Johnnie Kitchen. Miss Sinclair will provide a loving home for his cats.

Captain Marvel has donated his childhood home to the city of Portion to be used as the city sees fit. His only stipulation: that a young evergreen tree planted on the property be cared for and allowed to grow and prosper.

No services are planned. In lieu of flowers and donations, Captain Marvel's final wish is that people embrace society's outcasts.

"Forget not to show love unto strangers: for thereby some have entertained angels unawares." Hebrews 13:2 (ASV)

CHAPTER 43

✺

November 22, 2007
Thanksgiving Day

JOHNNIE SPRINKLED POULTRY SEASONING ON a small turkey. With Cade at basic training, D.J. in San Antonio visiting Steven Tuttle and his mother, and finals coming up, Johnnie wasn't in the mood to cook. But at least the aroma of sage would permeate her home for a few hours and fill the empty spaces. This would be the first Thanksgiving without the boys, and she was still reeling from Mr. Marvel's death. Good thing Whit offered to bring string beans and sweet potato pie. They'd at least have a vegetable and dessert to go with the turkey, and of course Granny Opal's annual cranberry congealed salad in a cornucopia mold.

The house phone rang as Johnnie shoved the turkey in the oven and glanced at the clock. Ten a.m.

She checked the Caller ID. Portion Regional Hospital.

The blood rushed from her head and pooled in a pit in her stomach. Had something happened to Dale or Callie Ann while they were out walking Brother Dog?

Fearing the worst, she plucked up the phone and tried to control her breathing.

A woman identified herself as Sandra somebody, but all

that registered in Johnnie's mind was, "I'm a nurse here at the hospital. Your grandmother asked me to call and let you know she's all right."

"All right? What's happened to her?" Relieved that her husband and daughter were okay, Johnnie switched her focus to Granny. Always strange, having to balance loved ones on the worry scale. Who was more worthy, who was less?

"She fell this morning while getting out of bed."

"Fell? Did she break anything?"

"Not any bones. Just a lamp she knocked over when she went down. She made a big deal about that."

"Oh, poor Granny! Are you sure she hasn't had a stroke? She's been having dizzy spells for months."

"No, ma'am. We don't think so, but we're running tests."

"But how did she fall?" Johnnie stared at the kitchen table, cluttered with her biology book and notes. It no longer mattered that she hadn't cleared the mess or set the table.

"She says she woke up and heard piano music coming from the living room."

Piano music?

A shiver ran up Johnnie's spine, and she gripped a kitchen chair for support.

"Are you sure she wasn't dreaming?"

"All I know is an ambulance brought her in a few hours ago."

Johnnie thanked the nurse then grabbed her purse and keys and sailed out the door. Halfway to the hospital she remembered to call Dale.

"Do you want me to come up there?" He sounded slightly out of breath. "We're two blocks from the house. Callie Ann can stay home and mind the turkey."

"No. Stay put. I'll call in a bit."

She didn't know what had rattled her more: the part about Granny falling, or the part about Granny hearing piano music.

Only one person in the family played the piano.

Mama.

JOHNNIE ROUNDED THE CORNER TO Room 202. Granny Opal appeared shrunken, lying against the stark white pillow of the hospital bed, but her red lips slid back in a loopy grin when Johnnie walked through the door.

"Hi, Gran ... you're wearing lipstick, so you must be feeling ...."

Halfway across the room, Johnnie felt the floor give way and the air rush out of her lungs. From the corner of her eye, she saw a woman seated in a chair off to the side. The woman shielded part of her face with one hand as if afraid to look up.

The woman looked just like Mama, only older.

Slowly, the woman removed her hand. "Hello, baby girl," she whispered, her voice scratchy and soft, all at the same time. The voice Johnnie had heard on the phone the night of her birthday. The voice she'd longed to hear for so many years.

Johnnie's throat closed up and she couldn't swallow. She opened her mouth but nothing came out.

Trembling, she turned and fled the room. Down the corridor she moved, mechanically placing one foot in front of the other. The tiled floor and walls blurred as in a dream, and she bumped into an orderly pushing a food cart.

Stunned, she stared into the young man's dark face. "Oh Lord, I'm so sorry. I'm such a klutz."

His quick smile put her at ease. "No problem, ma'am. You okay?"

Nodding, she offered another apology then moved on. She got as far as the nurses' station.

An older nurse wearing purple eyeglasses stepped from behind the counter. "Are you all right?"

Johnnie clung to the shoulder strap of her purse and took a couple of deep breaths. "Yeah, I'm fine. It's just that, well ... I think I just saw my mama for the first time in years. Except for a couple of times when I've spotted her around town. But those don't count."

"I see," the nurse said, removing her glasses. "Is she a patient here?"

"No, she's back there with my grandmother."

The nurse turned and looked in the direction of Room 202. "You must be Opal Grubbs' granddaughter. I'm Sandra, the nurse who called you."

Johnnie groped for words. "Oh. Uh, thank you. Do you know if my mama's been back there with her the whole time?"

"I believe she got here shortly after the ambulance arrived. Is there a problem?"

Johnnie closed her eyes, trying to absorb the shock.

"Oh, you don't know the half of it," she said, putting two and two together. Mama must have let herself in early that morning—Granny had never changed the locks—and decided to plop down right in front of the Steinway and plunk out a tune. "Why, isn't that just like my zany mama?" Johnnie laughed, shaking her head. "To show up after twenty-three years … and give a piano recital."

The nurse raised an eyebrow.

Heat surged through Johnnie's body, giving her the energy she needed to face Mama.

"Thank you for the phone call, Sandra. Guess I'll mosey back to Granny's room and ask the *gypsy* if she's staying for dinner."

A grin tugged at the corners of Johnnie's mouth as she pivoted and strode back toward Room 202. Turns out she had a little bit of Aunt Beryl in her after all.

SHE BENT TO KISS GRANNY. "Didn't mean to be rude earlier. How are you feeling?"

Granny cupped Johnnie's face in both hands. Her long elegant fingers covered in paper-thin skin formed a nest cool to the touch. "Couldn't be better, my dear, now that Victoria's back."

Even from five feet away, Johnnie inhaled Mama's scent—a mixture of cigarettes and motel soap.

Willing herself to breathe, Johnnie turned to say hello. "Nice to see you, Mama. How long are you in town for?" She tried to keep the bitterness out of her voice, but too many years and too many absences had come between them.

Mama stayed in the chair, fidgeting with a zipper on an old Army jacket folded across her lap. "I didn't mean to scare you to death," her nervous laugh turned into a hacking cough, "or run you off."

She looked smaller than Johnnie remembered, petite in a pale dress and pilled sweater, her slim calves crossed at the ankles, both feet wiggling in Mary Jane flats. Mama had always favored dresses over slacks, probably to show off her legs. Despite half-moon shadows under emerald eyes, her face radiated with the kind of beauty that time and circumstances couldn't destroy. Her auburn hair, streaked in silver, was pulled back with a ribbon—a style most women her age had outgrown.

"So, you just passing through? Or do you plan to stay?"

Mama sprang from the chair, almost effortless, like a bird. You'd never know she was fifty-eight. "Baby girl, I need a cigarette. Let's go outside."

Mama had never looked more fetching, but every time she opened her mouth, some of that charm fell away.

Gazing out the window, Johnnie spotted Granny's Lincoln in the parking lot. Mama must have driven it over behind the ambulance. Johnnie's thoughts turned to one floor up and a few rooms over—the place where Grandpa died. Mama had missed it all. Missed picking out the casket and making arrangements. Missed making sure Granny took her pills and paid her bills. Missed watching Granny come back to life, stronger than ever.

Johnnie swiveled, leaning against the windowsill, her eyes on the old woman in bed. *Don't you dare die on me now!*

Granny yawned, exposing her dentures. "Victoria?"

Pulling on her jacket, Mama lingered at the foot of Granny's bed. "Get some rest, Ma."

Granny's watery eyes gazed at her daughter, reflecting a mixture of love and sorrow. "Victoria …? I want you to tell our girl everything. Everything that happened."

Johnnie's mama stiffened as she took in a long breath through her nose. "In my own good time, Ma. In my own good time." In that brief moment, Johnnie thought her mother looked every bit her age.

Moving away from the window, Johnnie gripped her purse so tightly the strap dug into her shoulder. On her way out the door, she kissed Granny again, knowing each time she saw her might be her last.

Out in the corridor, away from Granny's ears, Johnnie turned to the woman who was both familiar and yet a total stranger. "So … where in the world have you been the last twenty-some years?"

Mama laughed, a deep laugh that seemed to come from a million dusty places. "Well, baby girl, it's like Hank Snow used to sing, 'I've been everywhere.'"

And done everything, Johnnie thought, but who was she to judge?

Her mama gestured with her head toward a door off to the right. "We can talk out there."

THEY STEPPED OUTSIDE INTO A small interior courtyard bordered by monkey grass on all sides. Fake butterflies and garden fairies on sticks hovered in one corner next to a small birdhouse on a pole.

Parking herself at a patio table next to a metal butt can, Mama fished in her coat pocket and drew out a pack of cigarettes and a plastic lighter. When she lit up, her face took on a hard cast, and Johnnie remembered the time Granny Opal told Mama she couldn't smoke inside the house. Mama got all huffy and started smoking in the bathroom with the exhaust fan running.

Johnnie plopped next to her, welcoming the late morning sun on her face. The shock of seeing her mama after all these years, plus the cool temperatures of the hospital, had left her shivering. The courtyard walls soaked up the rays, and Johnnie felt warmer out here than inside the building.

Mama puffed away on her cigarette, tilting her head back every time she blew smoke. With each hit her body seemed to relax.

"We looked everywhere for you," Johnnie began. "At first we thought you were out on one of your jaunts. But then you didn't return. A month went by. Then two. We called the cops. The morgues. The hospitals … you name it. I wanted to hire a private investigator after Grandpa died, but we didn't have the money. Then one day Dale said, 'Honey, sometimes people just don't want to be found.' So we quit looking."

Scissoring her cigarette between her fingers, Mama flicked her yellowed thumbnail against the nail of her ring finger. "Dale's a smart guy. Poppy always liked him."

"His crew's about finished with the Dooley Mansion. You should see what they've done with the place."

Mama nodded, her tongue working around her teeth. "That's some house. You ever been up in the attic? You can see most of Portion from there."

So Mama had been there, gazing out that dormer window. Johnnie stared at the cement. "How long have you been in town?"

Mama let out a breezy sigh. "Long enough. A few months."

"Where you staying?"

"A mom and pop motor lodge out by the lake. Rents by the week. No one hassles me."

"Why did you come back now? Why today? Why not ten years ago, or ten years from now?

Mama shrugged. "I don't know. I'm tired, though. I can tell ya that."

Something in Mama's voice reminded Johnnie of Mr. Marvel and how sick he was at the end. "What's wrong, Mama? Are you dying?"

Mama chuckled. "We're all dying a little bit every day."

An awkward silence came between them as she snuffed out her butt, grinding it into the gray matter.

"You know what today is, don't you?"

"You mean besides the obvious, Thanksgiving and the anniversary of JFK's death? Yeah, Mama, I do." Johnnie stared at one of the fake butterflies on a stick and waited. She wanted to hear her mama say it.

"Francis was killed in action thirty-seven years ago today." Mama snapped her fingers. "Gone in an instant. I went to Arlington once to visit his grave. But a tombstone doesn't keep a girl warm at night." Her voice cracked and she paused. "I've been with more men than I can count. He's the only one that mattered."

Stroking her neck, Johnnie turned to her. "Why did you keep his identity from me all those years?"

Mama shook her head and leaned back in the chair. "I kept his identity from a lot of people, not just you. He was three years older than me. He could've been charged with statutory rape, even though it was consensual. But mostly I had to protect him from Poppy. He went half-crazy back then. He would've ruined Francis's chance at West Point, not to mention his Army career afterwards."

"Dale found two old photos hidden at Granny's house—in the nightstand in Uncle Johnny's bedroom. You know anything about that?"

Mama looked away.

"He was going to come for us after the war. We were going to be a family. Get married. The whole bit." Her shoulders slumped, and her voice trailed off.

"You know you got a grandson who looks just like him?"

Mama nodded. "I about fell off the piano bench when I looked up and saw those dark eyes, that same knowing smile staring back at me. Ma says he's an artist."

You should see the painting D.J. did of you, Mama ....

"Your daughter's a real looker. I'd lock that girl up if I were you."

"Callie Ann's got a brain to go along with that body."

Mama crossed her feet. "Ma told me your other boy joined the Army."

"I tried to stop him, but Cade's got a mind of his own."

Mama picked at something in her teeth. "Doesn't he know it's dangerous?"

Johnnie heard herself laugh. "Why do you think he joined?"

They sat in silence for a moment. Then Johnnie spoke.

"About those photos Dale found. There's one with me and my dad taken at an Army post. The other is Uncle Johnny and my dad by the lake. Uncle Johnny's leg is in a cast. I didn't even know they knew each other ... until I saw that photo."

Bending over, Mama rested her elbows on her knees and shook her head. "That's where it gets twisted."

"I've got all day, Mama. I'm not leaving here until you tell me the truth."

Reaching in her pocket, Mama fumbled for her cigarettes. "If I tell you the story, promise you won't ever bring it up again?"

I may never see you again, Johnnie thought. "I promise."

Her hands trembled as she shook out a cigarette. "It all started the Saturday Johnny let me tag along with him to a matinee at The Palace Theatre. He'd just turned eighteen, and I was fixing to turn fifteen later that year."

At first Mama spoke in halting tones, then faster as the story unraveled.

"This boy with dreamy eyes strode in the door, a letter jacket from the Catholic high school tossed over his shoulder. He and my brother got to talking. Turns out they both had their sights set on West Point after graduation. Johnny had just received his acceptance letter and Francis was the alternate.

"After that day Francis was always at our house. I'd find every excuse to be in the same room with him. If Johnny told me to scram, Francis told him to be nice to his kid sister. We had our eyes locked on each other the moment we met. For the rest of that spring, we flirted like crazy. Poppy didn't like Francis from day one because he was Catholic. When Johnny broke his leg playing tackle football, Francis got his slot to West Point. For Poppy, that added insult to injury.

"Johnny took it better than Poppy, and the boys remained friends. Then one day Ma drove Johnny to the doctor. Francis dropped by while they were out, and the temptation was too much. We snuck down to the cove and one thing led to another and bingo … we went all the way."

For a second Mama smiled, closing her eyes as if remembering. She sighed.

Johnnie thought of her own tryst with Jeral Cagle, but she flicked it away like an irritating gnat. It was over and done with.

Then Mama's smile faded. "It only takes one time."

She pushed back from the chair, stood, and paced around the small courtyard.

"What happened next?" Johnnie asked.

Victoria stopped to catch her breath and lit another cigarette. She seemed more agitated at this point.

"A few weeks went by. Then one day Ma and I returned from the OBGYN. She marched into the kitchen and started slamming cupboard doors. Poppy came home from work and found me sitting at the table, bawling my eyes out. 'What's wrong, Victoria? Didn't you make cheerleader?' And I said, 'Yes, sir, Poppy, I sure did,' but I kept bawling. Ma had her back to us, and she chopped away on a cutting board that Johnny made for her in wood shop. Poppy set his briefcase down, loosened his tie, and looked over at Ma. 'Opal, what in the Sam Hill is wrong?' Ma spun around, waving a butcher knife in the air like a madwoman. 'Congratulations, Jonathan. You and I are going to be grandparents.'

"Poppy stared at Ma like she was a Martian. She set the knife down, untied her apron, and stormed out. Poppy placed his hands flat on the tablecloth in front of me and snarled in a voice that came straight from hell, 'Victoria, you've brought shame to this family. Don't even think you're going to bring that little *bastard* back here.'"

Bastard. The word seared Johnnie's soul. Who were these people her mama was describing? This Ma and Poppy from the early sixties? Surely they weren't the same loving grandparents who'd raised her?

Johnnie wanted to object, to interrupt, but instead she remained silent. Because once Mama stopped talking, she might not start up again.

Victoria continued. "I jumped on my bike and pedaled as fast as I could down to the cove. Lord, it was hot that August day. I didn't see Johnny fishing from the dock until it was too late. He had on Bermuda shorts; he was still in a cast. I bailed off my bike and charged into the water, hoping to end my pain. I'd lived by the lake my whole life but never learned to swim. It's not that I wanted to die. I just didn't want a baby.

"Johnny threw down his fishing rod and dived into the water, screaming for me to take hold of his arm. But we were sinking fast. The cast weighed him down. He couldn't bend that leg, much less swim with it.

"I screamed, 'I'm pregnant!' Oh, the look in his eyes ...." Victoria broke off to catch her breath.

Holding her head in her hands, Johnnie rocked back and forth in the chair. She could picture the whole thing, as if she were watching like a helpless bystander from the shore.

Victoria took a long drag on her cigarette and continued, "We thrashed about, fighting to stay afloat, but after a while he sunk below the surface. The next thing I knew somebody pulled me to shore. I was barfing water as the ambulance arrived.

"I'll never forget the look in my brother's eyes before he went under or the look on Poppy's face when they pulled Johnny from the water. In less than an hour, Poppy had aged twenty years."

Johnnie sat up straight. "That must have been so hard for you, Mama," she said, choking up.

Victoria stopped and stared in her direction. "Hell yes, it was hard," she said, her green eyes shining. "To watch someone you love leave this world, knowing you caused it. Well, that's more than a body can take." She paused, leaned over and ground out her cigarette. Her eyes flashed at Johnnie. "I didn't leave town because I wanted to. I left because I had to."

Her story over, she sashayed toward the door. Right before she went inside, Johnnie called out, "What song were you playing on the piano this morning when Granny fell out of bed?"

Mama took a few steps then said, as if in thought, "Oh, just some old hymn about a lost soul."

CHAPTER 44

❧

The Invitation

AFTER VICTORIA WENT BACK INSIDE, Johnnie pulled the journal from her purse and scribbled what was in her heart. Even though her fingers felt stiff, the pen glided across the page.

Dear Mama,

I could wrap my tongue around Granny Opal's mixing beaters and lick off all the icing, but I couldn't wrap my arms around you. I gorged myself on food because I got no nourishment from you. I wanted your sweetness, but the cake was there instead. You were always one meal away. One endless feast of broken promises.

Now you're back, and I've discovered something that's eluded me my whole life: all those years I thought I needed you, what I really needed was to find myself. And I did. I've recovered from a life-threatening eating disorder. Dale and I've built a beautiful life together, and we have amazing kids. I've even gone back to college. Not because it's expected of me, but because I want to.

Life's about second chances, Mama. I know you've had a

lousy go of it, but now's your chance to start over.

I'm here if you need me.

> Your daughter,
> Johnnie

She tore the sheet from her journal and folded it into fours. Clutching the note in her hand, she rose and went back inside. Right before she got to Granny's room, she phoned Dale.

"Everything all right?" he asked. "How's your grandmother?"

"She's fine. Just resting. Oh Dale, I have so much to tell you … but not over the phone. Can you meet me at the cove?"

"The cove? You mean right now?"

"Yes. And bring your hammer. A couple of boards on the dock need to be nailed back into place."

"Okay, but … Are you sure everything's fine?"

"Positive. Tell Callie Ann to hold down the fort and to keep Whit company if she arrives before I get back."

Johnnie dropped the phone in her purse and walked back into the room. Mama was nowhere in sight.

Granny dozed. Her wrinkled eyelids fluttered open when Johnnie bent to kiss her.

"I had a dream that Johnny came to see me," Granny whispered, her voice thick from sleep. "He was standing out back under the big pecan tree. He cracked open a pecan and held it out to me. 'Here, Ma, would you bake me a pie? The gooier the better.' Oh, how that boy loved my pecan pie! I rushed toward him, but I stumbled and fell. When I looked up, he was gone."

Johnnie fussed with Granny's blanket as if she were tucking in a small child. "I know what happened now. Mama told me."

A toilet flushed in the small adjacent bathroom. Granny dabbed at the corner of her eye then pressed a finger to her lips. "Shh, don't say anything to Victoria when she comes out. We don't want to upset her. I don't want her running off again."

Mama appeared, brushing at something on her dress. "Y'all

better not be talking about me." With the grace of a heron, she moved across the room in her Mary Jane flats and sat down, crossing her legs.

Johnnie moved from Granny's bedside to the window, overcome with the sensation that at this moment she was every age she'd ever been. From her earliest memories until now, alone in this room with these two women: the one who'd given her life, and the one who'd raised her.

"Come with me to the cove, Mama," she said, imagining how they would stand on the shore, hand in hand, and walk into the cold water together, up to their ankles. And Johnnie would pray for healing, and invoke the spirit of her dead uncle to look down on them and bless them. But what she said was, "Then we'll go back to the house for dinner. And you can meet your granddaughter."

Victoria scratched at something on the back of her neck then turned and looked out the window. "Another time, baby girl. I think I'll stay here and keep Ma company."

Granny Opal's tired eyes drifted from her daughter to her granddaughter. "Give my love to Dale and Callie Ann. And if you talk to the boys ...." Her voice trailed off, her eyelids drooping as she dozed.

Johnnie wiped her eyes and glanced at the crumpled note in her hand. "Don't read this until after I leave." She slipped the note in a pocket of her mama's jacket and walked out of the room.

They hadn't even touched.

CHAPTER 45

～⌇～

The Cove at High Noon

SQUASH-COLORED LEAVES LITTERED THE BANK where Johnnie sat on a quilt, watching Dale work on the dock. Repositioning a loose board, he picked up a nail and hammered away. The air smelled of wood smoke and the promise of winter, and the noon sun blazed high in the lake-blue sky. Her mind raced with everything her mama had told her.

She picked up her pen to write another letter, but could write nothing. For the first time in years, words failed her.

Stashing the journal in her purse, she focused again on the sketch Dale had shown her only moments earlier when they both arrived at the cove. After she filled Dale in on the details of the morning, they held each other for a long time, and then Dale led her to the cab of his pickup.

"I was going to show you this after dinner, but now seems like the perfect time. You know how D.J.'s been pushing me to update the name of my business, change the logo? Here's a sketch he's been working on. What do you think?"

Superimposed over the silhouette of a bungalow with a sleeping dog on the front porch were the words:

Dale's House of Restoration
Serving the Metroplex & Beyond
Restore Your Home
Restore Your Life

"D.J. even included Brother," Johnnie said, breathless.

Dale's eyes crinkled in a grin. "You like it?"

Tears welled up, and she wiped them with the heel of her hand. "That's our house ... the home you've been remodeling for years."

Dale grabbed his hammer and headed toward the dock. "Yep, it's like us, Johnnie Girl. A work in progress."

She glanced up from the sketch, once again admiring the way Dale filled out his jeans and flannel shirt. Except for a few lines here and there on his rugged face, he hadn't changed that much over the years.

Out of the corner of her eye, she caught a flash of crimson high up on a bare limb. A lone songbird filled the air with his sweet music.

Every cell in her body came alive with the rush. It was as if some powerful force was moving through her. She was aware of a presence, but she wasn't afraid. Choking back tears, she watched as the cardinal swooped down from the tree and moved out over the water, barely skimming the surface near the dock where Dale was working.

"John-nie ... John-nie ...."

The sound of a woman's smoky voice pierced the crisp fall air, competing with the *tap-tap-tapping* of Dale's hammer.

Johnnie whirled.

There was Mama, coming toward her.

* * *

Johnnie's Journal
December, 2007
Portion Lake

Dear Uncle Johnny,

I'm here at the dock, hanging a new Christmas wreath I bought on sale. The ribbon is bright red, like your favorite bird. I came by myself, because I needed to be alone to tell you something important.

I finally understand what you've been trying to tell me since I was a little girl, since that first time you came to me when Grandpa and I were walking along the shore.

Although you died before I was born, thank you for saving my life.

Your grateful niece,
Johnnie

PS: It's snowing.

The Lord has promised good to me,
His word my hope secures;
He will my shield and portion be
As long as life endures.

"Amazing Grace"
—John Newton (1725-1807)

KATHLEEN M. RODGERS' STORIES AND essays have appeared in *Family Circle Magazine, Military Times, Family: The Magazine for Military Families, Fort Worth Star-Telegram, Albuquerque Journal, Clovis News Journal, Her War Her Voice,* "Spouse Buzz" at Military.com, Women's Independent Press, and in the following anthologies: *Because I Fly* (McGraw-Hill), *Lessons From Our Children* (Health Communications, Inc.), *Stories Of Faith And Courage On The Home Front* (AMG Publishers), *Home of the Brave: Somewhere in the Sand* (Press 53), and *Red, White and True,* (University of Nebraska Press/Potomac Books).

Rodgers is a recipient of a Distinguished Alumna Award from Tarrant County College/NE Campus 2014. She lives in a suburb of North Texas with her husband, a retired fighter pilot/commercial airline pilot, and their dog, Denton.

Johnnie Come Lately is Rodgers' second novel. She is also the author of the award-winning novel, *The Final Salute*, featured in *USA Today*, *The Associated Press*, and *Military Times*. *The Final Salute* has been reissued by Deer Hawk Publications in 2014. She is currently working on a sequel to *Johnnie Come Lately, Seven Wings to Glory,* and is represented by Loiacono Literary Agency.

You can find Rodgers online at:

www.kathleenmrodgers.com.

Made in the USA
Lexington, KY
19 December 2014